The Marvelous Adventures and Rare Conceits of Master Tyll Owlglass

This edition published 2025
by Living Book Press
Copyright © Living Book Press, 2025

ISBN: 978-1-76153-766-0 (hardcover)
         978-1-76153-786-8 (softcover)

First published in German in 1515.

This edition is based on the 1860 printing by Trubner & Co.

A catalogue record for this book is available from the National Library of Australia

The Marvelous Adventures and Rare Conceits of
Master Tyll Owlglass

by

Kenneth Mackenzie

Folly
Goberneth
the
World

Contents

PREFACE.

"Wit, an't be thy will, put me into good fooling! Those wits that think they have thee do very oft prove fools; and I that am sure I lack thee, may pass for a wise man: For what says Quinapalus? Better a witty fool than a foolish wit."

Clown in "Twelfth Night," *Act I., Scene 5.*

Among the folkbooks of the German nation, not one has obtained so general a circulation as that now presented in an English form. It has been deemed worthy, as by the Appendix may be perceived, of being translated into French, Dutch, Danish, Polish, nay, even Hebrew, and honoured by being reprinted on every kind of paper, good and bad. A favourite among the young for its amusing and quaint adventures, and a study among those who strive, by the diligent comparison of different eras of national literature, to arrive at a due appreciation of national character, Eulenspiegel, or Owlglass the boor (peasant), possesses a peculiar value for the old. I well remember how, as a very little child, I first made the friendship of the lithe though clumsy hero; and to the present time do not feel that I can say I have lost my interest in the humourous quips and quiddities of the strolling vagabond. I little thought, when I then read the German book, that it would be my privilege to introduce him to other readers in my own language.

The Gil Blas of German mediæval story, there is deep instruction in the pungent jests and literal ways of the man who held up his mirror for owls to look in, and each of whose tricks might form the groundwork of a moral reflection. And for the early times in which it appeared, there was not a little courage in the author of it. Strange to say, this person appears to have been a Franciscan friar, Thomas Murner, who, in other matters, made not a little stir in his own day. He visited this country, and wrote a book in defence of our good King Hal the Bluff against that famous monk, Luther; and he received some assistance in a substantial gift from that monarch. An account of him will be found in the Appendix; we have here only to deal with the significance of the book itself.

Like the deep searching work of Rabelais, the book is a satire, not upon human life only, but upon special and dangerous topics. Very early editions contain the story of how Eulenspiegel procured an old skull from a churchyard, and turned the passion for worshipping relics to profitable account;[1] and the priests and would-be learned men of his time continually appear in ludicrous, undignified, or humiliating positions. Rank was not respected, nor was vice in high places passed by with (so-called) discreet silence. Yet with all the graver objects in the book, the immediate aim of amusement was never forgotten; and, letting us into the secrets of peasant life in Germany at an era when peasants had little to rejoice over, we almost imagine that we can hear the shouts of laughter with which the blunt outspoken jokes of this sly clown were received. But Mr. Hallam does justice to a higher appreciation of this kind of literature among the better classes of the time.

"They had a literary public, as we may call it," says this distinguished writer,[2] "not merely in their courts and universities, but in their respectable middle class, the burghers of the free cities, and perhaps in the artizans whom they employed. Their reading was almost always with a serious end: but no people so successfully cultivated the art of moral and satirical fable. These in many instances spread with great favour through Cisalpine

---

1   See Adventure the 36th, p. 63.
2   Introduction to the Literature of Europe, vol. i. p. 235 (Library ed.); vol. i. p. 240 (Cabinet ed.).

Europe. Among the works of this kind, in the fifteenth century, two deserve mention; the Eulenspiegel, popular afterwards in England by the name of Howleglass, and a superior and better known production,[3] the *Narrenschiff*, or Ship of Fools, by Sebastian Brandt of Strasburg.... It is a metrical satire on the follies of every class, and may possibly have suggested to Erasmus his *Encomium Moriæ*. But the idea was not absolutely new; the theatrical company established at Paris under the name of *Enfans de Sans Souci*, as well as the ancient office of jester or fool in our courts and castles, implied the same principle of satirising mankind with ridicule so general, that every man should feel more pleasure from the humiliation of his neighbours than pain from his own.... The influence such books of simple fiction and plain moral would possess over a people, may be judged by the delight they once gave to children, before we had learnt to vitiate the healthy appetite of ignorance by premature refinements and stimulating variety."[4]

Yet with all the repute which the book must have had among the boors and country louts of what people choose, with doubtful taste or insight, to call the "dark ages," Owlglass, if it had not contained within itself great vitality, might have lain in the obscurity which surrounds many a contemporary work. Of the three great philosophers then extant, I have somewhere read a kind of parallel, that Rabelais in his work satirised fantastically, and with peculiar reference to the more educated and scholarly readers of his time. Erasmus, on the other part, struck at the monks with vigorous hand in other fashion; while both Brandt

---

3 Matter of doubt to the present writer whether it be thus superior; in any case, it would be scarcely so interesting to people now-a-days. But see the Appendix.

4 Bouterwek, in his "History of German Poetry and Eloquence" (*Geschichte der deutschen Poesie und Beredsamkeit*), vol. ix. p. 336, confirms the observations of Hallam, and lends additional testimony to the popularity of the Eulenspiegel. Adolf Rosen von Kreutzheim, in the Preface to his poem, the *Esel-König* (Ass-King), alludes to the general dispersion of Eulenspiegel, Marcolphus, Katziporo, and other works, and abuses them in set terms as shameful, mischievous, and dangerous.

and Murner took a more popular form in their compositions: yet, while Brandt is now scarce remembered, Eulenspiegel remains, a striking and applicable book, setting forth, indeed, in a good light, the truth everywhere, that "the letter killeth but the spirit giveth life." In this may be found the reason of its wonderful popularity in Germany—in this is the secret of its constant reproduction in so many languages.

The fool in idle hour claims our attentive ear, charms, instructs, enchains the mind, when the sonorous voice and weighty arguments of the preacher would have no greater effect than the production of a yawn, or, at most, a fugitive repentance. The fact of the subjection of the letter to the spirit must be borne in mind throughout. Mighty times were those when, by sturdy hands and wise pates, the world was ridding itself of the rule of monks and literal interpreters of the universe and of the duties of society. Yet Murner, as has been mentioned, fought against Luther; nor, indeed, could Rabelais or Erasmus perceive, save somewhat dimly, whither their words tended. Perhaps, in secret, they saw, in fitful glimpses, the truth that history proceeds according to progressive laws of development; and when the monks, who at one time had done good service, were no longer useful to mankind, they decayed from inherent fitlessness, and so vanished, overcome by the light of such lamps as these.

A remarkable feature in the adventures of Owlglass must not be passed over without notice, viz., the very few allusions anywhere made to the occult sciences, or to similar subjects. In the story of the invisible picture there is one slight reference to alchymy; and in that where he is led forth to the gallows, the multitude regard Owlglass as a magician, who will rescue himself by the aid of demons. But so real is the character everywhere, that not even by the many editors has any tale been introduced connecting the hero with such matters. Yet the absence of such a colouring displays a greater skill and a deeper purpose in the author; from the tendency of the age in which it was written, any mention of occult science would have been excusable, nay, almost natural. If we remember that the era of its publication was rife with magicians, astrologers, and alchymists; that Cornelius Agrippa very shortly afterwards found it necessary to protest against the abuse of such subjects in his treatise "Of the Uncertainty and Vanity of the Sciences and Arts," that Trithemius was then Abbot of the Benedictine Monastery of Spanheim: all these considerations would have caused no surprise at the introduction of scenes of enchantment, or, at least, an employment of them allusively or by implication. But no; true to its mission of a folk-book, filled with the manners and customs of its time, Owlglass is thoroughly worldly, and for us, therefore, possesses greater interest and value.

It may be interesting for a moment to set side by side the jester exhibited in the pages of Shakspere and the good Master Owlglass. Historical Owlglass there certainly was at some time of the fourteenth century, his tomb yet standing at Möllen, as will be seen; but the pranks of many excellent jesters were all centred in the book telling of Owlglass; so that he has been overlaid with jokes, not in his own power to perform. Indeed, in the present edition, from a respect I have for chronology, I have been obliged to extrude two or three which would have involved anachronisms. However, they were somewhat dull, and therefore need not be regretted.

The first English version of Owlglass (as to which see the Appendix, p. 212) having been published early in the sixteenth century, in a "little dumpy quarto," by Master William Copland, its fame might, without much difficulty, have infiltrated the country parts of England; and, if we regard the clowns of Shakspere, Touchstone, in "As You Like It," for example, it might appear that Shakspere had seen this Black Letter of William Copland: yet, while the humour of Owlglass consists in his stolid performance of the exact words commanded him, there is clearly a quite other appreciation of wit in the English writer. It is, in fact, the polished foil beside the homely cudgel—both effective weapons, but one of them far more glittering, swift, and murderous. The cudgel may be warded off by a less skilful hand, the glancing steel hath made a wound, and been withdrawn in the very flash of its own rapidity. Dogberry and Verges, Costard perhaps, nay, even Sir Toby Belch, have points of character more resembling Owlglass than do the clowns of our great poet. The Fool in King Lear, has some kin to him, but is infinitely wiser. Indeed, we might perhaps rather class Bardolph, Pistol, and Nym, humourists in their way, with Master Owlglass than the subtle wits Shakspere brings upon the stage. Yet has Owlglass an existence beyond and outside all question of contrast, all opinion of similarity. Gervinus, in his comprehensive History of German Fiction[5] has well defined Owlglass to be "the personified quip and crank" (*der personificirte Schwank*). In fact, he is a Gothic Diogenes set in a Teutonic frame, living, moving, and having his being in an atmosphere as peculiarly distinct in its grotesque and massive proportions, as was the earlier Hellenic age, in its union of elegance and power. No previous time could have produced such an out-birth, and, with all our modern tendencies towards humour, fostered by the constant study of our quainter dramatists, another Owlglass would be a distortion, if not an impossibility.

That, even in grave England, and with quaint Ben Jonson, Master Owlglass was a favourite, we may see from two allusions which he makes to him; one in the "Poetaster," Act the Third, Scene the Fourth, where Tucca exclaims: "What, do you laugh, Owlglass?" And again in the "Masque of the Fortunate Isles," produced in 1626, Ben Jonson introduces Howleglass; and Johphiel says to Merefool:—

  Or what do you think
  Of Howleglass instead of him?

5 History of German Fiction, vol. ii. p. 298.

Merefool.— No him
       I have a mind to.
Johphiel.— O, but Ulen-spiegle,
       Were such a name—but you shall have your
       longing.

And later on, the remark is made:—
          Whether you would present him with an
       Hermes
       Or with an Howleglass?
    Skelton.—*An* Howleglass
       To come to pass
       On his father's ass;
       There never was,
       By day, nor night,
       A finer sight,
       With feathers upright
       In his horned cap,
       And crooked shape,
       Much like an ape,
       With owl on fist.
       And glass at his wrist.[6]

A most unjustifiable libel, by the way, is committed here, for Owlglass was always a "proper" gentleman, having no crook-back or ape-like appearance.[7]

One of the most thoughtful and philosophic writers of our day, Mr. Carlyle, has a few noteworthy sentences regarding this strange book, which we shall do well to transfer to these pages:—

"Lastly, in a third class, we find in full play that spirit of broad drollery, of rough saturnine humour, which the Germans claim as a special characteristic; among these, we must not omit to mention the *Schiltbürger* correspondent to our own *Wise Men of Gotham*;

6   Jonson's Works, p. 650.
7   An Howleglass is mentioned as being in the library of a Captain Cox. On which, see the Appendix, p. 212.

still less the far-famed *Tyll Eulenspiegel* (Tyll Owlglass), whose rogueries and waggeries belong in the fullest sense to this era.

"This last is a true German work; for both the man, Tyll Eulenspiegel, and the book which is his history, were produced there. Nevertheless, Tyll's fame has gone abroad into all lands; thus, the narrative of his exploits has been published in innumerable editions, even with all manner of learned glosses, and translated into Latin, English, French, Dutch, Polish; nay, in several languages, as in his own, an *Eulenspiegelerei* and *Espiéglerie*, or dog's trick, so named after him, still by consent of lexicographers, keeps his memory alive. We may say, that to few mortals has it been granted to earn such a place in universal history as Tyll; for now, after five centuries, when Wallace's birth-place is unknown even to the Scots; and the admirable Crichton still more rapidly is grown a shadow; and Edward Longshanks sleeps unregarded save by a few antiquarian English, Tyll's native village is pointed out with pride to the traveller, and his tombstone, with a sculptured pun on his name,—namely, an Owl and a Glass,—still stands, or pretends to stand, at Möllen, near Lübeck, where, since 1350, his once nimble bones have been at rest. Tyll, in the calling he had chosen, naturally led a wandering life, as place after place became too hot for him; by which means he saw into many things with his own eyes; having been not only over all Westphalia and Saxony, but even in Poland, and as far as Rome. That in his old days, like other great men, he became an autobiographer, and in trustful winter evenings, not on paper, but on air, and to the laughter-lovers of Möllen, composed this work himself, is purely a hypothesis; certain only that it came forth originally in the dialect of this region, namely, the *Platt-Deutsch*; and was therefrom translated, probably about a century afterwards, into its present High German, as Lessing conjectures, by one Thomas Murner, who, on other grounds, is not unknown to antiquaries. For the rest, write it who might, the book is here, 'abounding,' as a wise critic remarks, 'in inventive humour, in rough merriment, and broad drollery, not without a keen rugged shrewdness of insight; which properties must have made it irresistibly captivating to the popular sense; and with all its fantastic extravagancies, and roguish crotchets, in many points instructive.'"[8]

Mr. Carlyle then cites one adventure, that of the Easter Play, which has not been included in the present version; for although it illustrates well enough the interior of a parson's household of the fourteenth century, there is a smack of profanity about it which it is well to avoid. And, indeed, it is due to the reader of this volume, to inform him, that our present chronicle differs in one material point from all former editions. While it has been my object everywhere to tell the story of Owlglass in a quaint and simple manner, modern good taste required a special duty at the chronicler's hands: viz., that of purification and modification, for it may readily be believed that a book written *of* the fourteenth century, *for* the sixteenth century, would abound with homely wit, not quite consonant with the ideas of the nineteenth. Therefore several stories of a somewhat indelicate, and generally pointless, character have been omitted, and their place supplied with matter obtained by a collation of several editions in the German, French, and Flemish languages.

And another aim which I have had in view has been, where good taste and opportunity admitted, to apply, in a veiled manner, the axioms and quips of our knight-errant of roguery, to subjects and follies not banished from our own more polite age. The reader will thus be able to judge in how far this modern Owlglass differs from its predecessors. In no instance, however, have I permitted myself to lose sight of the object in view, which was to give as good a picture of the original as might be, and that in spirit rather than in letter. This spirit has been so justly estimated by M. Robin, a clever and dashing French critic, whose sad death may still be

[8]   Carlyle, Miscellaneous Essays, Edition 1857, Vol. II. pp. 287–288.

remembered by a few, that, at the risk of adding too much to this preface, I subjoin an epitome of his remarks:—

"It is quite true," says he, "that glory is nothing but vanity. I have seen in the sepulchral silence of libraries, names quite unknown, on the backs of gigantic volumes, the librarians could tell me nothing of these, except that they were the authors of these books. I have seen, on the pavement of ancient churches, pompous epitaphs, and heraldic arms, and the nails of the peasant's shoe tread them under foot. Be then in life a man of learning, knowing every language, be a noble of Spain, a Knight of the Golden Fleece, Viceroy of Mexico or Peru, say you have the right of keeping your hat on in the presence of the King, yet it will scarcely be known that you have lived, while a *vaurien*, a man who had neither hearth nor home, a practical joker, a drunkard, having the devil in his purse, living from hand to mouth, sleeping to-day in the streets, and to-morrow in the bed of his host, whom he never pays, and understanding too well the buffoonery of life ever to have thought of glory; as soon as this man is dead, and ignobly buried, he enters at once into immortality, bequeathing to the people a name which they will never forget, and, to the Attic language of the moderns, a word of which they stood much in need. Who can boast of having invented a word? Very few of the greatest writers can arrogate to themselves this most rare glory. But to leave one's name to the most grave and self-sufficient language in Europe, to force it to say *espiègle*, because one's name was Ulenspiegel; and to pass fifty years in practical joking and laughter; to be able to call oneself the father of the great family of Mystificators, surely this is no common fate, and doubtless the contemplator of it will cry out: 'Where doth Immortality dwell? Poor author, it was well worth thy pains to wear out thy brain in writing folios! Unfortunate hidalgo, it was well worth the trouble of being puffed up with pride at a long name unpronounceable in a breath, that this name should be forgotten, and that the name of a boorish jester should be transmitted almost intact to the most distant posterity."

The best test of the worth of a book, whether it be several centuries old, or, as it were, a production of our own day, is the proportion of times that it has been reproduced or imitated. Singularly enough, while, in most continental languages, such translations and imitations have been frequent, in two instances only has this celebrated folk-book appeared in an English dress; first, as has been already stated, in Black Letter, in 1528–1530, and again in a modified form in 1720. With a description of these two editions I will not trouble the reader here, as in the Appendix at the end an accurate account of them will be found; and I will merely add, in this place, that of the Black Letter translation only two copies are known to exist, both in the British Museum; and that of the second, a copy of which is now in my own possession, I have only been able to find one other, which is in the Douce Collection in the Bodleian.

It was originally in contemplation to reprint the scarce Black Letter edition; but, on a careful examination, I found this an impossibility, as the contents, for reasons already hinted at, would have shocked good taste; nor, in point of fact, would that edition have offered so great a variety as in this volume has been presented; which may be understood when it is explained, that of all kinds of stories, good and bad, the Black Letter gives but forty-eight; while in the present chronicle there are—such question-able adventures being omitted—no less than one hundred and eleven. Although the idea of such reprint was thus abandoned, there appeared no reason, however, why the old-fashioned form should not be adopted in the telling of the tale. For this and any other faults which the reader may detect I hold myself respon-sible; and I may mention, that so careful have I been to imitate the style of the time in which it is supposed to be written, that I have even followed the confusion between the use of the "thee" and "thou" and "you" and "ye" common in early books, especially at the transition era of the Stuarts.

The edition which I have adopted as a guide or clue-line, is the Low German original of 1519 in the excellent and exhaustive work of Dr. Lappenberg; and I need not here especially refer to any other, save that of M. Octave Delepierre, long time a zealous antiquary, who argues for a Flemish origin for our hero, an origin in which, giving every meed of praise to that gentleman for the singular ingenuity and complete localization which his book exhibits, I need scarcely say that I cannot coincide. Nay, it may even be suspected that he himself is but in jest with his argument.

I have also to draw the notice of the reader to the Appendices at the end of this volume, which enter into the bibliographical and other history of the book, and to mention that I am greatly indebted to the Rev. Dr. Bandinel, the venerable Librarian of the Bodleian Library at Oxford, and also to my friends, the Rev. Alfred Hackman, M.A., Precentor of Christ Church, and the Rev. John S. Sidebotham, M.A., Chaplain of New College, and Preacher at St. Martin's, Carfax, Oxford, for much valuable assistance in searching for Eulenspiegel literature amidst the treasures contained in that valuable library.

This is all, I think, which need here be said touching the task I have here completed; for the reader need not be asked to appreciate the artistic skill of my friend and coadjutor, Mr. Alfred Crowquill. If the reader does but experience in the perusal of this singular book—practically the first English edition of it—one tithe of the pleasure I have had in preparing it, all that was to be accomplished will have been duly fulfilled.

Kenneth Robert Henderson Mackenzie

35, Bernard Street, Russell Square, W.C.

October 3, 1859.

The Introduction touching Master Tyll Owlglass.

With what joy and inward content do I not greet ye, my masters, bringing with me for your sweet delectation and delightful comfort the history, the which I have most diligently written, and out of many learned and wise books gathered together, and which indeed telleth of the merry jests, rare conceits, and subtile cony-catching of that renowned Master Tyll Owlglass, who in the Brunswick land was born. And i' faith, ye do owe me not a little grace and thankfulness for that which I have now finished,—but as if my pains had been a thousandfold greater than they have been, I would not have spared myself. This is mine answer unto ye. And my desire hath been, that ye shall most merrily sit ye round the fire and laugh until that your sides shall ache, and your inner man be shaken with the continual reverberation

1

of your delighted spirit. For an ill heart is such an one that doth never rejoice, but trembleth ever and anon at the wonders with the which we be encompassed, so do ye now, without any other speech from me, accept this little book, and therein read, and ponder well the deeds of this noble master, who from low estate and boorish condition rose to be the companion of princes and dukes, and, by his infinitude of rare parts, remaineth well known and beloved of all men in divers countries and lands all over the fair domain of Christendom. And now do I bid ye farewell, and leave ye with a companion less tedious than am I, and in the reading of his life will ye not lose your labour, that know I well.

The First Adventure.

How Tyll Owlglass was born and was in one day three times christened.

As verily all creatures must have a beginning of their lives, so that they may come into this world to abide therein, so also must it be with the famous Master Owlglass, who lived in Germany many years, and of whom many notable adventures are told and noised about all over that country. In the land of Brunswick, in the deep wood named Melme, lieth a village named Kneitlingen, and there was born the pious child Owlglass. And the name of his father was Nicolaus, commonly said Claus, Owlglass, and his mother's name was Anna Wertbeck. It fortuned, that when the child was born that they made a great feast, and sent the child to be christened in the village of Amptlen; hard by the castle of Amptlen, which was after destroyed by the people of Magdeburg. And when the child was baptised, he was called Tyll Owlglass. Truly, however, after that the feast had come to an end, the godfathers and godmothers of the child having eaten and drunken right lustily (for it was the custom of that place most heartily to do these things), set forth on their way homeward, and the sun being hot, they were tired and they minded not their steps to be careful of them, and so it came to pass, that one of them carrying the child caught her foot upon a stone and fell into a ditch, so child and all were quickly covered with mud. But as weeds cannot so easily come to harm, the child was not hurt, but only thus christened in the mire.

When they got home, the child was washed clean in hot water. Thus was Owlglass in one day three times christened, first in the church, then in the mud of the ditch, and at last in warm water. So is it always shown with great and famous persons, that, in their infancy, strange and most wonderful things do foreshow their future greatness.

The Second Adventure.

How that Owlglass when that he was a child did give a marvellous answer to a man that asked the way.

Upon a time went the father and mother of Owlglass forth, and left Owlglass within the house. Then came a man riding by, and he rode his horse half into the house in the doorway, and asked: "Is there nobody within?" Then answered the child: "Yea, there is a man and a half, and the head of a horse." Then asked the man: "Where is thy father?" and the child made answer and said: "My father is of ill making worse; and my mother is gone for scathe or shame." And the man said to the child: "How understandest thou that?" And then the child said: "My father is making of ill worse, for he plougheth the field and maketh great holes, that men should fall therein when they ride. And my mother is gone to borrow bread, and when she giveth it again and giveth

less it is a shame, and when she giveth it and giveth more it is scathe." Then said the man: "Which is the way to ride?" And the child answered and said: "There where the geese go." And then rode the man his way to the geese, and when he came to the geese they flew into the water; then wist he not whither to ride, but turned again to the child and said: "The geese be flown into the water, and thus wot I not what to do nor whither to ride." Then answered the child: "Ye must ride where the geese go and not where they swim." Then departed the man and rode his way, and marvelled of the answer of the child. Thus from the mouths of babes cometh forth wisdom and ready conceit.

The Third Adventure.

How all the boors did cry out shame upon Owlglass for his knavery; and how he rode upon a horse behind his father.

Now when Owlglass had come to an age to run about, he began playing divers tricks and knavish actions among the boys of his village; and he fought and tumbled about upon the grass, that he looked more like a monkey than a boy. But when it came to pass that he was four years old, his malice waxed greater and greater, so that his father was ever being disputed with by the neighbours, who cried out shame upon Owlglass, as being so great a knave; and though it happened that his father did scold him with many words, Owlglass did always excuse himself by knavish answers. Thereat the father thought he would quickly learn the verity of these sayings of the neighbours, and at a time when the boors were all walking in the streets, he did set his son Owlglass behind him on his horse. Then, also, he commanded Owlglass that he should be most quiet and silent. What, then, did the pious and good child? He did silently play tricks and mocked the people, whereon they did most loudly cry out upon Owlglass: "Fie upon the little malicious knave!"

Now as Owlglass spake never a word in all this time, his father did not know how it came to pass that the people did cry out so loudly; and Owlglass complained to him, and said: "Hearest thou, father! Here sit I silently behind thee upon thy horse and say no word, and yet the people cry out against me for my knavery." Then the father sayeth but little, and taketh Owlglass and setteth him upon the horse in front of him. Then did Owlglass open his mouth wide, and did stretch forth his tongue, in mockery of the people. And the people did run forth, crying: "Out upon the little knave!" Yet did not the father see the knavery, but said: "Alas for thee, that thou shouldst have been born in an unhappy hour!" So much did he love Owlglass, that he then departed out of the land of Brunswick, and he did abide in the land of Magdeburg, hard by the river Saale.

In a little time thereafter, so sorrowful was he, that he gave up the ghost, and left his wife and child in great poverty. Thus it is that great men are often persecuted and smitten with many blows in their own land, nor do they find good comfort therein! Owlglass, although he knew not any handicraft, did grow up and wax older in knavery; and when that he was sixteen years old, did excel in tricks, quips, and quiddities.

The Fourth Adventure.

How Owlglass did learn to dance upon a rope, and did fall therefrom into the river Saale.

It hath been said of old time, by the wise and cunning: "When that the cat is out of the house, then play the mice." Thus fared it with Owlglass after that his father was dead. His mother had become old and full of years, and she could no longer have the mastery over Owlglass, and he did learn many greatly knavish conceits. And his mother was sorely troubled of Owlglass, and bore not with his knavery.

Now it fortuned, that the house where Owlglass and his mother did live, lay hard by the river Saale, and Owlglass did go up into the garret of the house, and there did learn to dance upon a rope, until that his mother did find him going to and fro upon the rope, and did so belabour him with a cudgel, that he fled through the window of the garret on to the roof, where she could not follow him. And this often came to pass, until he grew older, and she became weak and of no strength to have power over him. Then thought he, it was time that he should in open day render it manifest unto all, how great was his perfection in the art of dancing upon the rope, and he did stretch the rope across the river Saale, from one house even unto a house which lay over against them on the other side. And when that the people beheld such unwonted sport, they did run together, old and young, in a great crowd, and did marvel much that Owlglass should go hither and thither in so sure a manner upon the rope.

Happiness is, however, but for the few, and seldom doth evil fortune fail to sow sorrowful seeds in the midst of joyous doings; and thus fortuned it, that the mother of Owlglass did hear the shouting of the people at the feats of Owlglass, and that she might reprove with heavy punishment the knavery of her son, she hastened to the place where the rope was tied, and cut it through with a knife secretly. Then did good Master Owlglass plump into the water with much mockery and despite; and all the people did laugh greatly thereat, and Owlglass was vexed, so that he could speak no word; nor did he fear the bath and the peril of drowning as much as the jests of the people, who ran after him, blessing the bath with much outcry. Thus did Master Owlglass come evilly off in his first undertaking.

The Fifth Adventure.

How Owlglass did move two hundred young people, that they did give unto him their shoes, with the which he made rare sport upon his rope.

In no long space of time thereafter, Owlglass did desire to avenge him, concerning the mockery which befel him after the bath, therefore did he tie the rope across unto another house, and once again told the people that he would dance to and fro upon the rope. Soon did the people come together in great multitude, and there were in that place both old and young; then Owlglass spake unto the young people, and said that he would show unto them a most rare device upon the rope with their shoes. Then did they believe him, and with that put their shoes off their feet and gave them unto Owlglass, and he did put them all together upon a string and went up on to the rope; and all the people thought that he was going to make some wonderful stroke therewith. But the boys were sad, and would fain have received their shoes again.

When, therefore, Owlglass was sitting upon the rope and had ended his trickery, he cried out with a loud voice and spake these words: "Be ye now every one in readiness, and let him seek his shoes again;" and he cut the string and threw all the shoes upon the ground, in such wise that one shoe fell upon another into a great heap, and none could be distinguished. Then did the people, old and young, come in great crowds, and caught a shoe here and another there; and one spake and said this was his shoe, whereat another did make answer that it was his; and then fell they to fisticuffs, and with great blows they pulled out the hairs from their heads: one lay on the ground, and the other belaboured him with sturdy strokes; and one wept with a loud voice while another did laugh, and a third screamed like a peacock. Thus went things forward, until the old men began also to give many stripes to the crowd.

But Owlglass, sitting upon his rope, laughed until his stomach shook again, and cried out: "Right merry may ye be! Seek ye your shoes again in that wise in which I sought my way forth from the bath." Then did he come down from his rope, and left them in contention; nor did he again come forth, for fear of the people, but abode at home with his mother. Thereover did his mother greatly rejoice, and thought that now he was a wise and gentle person, and soon, therefore, would things go better with them all. Yet knew she not of his knavery, and wherefore he dared not go out. But the wisdom of Owlglass was great; for it is better to abide in darkness with a whole skin, than live in a palace of light and be beaten with many stripes. Thus did, therefore, our great example of wit and judgment.

The Sixth Adventure.

How that Owlglass his mother did move him that he should learn a handicraft.

The mother of Owlglass was right glad that her son was so still, and chid him only for that he would learn no handicraft. Yet answered he never a word unto all her reproofs, the which she was never tired of bestowing upon him. At last he opened his mouth and spake unto her, saying: "Dear mother, as it happeneth that one beginneth action, so also is the ending thereof." For he knew in his wisdom, that if he had begun with knavish doings, and should turn therefrom and live honestly, yet in the world would no one give heed unto him, but the rather regard him as a greater knave than before, esteeming him to be a hypocrite as well as a knave. "That believe I right truly," answered his mother; "and thus have I seen no bread in my house these four weeks gone by, nor have I had thereof any." "That toucheth not my speech," said Owlglass. "But with Saint Nicolaus must the poor man fast upon his even; and if perchance he should have bread, he may feast right merrily with Saint Martin on his day. Therefore will we also eat."

The Seventh Adventure.

*How Owlglass did deceive a baker at Strasfurt, and gat
bread for his mother.*

Then thought Owlglass: "God help us, how shall I compass
it that my mother may be rendered quiet? Where shall I get
me bread for her needs?" Thus went he forth from the village
where they abode, and departed on the way towards the town
of Strasfurt, and there beheld he a baker's shop. Then went he
in unto the baker, and asked him, saying: "Would he for a crown
send bread unto his lord?" Then named he the name of a lord
who abode in that town, and also the place where he lay, that
the baker might send with Owlglass a boy to carry the bread and
receive the money therefor.

Thereat answered the baker, that he would do everything
that he commanded, and Owlglass gave him a sack wherein to
count the loaves; but this sack had a secret hole, not to be seen.
The baker sent with him a lad to receive the money.

Now when Owlglass had gat him a bow-shot from the house
of the baker, he privily let a wheaten loaf fall down into the mire,
and thereat set he the bag down and said unto the baker's lad:
"Alas! the bread which is thus made dirty I can never bring in unto
my lord. Run quickly home and get for it another loaf, and I will
wait here till that thou dost come again." Then hasted the good
lad to his master's house, and did get another loaf for him; but
Owlglass secretly hid himself in a house outside the town until
that a cart came by, which did receive him and his bag; and he
returned unto the house of his mother.

When that the lad came back unto the place where Owlglass had let the loaf fall, he found that he was beguiled; and he went back and told his master, who speedily ran unto the inn where lay the worshipful lord of whom Owlglass spake, and he asked the serving-men of that lord for Owlglass; but they knew him not. Then the baker perceived that he was cheated of his bread, and so returned home. But Owlglass gave the bread to his mother, and bade her to feast with Saint Martin. Thus can a great man ever overcome the besetting evils of life.

The Eighth Adventure.

How Owlglass with other children, was forced to eat fat soup, and gat blows likewise.

There was in the village where Owlglass lived with his mother, a custom that when anyone killed a pig, the neighbour's children came to him in his house to eat a soup or broth, which was called the butcher-broth. Now there lived in this village a farmer who was avaricious, and yet he dared not to refuse the children the soup; then thought he of a cunning way by which he might make them sick of the soup-eating; and he cut into it the sour crumb of the bread.

When the boys and girls came, Owlglass also was among them, and he let them come in, and closed the doors and poured out the soup, and the broth was more than the children could eat; when one of them was full and was going away, the farmer had a rod with the which he struck him, so that each child was forced to eat more than it wished. The host knew well of the knavery of Owlglass, and therefore when that he was beating another child he always bestowed some hearty strokes upon him. And this did he for so long, as that they had ended all the eating, and that they felt like the dogs after grass-grazing. Thereafter would no one go unto the stingy farmer's house to eat the butcher-broth.

The Ninth Adventure.

How Owlglass brought it about that the stingy farmer's poultry drew for baits.

The next day, when he that had beaten the children went forth, Owlglass met him, and he said unto Owlglass: "Dear Owlglass, when wilt thou come again to eat the butcher-soup at my house?" "Yea, that will I," answered Owlglass, "when thy poultry draw for baits, and four and four together fight for a little bread." Then said the other: "Wilt thou be so long?" But Owlglass said: "An if I came ere the time of the fat soup hath come?" Then he went on his way and thought over it until the time that the man's poultry ran about the streets; then had Owlglass some twenty strings tied together at the midst, and at either end of the string was a morsel of bread hanging. These took he and threw to the poultry. When then the fowls here and there picked up and swallowed the bread, they could not keep hold, for at the other end another fowl was pulling, so that they were contending, and thus from the size of the bread they could not get rid of it, and so stood more than thirty fowls one over against the other and in throttling ran a wager.

The Tenth Adventure.

*How Owlglass was again moved of his mother to depart to
a foreign land, that he might learn a handicraft.*

After that Owlglass had played a bitter knavery somewhere, so that he might not dare show himself, he sat at home with his mother; and she, with many words, continually chid him, in that he would learn no craft to get money thereby. And she spake unto him saying, that he should depart into a foreign land, that he might there profit somewhat. But his mother had just killed a pig and so long as our good master Owlglass knew that any of it remained he would not quit. The mother of Owlglass thereat scolded him, until that he agreed to set forth, and made a small bundle of clothes and food, and, at length, went his way. Soon our wise master felt hungry, and thereat took forth from his wallet the provision he had, and did eat until there was none left. Thereafter did he not tarry long on thought, but when that it was dark, came again to the house of his mother. Then went he up to the garret and lay among the straw, where he slept lustily until the day had broken, then wake he up by reason of a noise he did hear in the neighbour's court. And Owlglass did look forth, and beheld a fox stealing the poultry from the roosting place. Then could Owlglass no longer keep silent, but cried with a loud voice: "Alas! thou cunning thief, an if I were not in a far country from this, it would go hard with thee but I would kill thee." Then heard the mother of Owlglass what he said, and came and marvelled not a little at beholding him.

The Eleventh Adventure.

How Owlglass crept into a bee-hive, how two thieves came by night to steal honey, what honey they did steal, and how Owlglass made it to come to pass, that the thieves did fight one with the other, and did leave the bee-hive standing.

Upon a time went Owlglass with his mother to the dedication of the church.[9] And at the feast there he drank so much, did our good Owlglass, that he was tired, and he sought a place where he might lie down to sleep in peace. Then found he a yard where stood many bee-hives, and some were empty, and into one of these crept he privily and thought to sleep awhile; behold he slept from midday till midnight, and his mother thought surely that he had departed homeward again, as she nowhere could see him. That same night came two thieves and they had it in mind to steal a hive of honey, and they conferred together, in that they heard it said that the heaviest is also the best.

Then did they lift up one after the other to see the which might be the most heavy, and at last came they to the one in which lay good master Owlglass; and it was the heaviest of all. Then spake the one to the other, saying: "Here is the best among the bee-hives." So took they that one and carried it away, but wist not what good burden they bare. Good Master Owlglass, feeling the motion, thereupon awoke up, and heard what they said about stealing honey; and he rejoiced in himself to think what honey

9   Feasts of the Dedication. These feasts, common in Germany, were also not uncommon, even to the present century, in parts of England. They were held in the churchyard on the anniversary of the day of the parish church being dedicated for divine service. See in *Tom Brown's School Days* (p. 30), a recent eloquent country-book, for a mention of this as applying to Berkshire.

HOW OWLGLASS CATCHETH THE THIEVES.

they had stolen. It was now so dark that ye could not see your hand before ye, an if ye even held it up to your eyes. Then put Owlglass his hand from out of the bee-hive, and caught hold of the foremost thief by the hair and pulled it until he roared. And the thief was very angry at the one who was behind, and thought it was he who had plucked him by the hair. Then spake the one who was behind him, saying: "Dost thou dream, or goest thou to sleep? How could I pluck thee by the hair? Hardly, is it possible for me to hold the bee-hive with both my hands." Then laughed Owlglass within himself at what the thief said, and thought that the game would go better in a while after, and waited till they had got a fine distance further forward. Then put he out his hand again, and plucked the hindmost smartly by the hair; and the hindmost man became yet more angry and said: "Thou sayest I pluck thee by the hair and I bear the bee-hive till I break my neck, and now thou pluckest me by the hair thyself." Then answered the foremost: "I pull thee by the hair? thou liest in thy throat. I cannot see my way before my face, and yet sayest thou: I pluck thine hair, quotha!" Thus with many revilings did they carry the hive along. And, as they were thus quarreling the one with the other in great choler and wrath, Owlglass plucked the foremost one by the hair again, and that so hard that he knocked his head against the hive. Thereat grew he angry, and let down the hive, and took his fellow by the head. That did also the other, and did manfully resist the blows of his comrade. Then fought they until they fell down in the dark and neither of them could behold the other, for the darkness continued very thick. Thus lost they their way and fled asunder with a great cry, and the bee-hive stood in the place where they had left it. Then Owlglass lay down again at ease to sleep until dawn; and when that it was light he thanked his stars that by this adventure it was shown him that he should see the world. And then gat he up from out of the bee-hive and did take a road, which lay before him, having a good heart that by his wit, wisdom, and knavery, he would live a merry and happy life in his time, and not die unhonoured of those that should come after him.

The Twelfth Adventure.

How Owlglass for little money did have a singing bird for his dinner.

In no long time thereafter, came Owlglass to Würzburg and there entered he into a good inn. Now the host of the inn had a singing bird hanging up in the house by the which he set great price, for it could sing divers merry ditties and songs of marvellous choiceness. Then said Owlglass unto him: "What take ye for this bird!" Then the host, who was of a miserly mind, answered him a great sum, the which Owlglass would not give him, yet at last they agreed that Owlglass should have the bird for four shillings. Then spake Owlglass: "Take ye the bird and roast it for my dinner, I would fain have a bit of him." Thereat marvelled the host, and did much pity the bird; but his miserly love overcame him. Then was the bird killed, plucked, and made ready. When that it was roasted, the landlord brought it on a dish to Owlglass; then spake Owlglass, and commanded the host that he should cut him therefrom a piece for six pennies; for he had not said he would pay for a whole bird, but only for a part thereof which he was fain to eat. Thereat marvelled the host still more, yet what could he say thereupon. He that is wise sayeth but little when the beguiler is nigh at hand, so the host held his tongue and the knave Owlglass departed thence in haste.

The Thirteenth Adventure.

How Owlglass did eat the roasted chicken from off the spit.

In the land of Brunswick there lieth a village, within the government of Magdeburg, and the name of it is called Budenstadt; thither came Owlglass and did present himself unto the priest there, and the priest, thinking our wise and pious master Owlglass a good and proper fellow, did then hire him for a servant in his house, but little did he know him. And the priest spake unto him, saying that he should have a good time of it and a good service. Also should he have meat and drink as good as his maid-servant, and all that he did should be done with half labour. Then did Master Owlglass agree with him, and said that he would do according to his word. Then he saw that the cook had but one eye. On that day took she two young chickens and she put them on the spit to roast over the fire. And she bade Owlglass turn, and so he did; and when the chickens were roasted, he brake one away off from the spit, and did eat it without any bread, for he remembered well what the priest had told him as to faring as well as himself and the maid-servant, and he thought it might be that he would lose his part of the dinner. And when that it was dinner-time, there came into the kitchen the one-eyed cook-maid to baste the chickens. Then beheld she but one chicken on the spit. Then spake she to Owlglass: "Behold, there were two chickens on the spit, and now there is but one, and tell me now where is the fellow that was beside it." Then answered Owlglass: "Woman, do but open your other eye, and you will behold the other chicken on the spit." Now when he thus spake of the want of her eye, she waxed wroth, and ran unto the priest, and said unto him that he might look how his new serving-man was doing. That she had put two chickens on the spit, and lo! there was but one at this time. And she said: "Then he mocked me, and said that I had but one eye." Thereat went the priest into the kitchen, and spake unto Owlglass, saying: "Hearest thou, Owlglass! wherefore didst thou mock my serving-maid? I see well that only one chicken is now upon the spit, and yet know I truly that there were two. Where then is now the other?" Then said Owlglass: "It is yet thereon; open both your eyes, and you will well see that there be the twain upon the spit. So said I also to thy maid, and thereat grew she quite angry and wroth." Then the priest laughed, and said: "The serving-maid cannot open both her eyes, for in good truth she hath but one." Owlglass made answer to the priest, saying: "That sayest thou, not I." But then said the priest: "Yet it is so; but the one chicken is in any wise gone." Owlglass spake then and said: "That chicken have I eaten myself, according unto thy words. For ye said unto me that I should fare as well as your maid-servant; and much grief would it have caused me had ye eaten the chickens without me, and made your words vain and a lie. Therefore for your honour's sake have I eaten the chicken, that ye might not fall into evil reputation for speaking that which is untruth." Then the priest was content and said: "Dear serving-man, I care not for the roasted chicken; but after this time do ye always according to the will of my cook." And Owlglass said: "Yea, holy father and worshipful master, be it so done as you will." Then whatsoever the cook-maid commanded Owlglass that he should do, that did he but in the half. An if she did bid him to bring a pail of water from the well, he brought but the half thereof, and if he should fetch two faggots from the wood pile then brought he but one. And so did he, and she saw well that it was all performed in that she might be spited thereat. Then spake the priest once again unto him, and said: "Lo, my well beloved serving-man Owlglass, let

me tell ye that my maid doth complain right grievously of thee."
Thereat said Owlglass: "Yea, master, yet have I never done except
according unto thy words. For thou didst say, that all I did should
be done with but half labour. Well would your serving maid
desire to see with both eyes and yet hath she but one—which is
but half-seeing, and therefore did I but half-labour." And thereat
was the priest right merry, and laughed much; but his servant
was full of wrath, and said: "Master, an if ye keep yon knavish
rogue any longer then will I depart from ye." Thus came it that
the priest was fain to send Owlglass away, yet forgat he him not;
and it fortuned that the parish clerk died, so he made Owlglass
clerk in his room. Thus, by foolishness and little knaveries, do
men come in this world to dignities and honours.

The Fourteenth Adventure.

*How that Owlglass did publish abroad that he would fly
from off the roof of the town-house at Magdeburg.*

After that Owlglass had some time been clerk of the parish
at Budenstadt, came he into the great and famous town of
Magdeburg, and there did he fix upon the church doors letters of
great import, so that the name of Owlglass became well known
and noised abroad through the streets of that city of Magdeburg;
and it was in the mouths of all the gossips, that the noble Master
Owlglass did purpose the doing of some marvellous strange feat.
And so it came to pass, that when the people were all full of great
wonder, that Owlglass spake unto them, saying: "I will flee down
through the air from the roof of the town-house." Thereat was
there a great outcry through the city; and both young and old did
in great multitude crowd unto the market-place, that by them
might this most marvellous wonder be seen; for, in the memory

of man, had not any person ever done so strange a thing before, nor had without wings so fled down through the air from that high place.

Then came Owlglass and stood upon the roof of the town-house, and did make motion with his arms, waving them hither and thither, as if he would flee down. And all the people gazed at his motion in great marvel, for they thought he would flee down presently. Thereat laughed Owlglass right merrily, and said unto the people: "Truly thought I, that nowhere in the world was there a fool so great as am I. Yet here in this city do I well see that ye are almost every one of ye fools; for when that ye did say that I could flee down from where I stand, then believed I ye not. I am not a goose, nor a bird, nor have I either feathers or wings to flee with, without the which can nobody flee. Therefore manifestly now do ye well see, that it is a deceit and a lie."

Then came he down away from the roof of the town-house in the same manner that he had gone up, and left the people standing. And some of them laughed, and others said: "Although he is both knave and fool, yet hath he spoken the truth." Thus is it with many besides the people of Magdeburg, who rush eagerly to believe that the which they might see is most plainly untrue; while what is possible and within their means to make them good sport, and serve them with good service, that neglect they with great scorn and contempt.

The Fifteenth Adventure.

How Owlglass did cure the sick folks in the hospital at Nürnberg in one day, and what came thereafter.

On a time came Owlglass to Nürnberg, where he did again set upon the church doors letters of great import, in the which he did publish abroad that he was a learned physician, more learned than in the world had yet been known; and that in all sicknesses, whosoever should turn to him should have content and his health again.

Now in the hospital at the town were there a multitude of people, who lay sick unto death, and of them did the master of that house crave in great truth to be relieved. Right verily would this benevolent man have given them their health and made them whole, and, if he could, have got ridden of them in the house. Then went he unto Owlglass, the learned physician, and spake with him, asking him whether he could, as in his letters he set forth, work such marvellous cures. And Owlglass answered and said: "Yea, if that the hospital-master would give unto him two hundred pieces." Then upon that conference did the master agree and promise him the money; and Owlglass said unto him, that he would not receive from him one penny, if the people did not all, within a few days, leave the hospital of their own desiring and action. Thereat was the master of the hospital very content, and gave unto Owlglass twenty pieces as a hansell.

Thereafter went Owlglass into the hospital, and took with him two servants; and he asked of each person that was sick, what it was that he lay sick of, and they answered. And at the last he said unto each, that he should not betray the secret which he should then tell unto them, and that swore they all. Then he spake unto each secretly, saying: "If that I should make ye whole, and give back unto all health and strength, then must I needs burn one of ye into powder, the which to mingle with your drink and give you to swallow, and with that will ye be made whole. Now I will take from among ye the one that is most sick, and him will I burn to powder. And I will stand at the door of the hospital, with the master of the hospital near at hand, and I will cry with a loud voice: 'He that is not sick, let him now go forth from the house quickly.' And that one which is last within the hospital door, him will I take. Forget ye not that in your sleep."

HOW OWLGLASS TURNETH DOCTOR.

Thus it came to pass, that all did remember his words; and when he stood with the master at the door, the sick and lame, and halt and dying, all came forth in haste, for none would be that one who should be burned in fire. So the hospital was quite empty, for many which had not for ten years arisen from their beds, now found their legs and departed thence.

Then did Owlglass demand from the master of the hospital that he should receive his reward, and the master with gracious thanks did present it unto him; then rode he forth from that city, and returned not again. In three days thereafter, came all the sick folk back again unto the hospital, and complained sorely of their sickness. Then said the master: "What will ye? Have I not brought unto ye a physician of skill, who did marvellously make you whole, that ye could all depart hence?" Then the sick folk discovered to the master the knavery that Owlglass had done, in that he had threatened them, that the last that should depart should be burned. So the master of the hospital perceived that he had been beguiled of Owlglass, and the sick folk abode in the house: yet was the money lost. Owlglass still was a great physician, for he had for three days cured them; and how many learned doctors are there who cure not in any wise?

The Sixteenth Adventure.

How Owlglass bought bread according to the proverb: "To him that hath bread is bread given."

Trusty faith giveth bread. And now that Owlglass had deceived the hospital-master, came he unto Halberstadt, and went round about the market, and saw that it was cold and winter time. Thought he, cold and hard is the winter, thereto bloweth a strong wind, and thou hast often heard that to him that hath bread is bread given. Then for a few pence buyeth Owlglass bread, borroweth also a table, and sitteth down in the front of St. Stephen's Dome. There held he up his knavery so long until a dog came by, the which caught me up a loaf from the table, and ran toward the cathedral court. While Owlglass ran after the dog, there passed by a sow with ten young pigs; these overthrew the table, and each, seizing a loaf, departed.

Then laughed Owlglass and said: "Now do I see that the words are not true: 'To him that hath bread is bread given;' for mine is taken." Thereat he departed from Halberstadt unto Brunswick.

The Seventeenth Adventure.

How Owlglass became a doctor, and did cure many folk.

The City of Frankfort is a great and handsome city, and in it do dwell many worshipful burghers, whose riches are many, and they eat and drink much, as is the custom with citizens; thus it fortunes that they are often ill. No marvel therefore that in Frankfort abide many doctors, who gain much money. Owlglass when that he came there, by his ready wit soon perceived the better part to take, and hired himself to be a doctor's man, and soon it was meet that he should go with his master to visit the patients. The good Owlglass would much have desired to know something of the names on the bottles which stood in the house of his master; but that could he not do, and therefore of all that his master did he could learn nothing but that when people were sick, they should drink warm water and be blooded. It fortuned in no long time thereafter, that his master had on a sudden to take a journey, in such wise that he had no time to tell the patients thereof. Then spake he unto Owlglass saying: "Go thou about the city unto the sick, and say unto them that in no long time shall I return unto them."

Yet the cunning Master Owlglass followed not his master's saying, but put on his head the wig of his master, and on his shoulders he bare his mantle. Then, with a grave and noble demeanour, he departed unto the houses of the sick patients who sent for him. When that he arrived, he sat gravely down with a serious face, felt their pulses, and after much heavy thought, he ordered them always to be blooded and to drink warm water. Thereafter he departed from them.

Then, marvellous to tell, all his patients grew wondrously well in no long time, and they paid him much money for his pains. When that his master returned, the knavery of Owlglass was soon discovered, and he was fain to depart. Yet such was the wisdom of good Master Owlglass, that it is related that his master thereafter followed no other art than had been thus invented by Owlglass; and after that time the doctor became famous, and wrote a large book upon the virtue of warm water and blood-letting.

The Eighteenth Adventure.

*How that Owlglass became a drawer of teeth and cured
all by a wondrous pill.*

As Owlglass was going along the road, he met upon the high-way, a man whose face was overcome with misery. Owl-glass thereat gazed upon him for a season, and after some time spake unto him these words: "Worthy fellow! thou dost seem so wrapped in melancholic humour, would'st tell me what aileth thee?" "Everything in the wide world," the other made answer: "for I have no money, which is the joy of all worldly business; for it maketh learned, maketh noble, maketh lovely, and merry. Also, maketh it an end of hunger and thirst which now sorely assail me." Then Owlglass bethought himself for a while, and presently took up from the next field some clay, whereof he made little pills, which he then wrapped in pieces of paper, and said to his comrade: "Be of good cheer, friend! Soon will we have money. Lo, in yonder city, the towers of which we can now see, are there fools in number great. Enter thou in before me, and there go for-ward till thou seest the best inn in the town, and therein do thou stay. At dinner stay thou as long as thou canst and be merry; yet after a while do thou cry out in great agony, as if thou hadst the tooth-ache. Then will I not be far from thee; and when I come in, be thou ready, and make answer to everything I say: 'Yea.' But do not thou let it be perceived that thou knowest me."

Then did the twain go forward into the town, and as Owlglass had commanded, so all things came to pass. Owlglass told the people that he was a dentist of great skill, and they called him to the man who was ill. Then took he from his pocket the pills which he had made of the clay, and laid one in the man's mouth. "Art not thou well now"? said he unto him. "Yea, truly," answered the other, "all the pain is gone." Then all the people in the inn came round the doctor in great multitude, and demanded that he should sell unto them his pills. And Owlglass sold what he had for a great sum of money, and an he had had clay enough he could have sold many more. Then shared he the gain with his comrade, and they departed hastily from that place.

The Nineteenth Adventure.

*How that Owlglass did at Brunswick hire him to a baker,
and did there bake owls and monkeys.*

It fortuned upon a time that Owlglass came into Brunswick city, and unto an inn where bakers met together; and hard by lived a baker, who called upon Owlglass to enter into his house, and made inquiry of him, as to the business he might follow. Then answered Owlglass to the baker, and spake, for our noble and well beloved master of jests was wily, and, indeed, all things unto all men: "I am a baker's man." Thereat said the baker: "Even now have I not any man in my house to serve me; wilt thou come to me, for I have need of thee?" Owlglass at that answered: "Yea." And when that he had been with him two days, the baker commanded him to bake at eventide, for that he could not help him until the morning. Then said Owlglass: "But what would ye have me to bake?" Thereat waxed the baker wroth, for he was a man soon hot i' the head, and he made answer in scorn, and said: "Art a baker's man, and askest thou what ye should bake? What do ye bake? Owls and monkeys bake ye?" And thereafter gat he him to bed.

Then departed Owlglass into the bake-room, and made the dough into nought but the shape of owls and monkeys, and these did he bake in the oven. At morning time arose the master baker, and went into the bake-room to aid his man. Then cometh he, and findeth neither rolls nor loaves, but rather a goodly mass of owls and monkeys. And he opened his mouth in great rage and said unto Owlglass: "What is it that thou hast baken?" And Owlglass did answer him and said: "Verily have I done that which thou didst tell me to do." And the baker, in great wroth, said: "What shall I do with this foolish knave? Such bread will no one have?" And therewith took he him by the head, and said unto him: "Pay me for the dough thou hast spoiled!" Then said Owlglass:

"And if I pay ye for the dough, will the goods be mine?" And the master answered: "What care I for such bread?" So Owlglass paid the baker for his dough, and he took the owls and monkeys in a basket, and he carried them away unto the inn, the sign of which was the Wild Man. And Owlglass thought within himself: "Thou hast often heard it said, that to Brunswick canst thou bring nothing novel or strange, but therefrom mayst thou draw great profit for thy pains." And it was Saint Nicholas' even. Then stood Owlglass with his store hard by the church gate; and he sold all his owls and monkeys at great price, and therefrom drew he a much greater profit than what he had paid unto the baker for his dough. This was noised about, and soon came it heard of the baker, who waxed very angry thereupon, and he ran unto Saint Nicolas' Church, and would have demanded either his share, or the charges of baking. But Owlglass had already departed with the money, and the baker might look far and wide for him. This feat of our good exemplar showeth plainly, that there is nothing so vain or foolish in this world, but that it hath profit contained within it for those who study to arrive thereat.

The Twentieth Adventure.

How Owlglass did again hire him unto a baker, and how he bolted meal in the moon's light.

Thereafter departed Owlglass, and wandered hither and thither in the land; and at last came he toward Oltzen, and entered into the village there. And when he was besought of the people to say what trade he exercised, he told them that he was a baker. Then did a master baker in the village hire him; and when that Owlglass was with him present in his house, his master did make ready that he should bake, and he spake unto Owlglass, and did enjoin him that he should bolt the meal, so that it might be prepared against the morning. Then Owlglass answered, and said: "Master, I would fain have a candle, that I may see with, and so diligently do your bidding." "Nay," answered the baker; "but that will I not do. No candle shalt thou have, nor have I at any time given unto my serving-men any such candle. Always did they bolt the meal in the moon's light, and verily must thou likewise do this. And this charge I thee to do." And Owlglass made answer, saying: "An if your former servants did bolt the meal in the moon's light, truly then will I also do it." At that was the master content, and he gat him to bed for a short while.

Thereafter taketh good Master Owlglass the bag, and he openeth the window and putteth forth the bag, until the moon's light doth shine thereupon, and then letteth he all the meal fall out on the ground where that the moon shone. And in the morning cometh the master, who desireth to bake, and he findeth Owlglass still casting out the meal. And the baker marvelled much when that he beheld Owlglass, for Owlglass was white with the meal. Then said the master, who was full of anger: "What do ye here, ye knave? Think ye that yon meal cost me nought, that ye throw it in the dirt there?"

Then answered Owlglass: "Did not ye command me that I should, without a candle, bolt the meal in the moon's shine, and have not I fulfilled this according to your words?" Then said the baker: "I said you should bolt the meal by the moon's light." And Owlglass answered him: "Be then of good cheer, master; verily thy meal is bolted both in and by the moon's light, and with much pains and weariness have I done this labouring. Nor is there much lost thereby; scarce a handful. Soon will I gather it up again, and the meal will not be in any wise made the worse." Thereat sayeth the baker: "In that time that thou dost gather up the meal, will it grow too late to make the dough, and then fall to baking." Then said Owlglass: "Behold, master, I know a piece of counsel, how we may bake as soon as our neighbour yonder. His dough lieth ready in the trough, and I will go thither and quickly fetch it, and carry our meal thither in place thereof." Thereat grew the master of Owlglass right angry, and said unto him: "May the evil one have thee! Get thee to the gallows-tree, thou knave, and fetch thee thence the first thing that thou dost find; and let the neighbour's dough lie where it be." "Yea," answered Owlglass.

Then departed he out of the house and went unto the gallows-tree, and there lay the skull of a thief, which had fallen down. This took Owlglass and bare it unto his master, and brought it into his house and said: "Here bring I from the gallows-tree the first thing that I did find. Wherefore would ye have this? Of a truth know I not what may be the best thing it is fit for." And then the baker spake in anger, and said: "Lo! bringest thou me nothing more than this?" Then Owlglass answered and said: "If that any other thing had been there, I would also have brought it for thee; but no other thing was lying there." Then waxed the baker more wroth, and said unto Owlglass: "Behold, thou hast robbed the law and the gallows; that will I tell unto the burghmaster, and thou shalt answer it."

And the baker departed from out of the house to the market-place, and Owlglass followed him. So hastily, howsoever, went the baker, that he looked not round, and knew not that Owlglass was following him. Then stood the baker before the burghmaster, who was on the market-place, and he began to make complaint against Owlglass. And Owlglass was lithe and nimble, and when that the baker began his words, he stood hard by and opened his eyes very wide. And when the baker beheld Owlglass, he clean forgat, in his anger, what it might be that he would make complaint of, and said to Owlglass, with great malice: "What wilt thou have?" Owlglass made answer to him: "I desire not to have anything, than that I should behold what complaint you make against me to the burghmaster. And that I might see your words, do I open mine eyes very wide, for words are most difficult to see." Then said the baker: "Get out of my sight, thou knavish beguiler, I desire nought else!" Owlglass then said: "If that I should get out of thy sight, then needs must I get my body into thine eyes; and if ye shut your eyes, must I come through thy nostrils." Then went the burghmaster on his way, for he perceived that it was but foolishness; and he left them both standing. And when Owlglass saw that, he followed the baker, and spake unto him, saying: "Master, when shall we bake? It is time now, for the sun shineth no more." Then departed he, and left the baker standing in the market-place.

The Twenty and First Adventure.

Telleth of what manner of thinking was Owlglass, and how he formed his life according unto principles of virtue and goodness.

Of our most noble and beloved Master Owlglass, have I now told ye not a few truthful and diverting histories and adventures; but, yet have I not said any word in respect of his ways of thinking, gathered by great experience out of many lands, in his continual travel to and fro, up and down in his country. Now he loved much to be always among friends and in company, and as long as he lived were there three things, which with great avoidance he did always run from and leave undone. The first thing was, that he never did ride a horse which was gray, but at all times a bay horse, for the gray horse did mind him of an ass, the which animal held he in great scorn. The second thing which he could not bear to be with him was the company of little children, for that wheresoever he found them, there was more care taken of them than of his own noble person. The third thing was, that he would never lie in an inn where that he found an old mild host; for a host that was old and mild held Owlglass in but little esteem, and was thereto also for the most part nought but a fool.

Every morn when that he rose up from his bed, he blessed himself against healthy victual, great happiness, and strong drink, in which three blessings none can deny that he was a wise man. And when it fortuned that he passed by an apothecary's house, did he bless himself against healthy victual, for it mote truly be a healthy place whence victual might issue; yet it was a sign of sickness before. Good fortune was it when a stone fell from the house top and struck him not down; for then might he of a truth cry, with great praise: "If that I had myself been standing on that place, so would it have fallen upon me and killed me;" and such fortune would he most willingly not have. The strong drink against which he blessed himself, was water, for it be so strong as soon to drive round great mill-wheels, and to the good fellow that drinketh thereof cometh death. It was also told of Owlglass that he wept always when that he did go down a hill, and he laughed when he climbed one. For truly wist he, in the descending, that soon would he come again unto a mountain, while in climbing knew he that soon would he come again to the top, whence to pass down into the valley. In fine weather, or at a time when summer began, then did he also weep with many tears, and when that winter approached, laughed he. And ye that read herein may, in your wisdom, answer the reason why he did this thing.

The Twenty and Second Adventure.

How that Owlglass did hire him to the Count of Anhalt to blow the horn on a tower, and when that enemies did approach, then blew he not; and when that they came not, then blew he.

Not long thereafter, came Owlglass unto the Count of Anhalt, and he did hire him unto the count as a tower watchman. And the count at that time had enemies in great multitude, so that he had with him in number not small, both horsemen and foot folk, unto whom he must needs give meat and drink every day. And Owlglass sat up on the tower, and he was clean forgat of them that should give him provision. And on that day it came to pass, that the enemy did, in strong force, come unto the town and castle of the count's grace, and they took therefrom all the cattle, and drave them off. Owlglass then lay still upon the tower, and he looked through the window and made not any outcry, either in that he blew, or in that he did cry aloud. But it did come unto the ears of the count that he heard the enemy, and with his folk he quickly gat him forth, and pursued them and drave them before his face. Then saw some of the folk, that Owlglass lay in the window of the tower, and laughed. Thereat did the count cry out unto him: "Wherefore liest thou on the tower and art so still?" And Owlglass made answer unto the count, saying: "Ere dinner time do I not with grace and comfort ever delight in crying out." Then cried the count back unto him: "Wilt thou, when the enemy cometh, blow thy horn?" Thereat said Owlglass: "Enemies dare I

not blow, or would the field be full, and with the cows would they depart. And if I blew enemies a second time, in such multitude would they come, that they would fight with thee, and overcome thee even in thine own gate." Therewith ended they their conference. Then departed the count in great haste after his enemies, and contended with them with much strife; and Owlglass was again forgotten as he lay upon his tower.

But the count was greatly content with his prowess, and with him brought back from the field of battle a goodly heap of pork, the which did they thereafter cut up, and some roasted they and other did they boil. And Owlglass would most willingly have had thereof as he sat on his tower. Then did he begin to plan how that he might get thereof, and he did watch when that it should be dinner time. And when that it had become dinner time, he began to blow his horn, and to cry with a loud voice: "The foe cometh! The foe cometh!" Then the count gat him up with his arms, and put on his harness, and took his weapons, and departed quickly forth from the castle into the field. Thereat rejoiced our noble Master Owlglass, and quickly did he get him down from the tower, and came unto the count's table, and took therefrom boiled and roast, in the which delighted he, and he returned back on his steps, and gat him to the tower. And, when that the horsemen and foot folk came again unto the castle, and of enemies had found not a hair, then murmured they one to the other, saying: "This hath the watchman done to mock us with great scorn and knavery." And the count cried aloud unto Owlglass, and said unto him: "Wherefore hast thou become foolish and mad?" And Owlglass said: "If that hunger and thirst drive mad, then do I not marvel at my madness." Thereat said the count: "Why didst thou blow on thy horn for enemies, and there were none?" Then spake Owlglass, and made answer unto the count, saying: "Whereas it fortuned that no enemies were present, I thought in my mind that it would be well to blow on my horn, for that they might come." Then said the count unto him: "Thou goest about to deceive us with knavish beguiling. When that the enemy cometh, thou wilt not blow; yet when no enemy is nigh at hand, then blowest thou. Of a truth, it is a matter of treachery." Therewith relieved he Owlglass of lying in the tower, and appointed thereunto another watchman.

Then came it to pass, that Owlglass should run with the foot folk to strive in battle with the enemy. And thereat was good Master Owlglass moved to anger, and cast about in his mind to discover how he might be relieved, and obtain other service. And when the count's folk departed out from the castle to fight with the foe, then was Owlglass always the last man; and when they returned back unto the castle, was he truly likewise the first man to enter therein. Then spake the count unto him, saying: "How shall I understand this thing? Wherefore art thou always last to depart from the castle, and the first to return back again?" And Owlglass answered and said: "Let not thine anger fall upon me, noble lord; for when that thou and all thy people sat and ate and drank, with great feasting, then lay I upon the tower and fasted so that I fainted thereby, and lost much strength. If therefore ye should be minded, that I should be the first in the field to encounter the foe, I pray thee that ye do let me eat now that with strength may I be filled, and then will I do it, and ye shall perceive that I shall be the first against the enemy and the last to depart from him." "I mark well," spake the count, "that thou wilt be a long time in doing this thing, and as long as thou didst sit on the tower." Thereat said Owlglass: "That which belongeth of right unto a man do others take from him most willingly." And the count said: "Long shalt thou not be my servant," and therewith gave him leave to depart. And thereat rejoiced Owlglass, for he cared not every day to fight with the enemy.

The Twenty and Third Adventure.

How that Owlglass did have golden shoes struck unto his horse's feet.

Owlglass was one of those men that the fame of his holy doings came unto the ears of many great lords. The princes, also, loved him much, and did give unto him garments, horses, money, and provision. And he came unto the King of Denmark, who said unto him, that he should do for him a wondrous strange thing, having his horse shod with the best shoes that could be found. Then answered Owlglass to the king, and spake unto him and asked him: "If that he should believe him?" And the king answered and said: "Yea, and if he did according unto his word, it should come to pass as he had promised him." Then Owlglass did ride his horse unto the goldsmith's house, and there had golden shoes, with nails of silver, struck unto his horse's feet, and gat him home again unto the king's presence, and asked him if that he would pay for the shoeing of his horse? The king said: "Yea, that would be right truly;" and said unto his treasurer, and commanded him, that he should pay for the shoeing of the horse of Owlglass. The treasurer thought that it had been done by a blacksmith. And Owlglass led him unto the goldsmith's house, and the goldsmith demanded of him one hundred golden marks therefor. The treasurer would not pay this; but went and told the king thereof. Then sent the king for Owlglass, and said unto him: "Owlglass, how dear hast thou made this horse shoeing to be? If that all my horses were shod as thou hast had thine, soon should I have to sell my country and my people!" Then Owlglass answered and spake unto him: "My gracious lord and king, thou didst say I should have my horse to be shod with the best shoes, and have I not done according unto thy words, for would ye have better shoeing than silver and gold." Then said the king: "Thou art my dearest servant, thou dost that I tell thee to do." And the king laughed at the merry jest, and did pay the hundred marks. Then Owlglass brake off the golden shoes from his horse's feet, and had shoes of iron struck on, and he abode with the king unto the day of his death.

The Twenty and Fourth Adventure.

*How that Owlglass did have a great contention before the
King of Poland with two other fools.*

While that the noble Prince Casimir, King of Poland, yet lived, there came unto him at his court, good Master Owlglass. And Casimir (blessed be his memory!) did have two fools there, who, in knavery, could not be overcome. And the king of Poland had heard much said of Owlglass, that, in truth, he was not in any way to be quipped or deceived. Nor did Owlglass agree with the fools of the king, and that beheld the king right soon. Then spake the king unto Owlglass and the two fools, saying: "Behold! unto that one of ye the which can wish the greatest wish will I give a coat and twenty gold pieces thereto, and this shall be within my presence." Then said the first fool: "I would have that heaven were nothing but paper, and the sea nothing but ink, that therewith might I in figures write down how much money I would have, and that it came unto me." The second spake, saying: "I would have as many towers and castles as there be stars in heaven, so that therein might I hold all the money that my fellow here would have." Then was it time that Owlglass should speak, and the king thought that in truth he could not wish anything greater. But Owlglass opened his mouth and spake, saying: "I, in truth, would desire that after ye two have made me your heir, that the king would yet on this day hang ye both." Thereat laughed the king right merrily, and Owlglass won the coat and the twenty gold pieces, with the which he departed in joy.

The Twenty and Fifth Adventure.

How Owlglass did make confession to a priest, and took from him a silver box.

On a time it happened that Owlglass thought to go to confession, for his sins were many, and therewith was his soul sore laden, so that he meditated much on the badness of his ways. Then came he to the church, where sate the priest in the confessional, and before him stood a silver box, by which he set great store. Then Owlglass began a long speech, in the which he told the good priest his heavy sins, so great in number; and at last, the saying of Owlglass was so long, that the priest did lean back and slept, for he was weary of the knaveries of Owlglass. Then Owlglass took the box away, and did put it in pouch.

When that the priest again awoke he did rub his eyes with his fingers, and spake unto Owlglass, saying: "Where stood we, my son?" Then answered Owlglass, and said unto the priest: "We stood at the eighth commandment, father." Then said the priest: "Speak on, my son; fear not, nor in any wise conceal what lieth upon thy conscience." Then continued Owlglass, saying: "Alas! holy father, on a time I did steal a silver box from a person, and I will now give it unto thee." Then said the priest: "Nay, my son, stolen goods will I not have; give the box unto him that owneth it." "That would I already do," answered Owlglass; "but he refused me, saying that he would not receive it." Thereat spake the priest, and said: "Then canst thou keep it with a good conscience; go in peace, thy sins are forgiven thee."

Then Owlglass departed, and sold the box unto a Jew for several pieces of silver. But the priest slept not again in confession; and thus Owlglass gat for others more sins forgiven than before, which did great good unto all men.

The Twenty and Sixth Adventure.

How that Owlglass was forbidden the dukedom of Lunenburg, and how he did cut open his horse and stand therein.

In the land of Lunenburg, near unto Zell, did Owlglass work some great knavery on a time. Therefore did the Duke of Lunenburg forbid him the land; and he gave commandment to his servants, if that Owlglass should be found therein they should seize him, and, without any mercy or shrift, hang him up. Yet did not Owlglass in any manner forsake the land, or in his journeyings avoid it, so as to come round through any other country; but when that it came in his way to be convenient to pass through Lunenburg, did he nevertheless ride or walk through it when he would.

Thus it came to pass on a time, that Owlglass had much reason to ride through Lunenburg, and it fortuned that as he was riding along, he saw the duke with many folk riding the same way. Then thought he within himself: "Lo! it is the duke; and if that thou dost hasten away to fly from before his face, then with their horses will they soon come up with thee, and they will take thee; then will the duke with great anger come and command them to hang thee up unto a tree." Then did he confer within himself what thing it were best that he should do; and he gat him down from his horse, and took a knife, and quickly cut open the horse's belly, casting forth the entrails, and then gat he in and stood within the four legs in the midst. Then when the duke came riding by with his horsemen, and gat to the place where sat Owlglass in his horse's belly, then the servants of the duke spake unto him, saying: "Behold, gracious lord, here sitteth Owlglass within his horse." Thereat did the duke ride up to Owlglass, and say unto him: "Art thou there, Owlglass? What bringeth thee into my country when that I did warn thee with great punishment not to come thither? Did I not say, if ye came therein I would have thee hanged on a tree?" Then said Owlglass to the duke: "Noble and gracious lord, I pray thee that thou wilt be pleased to spare my life, for I have not done so evilly as to be punished with death." Then said the duke unto Owlglass: "Come thee hither unto me, and do thou make thy innocence plain unto me, or what meanest thou that thou dost so stand in the belly of thy horse?" And Owlglass answered, and said: "Most high and gracious lord! have I not heard it always said of all that from old time between his own four posts is a man safe? Now do I stand in such wise between my four posts, as ye can see; for I feared the displeasure with the which I knew in my heart that ye would visit me," Then did the duke laugh right merrily, and said unto Owlglass: "Yea, this time will I excuse thee. But wilt thou henceforward stay far away from my land, nor enter it at any time?" And Owlglass answered and said: "Gracious lord, so mote it be as ye would have." Thereat rode the duke away from him, saying: "Stay as ye now be." But Owlglass leaped quickly forth from his horse's skin, and spake unto the dead horse: "I thank thee, my good beast, for thou hast preserved my neck from great danger of the halter, and through thy death am I made alive. From a hunted donzel hast thou changed me into a gentleman; therefore, lie thou there, for it is better that the crows eat thee than that they should tear me." Then departed he out of the land on foot.

The Twenty and Seventh Adventure.

How that Owlglass did buy an inheritance in land from a boor, and how he sate therein in a cart.

In no long time thereafter came Owlglass again into the land of Lunenburg, and he tarried in a village near unto Zell, until the time came in the which the Duke should again ride that way. And it came to pass that a boor did come by Owlglass as he went along to plough his land. And by that time had Owlglass gotten him another horse, and a cart therewith, and he came unto the boor, and spake unto him, saying: "Whose land is this that thou ploughest?" Then answered the boor and said: "Truly is it mine, and I did have it in inheritance from my forbears." Thereat said Owlglass unto the boor: "What money wilt thou have for as much earth as would fill my cart?" Then said the boor: "Truly will I have a shilling therefor." And Owlglass gave unto him what he demanded, and filled his cart therewith, and crept into it, and drove his cart into Zell unto the castle there, unto the Aller water. And when that it came to pass that the duke rode by, did he behold Owlglass as he sate in the cart with the earth up to his shoulders. Then spake the duke unto Owlglass, and said unto him: "How comest thou here again? Have I not forbidden thee to come into my land, and did not I say thou shouldst suffer death? And now, after that I pardoned thee when thou didst stand in thy horse, thou dost again tempt my wrath with thee?" Then spake Owlglass unto the duke in answer, saying: "My gracious lord, I am not in your land but in mine own, wherein do I sit; and I bought it of a boor for a shilling, and rightfully could he sell it, for from his forbears hath he inherited it. So is this truly my land." Then spake the duke, and laughed the while: "Depart ye now straightway with thy land out of my land, and come not again, or will I have thee hung up, with thy horse and thy cart beside." Then leaped Owlglass on to his horse from out of the cart, and left the cart with his land standing before the castle.

The Twenty and Eighth Adventure.

How that Owlglass painted the forbears of the Landgrave of Hessen, and told him that an if he were ignobly born, he might not behold his painting.

Many marvellous things did Owlglass bring to pass in the land of Hessen. After that he had journeyed up and down in the country of Saxony, and his fame had spread so abroad that no longer dare he work his knaveries and beguilings in that land, came our worshipful Master forth from Saxony, and did enter into the land of Hessen, and came therein unto Marburg, unto the Landgrave where that he kept his court. Then inquired the landgrave of Owlglass, what manner of man he was and what he could do. Then answered Owlglass, and said: "Lord, I know the arts, and that manner of man am I, and your humble servant." Thereat rejoiced the landgrave greatly, for he thought that Owlglass was an alchymist, and in alchymy had the landgrave much delight. Then spake he unto him, saying: "Art thou an alchymist?" And Owlglass answered: "Nay, that am I not, in good sooth, for of dross make not I gold, but rather quite the other thing. Yet am I a painter, the equal unto whom can be nowhere found in any country, for my work is far better than the work of any other painter." Then said the landgrave: "Come, let us now look upon some of thy work." And Owlglass said: "Yea, my lord." And he had with him some paintings cunningly devised, the which he had brought out of Flanders. These took he from his wallet, and displayed them before that prince. These pleased the lord much, and he said unto Owlglass: "Worshipful sir painter, what money will ye have if that ye would paint on the wall of our castle hall the story of the family of the landgraves of Hessen, and how that through them I became friendly unto and with the King of Hungary, and other lords and princes, and how long the land of Hessen hath been established? And that must ye tell me in the wise that will be most costly and precious." Then answered Owlglass: "Behold, most gracious prince, if that ye would have it so rarely done, it might truly cost not less than four hundred marks." Then answered the landgrave, and said unto Owlglass: "Master, an if you do but make it rarely, the money shall not fail, nor will we forget to reward thee as ye shall deserve." Then did Owlglass consent to become the painter of the picture; and thereat gave the landgrave unto Owlglass one hundred marks so that he might buy colours therewith.

But when that Owlglass came with three servants he had found, to see what the work was which was to be done, he gat him unto the landgrave, and spake unto him, and entreated him, saying: "Behold, noble prince, I would crave a grace from ye, which I would ask that ye should grant unto me." Then spake the landgrave: "Yea, that I will grant thee. Speak on." And Owlglass answered, and said: "The grace I crave from thee is, that, while my work is going forward, no one shall enter without that they ask of me whether they may enter therein." And therewith the landgrave granted Owlglass the grace he desired. Then conferred Owlglass with his men, and said unto them, that they must take an oath unto him not to betray him; and so did they. And he said unto them, that they need not do any kind of labour, but they might play at tables and chess and other merry pastimes. And thereat were the men content; nor was it greatly marvellous that in such wise they should be, for Owlglass did promise to pay them for serving him after this manner.

Then it came to pass, after some three or four weeks had gone by, that the landgrave craved much to see in what measure the

painting of Owlglass was ready, and whether, of a truth, it did resemble the ensamples which Owlglass had shewn unto him, which were so goodly and fair. Thereat gat he him to Owlglass, and said unto him: "Alas, most worshipful master, I would fain come into the hall and see in what measure my picture doth grow ready." Then Owlglass spake unto the landgrave, and answered him, and said: "Yea, and that shall ye also do. But I must tell unto thee a marvellous secret which doth touch all my painting, in that no one, if he be ignobly born, or not according unto the ordinance of Holy Church, can behold my painting to see it." The landgrave said thereafter: "Truly that is a marvellous thing." Yet, my masters, ye may perceive in that the landgrave was an alchymist, so had he also more belief in such affairs than cometh unto the lot of all men. And then went he with Owlglass into the hall, and there had Owlglass hanged up a white cloth, that he should have painted. And with a white wand did he point to the wall when that he had with his hand put the cloth somewhat aside, and then spake he to the landgrave, and said unto him: "Most noble landgrave, look upon this painting, so marvellous well done and with fair colours, and behold here in this corner he that was first lord of Hessen and earl of the land. And here perceive ye one that was an earl of Rome thereunto, and he had a princess and a wife, who was duchess of Bavaria and a daughter of the mild and good Justinian, who afterwards became emperor. And look ye, noble lord; of them was born Adolphus. And of Adolphus came William the Swart; and this William had a son Ludwig, who was named the Pious; and so forward until that we come down unto your lordship's grace. And I know well that there is no person living that can reprove my work, so curiously have I made it, and with such fair and goodly colours." Yet saw the lord nought before his face but the white wall, and he thought unto himself: "Though I see nothing but the wall, yet will I say nought unto the master, else will he know full well that I am not nobly born, but basely and vilely." Therefore said the landgrave unto Owlglass: "Learned and cunning master painter, your work pleaseth me marvellously well, yet is my understanding very small therein." Therefore departed he out of the hall.

And when that he did come unto the princess his wife, she spake unto him, and asked him, saying: "How goeth it with the master painter? Ye have seen his work and devices, and how are ye pleased therewith? Truly have I but small belief in him; for he seemeth unto me a rare and most cunning knave and beguiler." And the landgrave answered her: "I have shrewd trust in him; and therein is displayed great cunning and mastery: I like it well. Would it please thee also to look thereon?" And she said: "Yea, that it would." And the landgrave said: "Then, with the master's consent, shall ye do it." Then sent she for Owlglass, and said unto him, that she did desire to behold his painting. And that did Owlglass grant unto her; but he told her likewise the marvellous secret which did hang upon his painting. And they entered in, and with the princess came eight maidens of her women and her woman-fool, which did everywhere be in her company. And Owlglass put back the cloth with his hand, and with his wand told them the same story which he had told unto the landgrave. Yet perceived they nothing; but being ashamed, spake not any word, neither praising nor blaming the picture. But then did the woman-fool open her mouth, and spake, and said unto Owlglass: "Worshipful master, an if it be that I am basely born, yet see I nothing of thy device upon the wall." And Owlglass thought: "Now goeth the matter not so rarely on as before; for if the fools speak truth, then truly must I depart hence:" and laughed thereat within himself.

Thereafter departed the princess, and went unto her lord and husband, and he spake unto her, and asked her how that the work liked[10] her. And she answered and said: "Most gracious lord, it liketh me as well as it did you, and truly is most rare. But my woman-fool it liketh not; and she saith that she cannot see any painting there at all. And she and my maidens think that there lieth hid some knavish practice therein." Thereat began the landgrave to take counsel within himself, if it might be that he was beguiled; but he sent word unto Owlglass that he should make ready his work, for that all his court was coming to behold the picture, and that if any among them fortuned to be base-born, then should their lands be escheated unto the landgrave. Thereat gat him Owlglass unto his fellows and discharged them, and gave them money, and they departed. And then went he unto the treasurer, and of him gat he other hundred marks; and then went he forth from the castle, and so departed on his way.

And it came to pass that on the morrow the landgrave demanded where that his painter might be—but he had departed. Thereat went he with all his lords into the hall where that the master had exercised his cunning device, but there saw they no painting; so they spake no words, but kept their mouths shut. Thereat said the landgrave, for he beheld the sign which Owlglass did always write where that he had worked any knavery, which was that he wrote up the device of an owl and a glass: "Now do we know that we are beguiled; and with Owlglass have we but little for to be moved, but rather for the two hundred marks, but the loss thereof can we likewise bear. But a great knave is he, and must henceforth remain far from our lands."

Thus did our noble Master Owlglass everywhere teach wisdom unto the lieges; but from Marburg had he gat him forth, nor would he again have to do with the painter's mastery.

10. *i.e.* Pleased.

The Twenty and Ninth Adventure.

How that Owlglass was for little money well entertained
of two innkeepers.

It fortuned that in a village were there two innkeepers, who did with great hatred pursue each other, and they could not bear to live in friendship, or as neighbours should. And if it came to pass, that the one did have in his house more custom than the other, then was there much anger and envy therefrom, and they grew ever more enemies thereafter.

On a time it came to pass, that Owlglass came thither, although thereby he ran great danger. And he entered into the house of one of these twain, and he spake unto the host, and asked of him, whether for twelve pennies he might have wine? "Yea," answered the host, "that he might in good truth;" and went and brought him speedily a measure of wine. Thereafter asked Owlglass again, whether he might for twelve pennies have beef and salad? "Yea," said the host; and brought beef and salad, the which did Owlglass eat with rare enjoyment. And as he was eating, the cook carried a fowl by on a plate, and Owlglass saw it, and he called for the host, and asked him, if for twelve pennies he might have a part thereof? "Most truly," said the host. And behold his measure of wine was empty, and Owlglass moreover called the host unto him, and said: "Can I for twelve pennies again have wine?" "Yea," answered the host, and rejoiced in his good visitor, and brought him a fresh measure of wine. And Owlglass was full and fairly provisioned within, and he prepared to depart, and rose up, and he laid twelve pennies on the table, and then he would have departed out of the door. Thereat the host held him back, and said unto him, that the money was not enough, and that he must pay four times as much. "What mean ye?" said Owlglass. "Did not I ask ye every time, if that I might have for twelve pennies that which I required? And now would ye have much more? How mean ye? There is my debt, and is it to be laid unto my charges that ye have not understood me?" Then saw the host that it was most plain he had been beguiled; and he spake unto Owlglass, that he would forgive him the debt and add thereto the present of a piece of money, if that he would go unto his neighbour hard by and there work the same thing. Then Owlglass put the piece of money in his doublet, and laughed, and said unto the host: "Verily have I already done thus at your neighbour's house, and he it was that did give me a piece of money an if I would but come to you." And therewith departed our well beloved brother Owlglass, and the host marvelled with great marvel.

The Thirtieth Adventure.

How that Owlglass did tell his master how he might scape giving pork unto his neighbours.

On a time Owlglass was servant unto a boor, who was a man of great avarice, and did never like to give unto others anything he might have. Now it fortuned that he killed a pig, and as he had received from others pieces of bacon when that they killed, so now would they expect that he would give unto them in return. Then he spake unto Owlglass, saying: "Truly art thou of a quick wit and ready invention. Tell me how shall I escape giving unto my neighbours." Thereat said Owlglass: "In truth, nothing is more easy. Behold, when it is night-time hang thy pig without thy door upon a hook, and when that it cometh unto midnight take it secretly away, and make great complaint that it hath been stolen." And the boor did according unto the words of Owlglass, for he was content.

When that he came in the night to take his pig secretly away, he found it not, and did cry out woundily that robbers had taken it. And truly our good Master Owlglass had conveyed the pig away himself. And when he heard the boor cry, he came up to him, and asked what might have happened. And the boor answered Owlglass, and said: "The thieves have come and taken away my pig." Then answered Owlglass: "Excellently spake! So tell thou unto all thy neighbours." But the other said: "Nay; but the matter hath not ended as I desired. The pig hath truly been stolen." And Owlglass answered him: "An if ye speak thus well, all the town will believe you. Most excellent, by my halidom!" And although the boor would have persuaded Owlglass of the truth, did that great master only laugh. And thereafter did he tell unto the neighbours what he had advised; and no one would believe the boor.

The Thirty and First Adventure.

How that Owlglass conferred with the rector and masters of the University of Prague in Bohemia, and how he did make answer unto their questions, and therein came off most wisely.

And Owlglass departed and came unto the city of Prague in Bohemia, and there he set letters upon the church-doors, and therein said unto all that might read, that of a truth was he a most famous master, and one that could make answer unto all questions. And the rector and masters of the university heard that this learned man had come; and they were troubled thereat, and they took counsel how that they might put such questions unto him as he could not resolve, and thus might they cause him to be cast forth from the town with much mockery and shame. And so did they agree. And they sent the bedell of the university unto the inn where Owlglass lay, and charged the host that he should bring his guest into the chamber of the rector and masters; and he promised to do this thing. And they charged Owlglass that the next day he should give answers unto the questions which they had writ down, and if he could not answer, then should he be declared unworthy. And Owlglass answered, and said: "Tell the most learned rector and masters that I will do it straightway as they do require of me; and I trust to prove myself a pious man as from old time have I done."

And on the next day the rector and masters and students of the university assembled together, and Owlglass came with his host and some few of the citizens, so that all might proceed with good content. And when that he had entered into the assembly, they signified unto him that he should stand upon the stool, and make reply unto the questions so demanded of him. Then the rector opened his mouth, and spake unto Owlglass, and asked him, how many gallons of water there were in the sea; and he charged him to speak the truth and to conceal nothing from him, for an if he could not answer, then would he punish him as an ignorant beguiler, and cast him forth. And Owlglass thereupon answered him and said: "Four hundred and eighty million seven hundred and thirty thousand two hundred and sixty-four gallons and two-thirds of good measure. An ye will not believe what I say, cause ye the rivers and lakes and streams which run therein to stand still, and I will mete it, and if it prove not as I say, then will I confess that I am unwise." And the rector could not do this thing, and therefore he was obliged to admit the answer of Owlglass; and he next asked him this following question: "Tell me how many days have passed by from Adam's time until this present hour?" And

Owlglass spake unto him, saying: "Most worshipful master rector, the number is not great; only seven have so passed—Sunday, Monday, Tuesday, Wednesday, Thursday, Friday, and Saturday; and when that they have passed, then begin other seven days, and so will it go forward until the end of the world." Then said the rector: "Now answer me exactly, and say where is the middle of the world?" Then Owlglass answered: "That is here where we now stand; and if ye believe me not, do ye take a cord and mete it, and if it be a hair's breadth less, then will I stand ashamed." Then the rector waxed wroth, and asked Owlglass the fourth question: "How far is it from earth to heaven?" And Owlglass made answer: "When that one speaketh in heaven it is easy to hear it down here; therefore get ye one of ye up thither, and I will cry aloud, and if ye hear me not, then will I confess my wrong." And the rector waxed tired of questioning Owlglass, and asked him: "How great was heaven?" And Owlglass said unto him: "It is a thousand fathoms wide, and a thousand cubits high; and if ye believe me not, take the sun and moon and stars from heaven, and mete it, and ye will find I am right therein."

And, my masters, I charge ye to tell me, what could the worthy folks answer unto Owlglass? In all things was he too cunning for them; and by knavery had he beguiled them all. Then did he strip off his long coat, and departed from Prague.

The Thirty and Second Adventure.

How that Owlglass did on a time mix him up in a marriage strife, and did soon end it with great renown.

It came to pass on a time, that Owlglass entered into a town where much wine was made, and where the folk of the town did oftentimes drink themselves drunken thereupon. And, my masters, well do you know that when on a time ye have peeped into the glass, so that ye have been not as it would like me an if ye always were; and after that ye come home, ye do not find that your wives receive ye in so goodly and excellent a wise as at other times, so happened it that our noble and beloved Master Owlglass, as he was passing along the street to get him to the inn where he lay, did hear a brawling within a house hard by, as of people disputing the one with the other in great anger. So our good friend therewith stood still, and he hearkened, and perceived that it was the wife of a cobbler who, unto her husband, the which had come back from the winehouse well drunken, was reading the evening blessing, the which doeth such great and excellent good unto all husbands. And with many words contended they until that it was supper time; then the husband took his wife by the head, and said unto her: "Wilt thou cook for me my supper?" And she said: "Nay, that would she not," and then went they to quarreling again with much contention. At last said the cobbler: "I would have that the devil should come and fly away with thee!" And when that Owlglass heard these words, he took up a large stone which lay in the street, and threw it at the window, so that the frame and glass all fell together, and brake with a loud noise. And the twain who were contending within, thought in truth that the devil had come thither, and were stricken with great terror. But Owlglass gat him away, for that he might not have the charges of the broken window demanded of him. Yet went the story forth with great renown, and even unto this day do the town folk believe that the devil appeared in shape like unto a great stone; and if that ye believe not my saying, get ye thither and ask it of them yourselves.

The Thirty and Third Adventure.

How that Owlglass did cause an ass to read certain words out of a book at the great university of Erfurt.

Now after that Owlglass had departed, and had gat him away, it came to pass that he journeyed until he entered the city of Erfurt, at the which place is a most learned university. And our well-beloved Master Owlglass, like unto some wise men of our days, could not hide his wisdom under a bushel; but wheresoever it fortuned for him to sojourn, there must he teach the people some cunning thing. And after that he had come unto Erfurt, he gat him unto a notary, and with fine writing had he letters marvellously done in goodly and fair manuscript, setting forth therein his wondrous parts. And such letters of challenge he set upon the church doors. And the great fame of Owlglass had come unto Erfurt, where the rector and learned doctors had heard not a little of his knavish beguilings and conceits; thereat conferred they together as to how they might so enjoin him to do a thing the which he might not be able to perform, but have great shame thereby, and that they themselves might not be deceived and mocked. And then they agreed that they would give unto Owlglass an ass to be his scholar, the which he should teach that he might in time become a reader and a wise beast, for of asses were there great plenty in that university.

Thereat went they unto Owlglass, and they spake unto him, saying: "Worshipful master, well know we that you have set letters of art upon the doors of the church, by the which ye say ye can teach unto any beast, both that he shall learn to write and to

read; now, therefore, have the doctors of the university resolved, in that among us be no lack of asses, that ye shall receive one to be a scholar and student under thee, and that he shall learn to read. Will ye have him to be a scholar, and receive him and therewith, when that ye have taught him, a great reward?" Then answered Owlglass and said: "Yea, that will I; but thereunto must I have time, for an ass is an animal not wise nor easy to be taught." So they conferred together, and agreed that he was to be allowed twenty years in the which to teach him. Then thought Owlglass in his own mind: "So there are three of us unto this bargain. If that the rector should die, then am I free. And if it should come to pass that I should die, then can I break the contract. But if my scholar should not live, then am I also quit." And he agreed with them, and of the money he received some in part. Then he gat him into the inn of the town, and the master of the house was a man of singular mind. And for his scholar did Owlglass hire him a stable, and he gat him a great old book, and laid it into the manger before him, and between each leaf of the book he laid oats, and the ass soon beheld that, and he turned over the leaves with his tongue to eat the oats, and when that the oats were all gone, he cried out with a loud voice: "E, A—E, A!"

And when that Owlglass perceived this, he rose up and gat him unto the rector, and came into his presence, and said unto him: "Worshipful master rector, when will it please ye to come unto me to see how my disciple doth get forward with his book?" Then said the rector: "Doth he agree unto that which thou teachest him?" And Owlglass answered him, and said: "Truly he is a difficult disciple, and one that loveth not his book; yet have I brought it about that by much labour he pronounceth two vowel sounds very well, that is to say, E and A. Will it not make ye pleasure to come and hear him?" And all this time had the good scholar fasted. And when that Owlglass came with the rector, and some of the doctors of the university, he took a book and laid it in the manger before him, and when that the ass beheld it, he turned over the leaves backward and forward, hither and thither, with his tongue to find the oats, but, as he found nothing therein, he cried with a loud voice: "E, A—E, A!" Then said Owlglass: "Behold, most learned doctors, my disciple doth now pronounce well, although yet somewhat broadly, the two vowels E and A, and that can he do. I have great hope of him that he will soon get farther." In no long time after died the rector; and then Owlglass abode no longer with his disciple, but with his money departed, thinking that in truth it would demand great industry to make all the asses in Erfurt wise. Therefore he did it not; and they be all asses in that city unto this day.

The Thirty and Fourth Adventure.

How that Owlglass did kill a hog, and answered for his evil doing unto the burghmaster.

Now it fortuned, that Owlglass once came unto a village, and did hire him unto a boor to be his serving man. And this boor rejoiced greatly in all the wise sayings of Owlglass; and in no long time was Owlglass the best man in the house. And it came to pass upon one even that the boor made complaint unto Owlglass, and said unto him that he had an evil neighbour who endeavoured with all his might to afflict him in all ways that he might, and who, as the old saw saith, would have given an eye that the boor might be blind. Then Owlglass thought within him: "That will I soon repay with marvellous heavy interest. And so that my master doth thereat have joy and goodly satisfaction, then shall I be content." And when that he entered into the farm-yard on the next morning to depart about his labour, Owlglass beheld that the neighbour's hog had broken into that place, and was rolling on the dunghill in the yard; and hard upon the dunghill was there a pond of water, which stood still, and was covered with green. Then took Owlglass a cudgel and did strike the hog therewith, until that the hog ran into the pool and was therein drowned. But privily had the neighbour watched Owlglass, and beheld that which was done; and he cried aloud, and ran unto Owlglass, and demanded money for the hog which he had thus lost. And as Owlglass heeded him not, he came unto his master and desired the same thing. But the master of Owlglass said: "Truly, therewith have I nought to do. My servant man did this thing; go ye therefore unto the burghmaster and speak thereof unto him, and let my man answer it." Thereat the owner of the hog gat him unto the burghmaster, and complained unto him of what Owlglass had done. Then the burghmaster sent for Owlglass, and spake unto him, and demanded that he should answer it.

And Owlglass did rise up early in the morning, and he saddled a horse, and gave him to eat, and then departed, and gat him unto the house of the burghmaster. And the burghmaster, at that time, fortuned to be at his breakfast, and had before him a porringer of barley broth. And the burghmaster questioned Owlglass how that it had come to pass that he had killed the hog. Then Owlglass answered cunningly, and told him how that the hog brake his way into the yard and wallowed upon the dunghill; and, moreover, he told him how he had struck the hog, that he departed into the pool, and was there drowned. But the burghmaster was a man of slow understanding,—as is in truth not a thing marvellous strange amid people set in authority,—and he demanded of Owlglass that he should tell him the story more plainly. Whereat replied Owlglass and said: "Most worshipful sir, I will set forth unto you this thing very plain and easy to be comprehended of you. Look you, suppose ye that ye were yourself the hog, and your porringer of barley the pool, and suppose that I came after this wise, and with my hand smote you thus"—and therewith fetched Owlglass the burghmaster a great blow over the head—"thou mightest fall therein." Thereat cried the burghmaster aloud, and would have held Owlglass; but he ran forth and leapt upon his horse and departed thence with great haste.

The Thirty and Fifth Adventure.

How that Owlglass at Nugenstädten, in the land of Thuringia, did wash the women's furs.

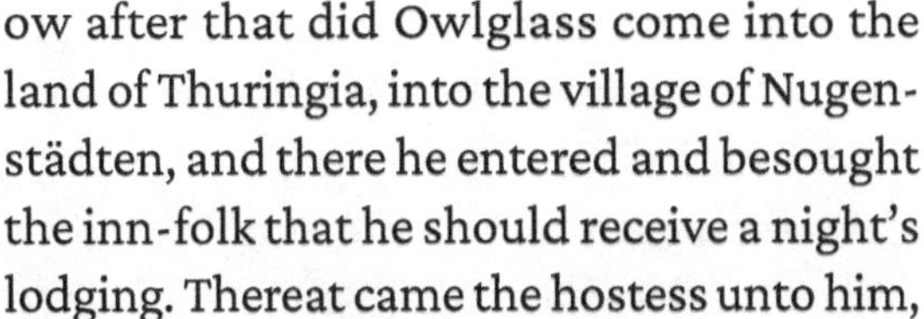

OW after that did Owlglass come into the land of Thuringia, into the village of Nugenstädten, and there he entered and besought the inn-folk that he should receive a night's lodging. Thereat came the hostess unto him, and asked him, saying: "What manner of trade followest thou?"

And Owlglass answered and said unto her: "Truly am I of no trade, but do in all things accustom myself to speak the truth." Then said the hostess: "Such do I most gladly receive into my house, and truth-speakers are welcome." And Owlglass looked round him, and he perceived that the hostess did squint; therefore he said: "Squint-wife, squint-wife, where doth it please ye that I shall sit, and where would ye have me to lay my staff and wallet?" Thereat waxed the hostess very wroth, and said unto him: "May nought good ever happen unto thee; in all my life did no one ever say unto me that I squinted!" But Owlglass answered and said unto her: "Dear hostess, be not angry with me, for an if I do speak the truth, then must I do it at all times, and in all things." And thereat was her wrath turned away, and she, being merry, laughed and was content.

Now after that Owlglass had abode that night in her inn, they conferred together, and he told her that he could wash old furs so that they became new again. Thereat rejoiced the hostess greatly, and begged that he would do this, and she would tell all her neighbours that they should also bring their furs to be washed. And Owlglass said: "Yea, verily, that would he do." Then all the women in the village brought unto Owlglass their furs, that they might be washed. And Owlglass said unto them: "Ye must have milk." And all the women desired greatly to have new furs, and they each gat them home, and brought unto Owlglass all the milk that they had there. And Owlglass set two cauldrons upon the fire, and he poured the milk into them, and then put the furs into the milk, and they were boiled therein.

And it came to pass, that when he thought that they had boiled enough, he said unto the women: "Now must ye bring me young white elm twigs, and peel ye them, and when that ye come again unto me, I will take out the furs, for then will they be boiled enough, and I will wring them; yet must I have wood to do this." And the women departed right joyfully to fetch the wood, and the children ran with them, and sang and danced, and said: "O beautiful new fur cloaks! O beautiful new fur cloaks!" Then stood Owlglass and laughed, and said: "Wait ye yet a while, the furs be not right yet." And while they were gone for the twigs, Owlglass piled more wood on the fire, and left the furs boiling, and departed out of the village. And yet hath he not returned to wash the furs. When that the women folk came back, they began to quarrel, and strive one with the other, for each would have her fur first forth from the cauldron; but when that they looked how they were proceeding, lo! they were all boiled to rags and fell to pieces. And Owlglass rejoiced that he had so happily gone forth.

The Thirty and Sixth Adventure.

*Telleth how that Owlglass journeyed about the land with
a saint's head, and did beguile many therewith.*

Now the malice of Owlglass had been so great that everywhere
was he known, and his knavery noised abroad, so that where
he once came at any time, to that place durst he not go again,
unless it mote be that he disguised himself in strange appearance that others might not know him. And although, with his
idleness, he could never have much content, yet from his youth
up had he always been one that loved good living, and by his
divers beguilings he always had by him good store of money.
But by his knavishness he had fallen into such evil repute, that
nowhere might he get money, and he began to see the bottom of
his money-pouch oftener than it pleased him to do. So he began
to consider within himself, how that he might without labour get
more money, for he knew that often more money is gained by idle
courses than by hard work. Then thought he that he would become
a pardoner, and journey to and fro with a holy relic, therewith to
persuade the people that they should give him money. Therefore
he gat him the long gown of a priest's scholar, and went unto the
sexton, who gave unto him a skull; therewith he departed unto
the silversmith, who set it about fairly with brave workmanship
in silver. Then came he into the land of Pomerania, where have I
also been, my masters. And there are the people right honest and
good, brave men and true, believing that which ye say unto them;
and their piety is as great as their faith. Yet in that land Owlglass
found that the priests cared more for drinking than preaching;

and when that a church feast, a wedding, or any other assembly came to pass in a village, then did Owlglass go unto the priest, and entreat of him that he might preach, and shew unto the boors the holy relic which he bare with him; and Owlglass promised to give unto the priest half of whatever offerings the village folk made thereto. The unlearned priest was content enough if that he might only receive money thereby.

And when that there were many folk in the church, Owlglass gat him up into the pulpit, and spake somewhat to them of the old covenant and of the new covenant, of the ark and the golden vessels where lay the holy bread. Thereafter spake he of the head of the holy Saint Brandonus, he that was a sanctified man, and that to his honour was it now resolved, that a church should be builded, and that with money not got by knavery; nor would he receive aught from any that loved not their husbands. Then gave he the head unto the peasants to kiss, and it might have been the head of a thief for what Owlglass knew; and after that he blessed them, and gat him down, and went to the altar, and there began he to sing, and ring the bells. Then came all the women, good and bad, unto him with their offerings; and the bad came twice and thrice, and he received all, nor turned away any. And the women believed in his saying, and thought that one that came not should be reproved. And any woman who had no money brought unto him a golden ring, and they strove together which should offer more often than another, for therewith was their virtue confirmed. And many offered so that all folks might behold it, for charity covereth a multitude of sins. Thus did Owlglass get the fairest offering which in that land had been offered, and all the women of the land held Owlglass in great reverence for his piety. And Owlglass knew how to practise malice with gain. Nor do the folks even unto this day omit with much openness to give unto charitable uses a trifle from their substance, and their names are written in great letters; and some that respect charity

have an awe for them, but a few there be that think ye should
work goodness in secret.

The Thirty and Seventh Adventure.

*How that Owlglass did make the town-watch of Nürnberg
to fall into the water which is called the Pegnitz.*

Owlglass was most wise in knavery. And when that he had
journeyed far and wide with the holy head of Saint Brandonus, and had beguiled the people, so that he felt it in his pocket
as a heavier weight than it lay upon his soul, he came unto Nürnberg, where he purposed to make good cheer with the money
which the head gat for him. And after that he had lain there for
a while, he could no longer live unless that he committed some
vile knavery; therefore he looked round as to what he might do.
And, behold, it came to pass that the town watchmen slept in a
great watch-box, beneath the town-hall, in their armour, and
this saw Owlglass. Now Owlglass had learned all the highways
and byways at Nürnberg, and he craftily took heed of the small
bridge which is called the Hangman's Bridge, and which leads
between the Pig-market and the Little House, where of a night
it is ill to pass; and many a one who hath gone thereby to fetch a
measure of wine, hath had too great a drink of water. Thereafter
waited Owlglass with his knavery, until the people had begun to
sleep—and truly watchmen sleep always early; and when that it
was quite still brake he craftily from the bridge three planks, and
cast them into the Pegnitz, and then departed on his way to the
town-hall, and there 'gan he to swear, and with an old knife which
he had he struck the stones of the street, that fire flew far round.
Now the watch awoke thereat, and they heard him, and gat them
up, and followed after him. So Owlglass fled before them, and ran

in the way which led to the Pig-market, and when he came unto the bridge he helped himself diligently across as best he might where that he brake away the planks; and after that he had come thereover, he lifted up his voice, and cried unto them: "Ho! ho! ye shamefaced knaves! where be ye that ye follow not?" And thereat were the watchmen angry, and they pursued him yet faster, and each desired to be the first to catch the mocking beguiler. Then fell they one after the other into the Pegnitz; and it fortuned that the hole was so narrow, that they dashed their teeth out as they fell against the other side. Then spake Owlglass unto them, and said: "Ho! ho! come ye not forward yet? To-morrow follow after me yet more hastily." And one there was of them who brake his leg, and another his arm, and the third knocked a hole in his skull; thus no one came off without some hurt. Now, after that Owlglass had thus accomplished his knavery, he abode no longer in the town of Nürnberg, but gat him forth, and departed; for he was sore afraid, that, if it should be discovered, the lords of the city of Nürnberg might cause him to suffer therefor.

The Thirty and Eighth Adventure.

How that Owlglass did at Bamberg eat for money.

On a time, did Owlglass receive money through his cunning, when that he had departed from Nürnberg and came unto Bamberg, where that he found that he was an hungered. And in that city of Bamberg entered he into an inn, and the hostess thereof was a good soul and a merry, and she bade him welcome with gay words, for by his clothes perceived she that he was a guest of rare quality. When that the time came in the morning that they should eat, she spake unto Owlglass, and asked him, saying: "Whether would he sit at table to eat, or have a portion for so much money?"

And Owlglass answered, and said unto her "I am a poor man and a needy." Then entreated he her, that she should, for God his sake, give unto him to eat. Thereat said the hostess: "Friend, an if I gave unto thee to eat, I should lose thereby, for the flesher and the baker will demand to have money of me for their wares. Therefore, for eating must I also receive money." Then said Owlglass: "Alas! my dear woman, to eat for money doth also content me: tell me now how much shall I eat for?" And the woman spake unto him, saying: "At the gentles' table, four and twenty pence; and the next table thereunto, for eighteen pence; and with my serving people, twelve pence." Then answered Owlglass unto her words, and said: "Hostess, the table for four and twenty pence is the most, and will best convene unto me." Therefore sat he down to the gentles' table, and did eat as much as ever he could. And when that he had eaten and drunken very heartily, he said unto the hostess, and besought her that she would settle with him, for that by poverty it was necessary he should depart. Then answered she unto Owlglass, saying: "Gentle guest, an if ye give unto me twenty-four pence, ye may, in God's name, depart whither it please ye." But thereat said Owlglass: "Nay, but ye should give unto me twenty-four pence, for ye said unto me, that for four and twenty pence should I eat; and therefore apprehended I, that ye meant to cause that I should earn money, and most heavily did I earn it, for if life and strength had touched the matter, then could I not have eaten more. Therefore pray I ye, render unto me my hard earnings." Then said the hostess: "Friend, thou speakest truly, for thou hast eaten as much as any three could have done; but that I should give unto thee money cometh not within my thought. Yet, in so far as toucheth the dinner, that will I excuse thee; go therewith in peace; but I give ye no money, be ye assured. Nor will I demand it of ye; but come not hitherward again, for if that I should with every guest have such, little would come therefrom but loss to me." Then departed Owlglass, and little thanks gat he.

The Thirty and Ninth Adventure.

How that Owlglass did make a wager with a Jew about a horse, and did deceive him.

In no long time thereafter came Owlglass into Mechlenburg, and there he gat him a horse of excellent goodness. And as he would have departed on his way thence, and rode by an inn, the horse would no longer go forward, for it had an evil habit that at every inn would it stop. Thereat said Owlglass: "In truth, thou canst also drink thee a measure of liquor, for it is hot;" and therefore he gat down from the horse, and tied him up unto the gateway. Then entered he into the inn, and the guest-chamber thereof, and there sat several guests within, making merry. At the table there sat a Jew, who was a dealer in horses; and the Jew had perceived the horse of Owlglass as he came up unto the house. And he spake unto Owlglass, saying: "Wilt thou sell thy horse, and what wouldst thou have in money therefor?" Then Owlglass answered, and said unto the Jew: "This horse canst thou not buy, Jew; it is a Mechlenburg horse, and of a most rare breed, and three hundred nobles would scarce pay for it." Then said the Jew: "Nay, but what think ye, gracious sir, for twenty nobles would I buy thee such a horse. Wilt thou set a wager upon it?" "Most contemptible son of Moses," said Owlglass, "thou couldst not. He hath not one fault, and is as gentle as a tender lamb." "Well," answered the Jew: "wilt thou take twenty nobles therefor?" Then Owlglass spake unto him, and said: "Look you, Hebrew Jew, an if thou wilt take three strokes from my riding-whip, then will I give thee the horse, and he shall be fairly thine own." Thereat said the Jew: "Ye would fain jest with me, noble sir; may I trust your word?" And Owlglass said: "Hast thou not heard it?" Then cried the Jew: "Yea; and the gentlefolk yonder will be witnesses thereunto." Then said Owlglass: "Good: when wilt thou have the three strokes? Wilt thou have it that I begin now at this place and time?" Thereupon the Jew answered Owlglass, and said: "An if that I must have them, it may as well now be as at any other time." Then Owlglass commanded that the Jew should be tied up, and said unto him: "Now do thou remember. Thou hast to receive from me three strokes, and when thou hast received them, then shalt thou truly become possessor of my horse."

Then he took his whip, and lifted it, and came down with a great stroke upon the back of the Jew, so that he cried aloud with marvellous pain. Then said Owlglass: "Son of Abraham, art thou content, or wilt thou straightway receive the next stroke?" And the Jew answered, and said: "Gracious sir, the other will I have now; but I entreat thee, for pity's sake, not to strike me so sore." And Owlglass spake unto him, and said: "Then make thou thyself ready:" and therewith gave he unto the Jew a yet sorer stroke. The poor Jew thereat bit his tongue woundily with the pain, and cried to Owlglass that he should speedily give him the third stroke. Then said Owlglass: "Nay; but for the third stroke may-est thou stay a while, so long as thou receivest it not is the horse mine. Behold, here are the witnesses." Thereat, although the Jew scarce could stand with the pain, he entreated Owlglass that he should then give him the third stroke; but Owlglass would not. Then lamented the Jew, and Owlglass gave unto him a measure of wine; but he ceased not to complain in that he had been beguiled of Owlglass. Yet was the Jew justly served, in that, with small pains and labour, he would have received the horse of Owlglass.

O most worthy teacher of wisdom unto the ignorant and sin-ful, why camest thou not in the days in which I do here chronicle thy marvellous deeds?

The Fortieth Adventure.

How Owlglass did have much money for an old hat.

Money remaineth not always with any of us, my masters; and so truly did Owlglass find, when that he was in the town of Cologne. And he was so poor, that of all his money he possessed only four shillings; and on his head he wore an old hat, with three corners, and thereat did all people laugh. Then Owlglass thought that he would therewith have rare sport and profit. And as he was going along the street of the town, he beheld two officers of the soldiers; and he knew that they had pouches well lined with gold pieces. And they laughed at his hat. Then spake Owlglass unto them: "Behold, ye do laugh at my hat. Verily will I shew unto ye that in no wise is it to be accounted nought, but hath great virtue; and to content you therein, I bid ye both dine with me on this day." And the soldiers consented, and so gat them with Owlglass. When that they came unto the gate of the best inn, Owlglass said: "What say ye? where shall we dine?" Then they answered and said: "Let us enter herein and dine, if that ye have a good pouch of money?" And Owlglass said: "Be of good cheer, that maketh no matter, let us enter therein." Then entered they; and Owlglass secretly conferred with the hostess, and gave her the four shillings, therewith to satisfy her for the dinner.

And when that the dinner was served, the officers waxed merry, for it was a very excellent dinner, and they were content. Thereafter did Owlglass say unto the hostess: "What money dost thou want to satisfy thee for thy dinner?" And she answered and said: "Four shillings." "Four shillings, sayest thou?" answered

Owlglass, and therewith he took his little hat and he turned it
four times about upon his finger, and asked her if that she were
content. And she said: "Yea; and fair thanks unto ye likewise."
And therewith departed she. But the officers, when that they
beheld it, said: "But how marvellous is this thing!" And they
were most astonished. "Alas! my masters," said Owlglass unto
them: "do not ye now see how great is the value of the hat? With
the money that more than twenty times hath been offered me
therefor, should I be rich."

Then said one of his guests: "If that I offered unto thee a good
sum, would not ye sell it? For poor soldiers as be we, so great a
marvel would be accounted very useful unto us, for then should
we never die of hunger." And Owlglass was persuaded, and he
gave them the hat for four hundred marks. And the next day, he
who bought it desired to make trial of it; and he went unto the
inn and had a great banquet made ready, and he assembled his
friends together to eat thereof. Then when the time came for
paying the host, he sought to pay the charges by turning the hat
about; but the host understood it not. And so the soldier had to
pay many marks therefor; and when he looked after Owlglass
he found him not.

The Forty and First Adventure.

*How that Owlglass journeyed unto Rome to see the Pope,
and how his Holiness considered that Owlglass was an
heretic.*

It hath been every where seen, that Owlglass was a most knavish
wight. And when it had come to pass that he had worked these
such deceiving actions, he thought of the old proverb which saith:

> "If that thou a knave wouldst see,
> At Rome eftsoon thou'lt fitted be."

And Owlglass was aweary of his own devices, and thereat wished that he might find another like unto him. So departed he, and he journeyed forward, and at last came unto Rome. There entered he into an inn, which a widow kept, and she saw that he was a goodly man to look upon, and she spake unto him, and asked him of what country was he. And Owlglass told her that he was of the land of Saxony, and that he had come unto Rome because that he craved to confer with the Pope touching a certain business. Then answered the widow and said unto him: "The Pope canst thou see, but as to speaking with him that mayest thou not do. I have been bred and born in this place, and of gentle birth also, yet have I never spoken with the Pope. How then, think ye, that ye will do this thing? Truly would I give a hundred ducats an if that I could have speech of him." And Owlglass answered and said: "My good hostess an if I gat ye speech of him would ye give me the hundred ducats?" The woman said: "Marry that would I," and straightway promised them unto him. But she thought that it could never be that Owlglass would do this thing; for she knew that it was a heavy and long labour to bring it about. But Owlglass said unto her that if he did cause it to come to pass, then would he demand the hundred ducats; and therewith were they both content.

And Owlglass tarried until it fortuned that the Sunday came round, on which the Pope read the mass in the chapel called Jerusalem, in the church of the holy Saint John Lateran, the which he did once in every four weeks. Then gat him Owlglass to the chapel, and thrust himself in as near as might be unto the Pope's person, and stood there; and when that the host was lifted up, or a blessing given from the altar, then did Owlglass turn his back thereunto, the which was a thing not fit to be done. And thereafter was the Pope told of this, that a very proper handsome man had stood at the mass and so acted. Then said his Holiness that such a thing was an abomination, and that he feared the man who had done so was in unbelief and an heretic. If that this were not punished, it would be a great scandal. Then sent the Pope for Owlglass, and the messengers came unto him and carried him before the Pope. Then said the Pope unto Owlglass: "What manner of man art thou?" And Owlglass answered and said: "I am a good Christian." Then said the Pope: "What belief hast thou?" To which Owlglass made reply: "That he was of the same belief as his hostess," and named her by name, and she was a woman well-known. And the Pope commanded that she should be brought to him; and he asked her, saying: "What belief hast thou, woman?" And she made answer unto the Pope and said: "I am a thorough Christian, and a believer in that which the Holy Church ordaineth is to be believed, and no other belief have I." In the which the good woman did marvellously resemble divers other excellent Christians, which take from the mouth of ignorance the confirming grace of wisdom.

Then stood Owlglass by, and with much humility, did seem to be very pious, and said: "Most gracious Father! this true faith hold I also, and that most firmly, and am a good Christian man." Then said the Pope unto him: "Wherefore dost thou turn thy back to the altar?" And Owlglass answered and said: "That did I, forasmuch as I am a grievous sinner, and one not worthy to behold the altar, as I have not received absolution for my crimes." Thereat was the Pope content, and giving him absolution, he let Owlglass go; and he returned unto his inn, and demanded the hundred ducats, the which the widow gave unto him. Yet found not Owlglass the knave he sought, and himself was not a whit more honest than before; so that his Roman journey did him no great good.

HOW OWLGLASS MAKETH THE COCK THE SECURITY FOR THE HENS.

The Forty and Second Adventure.

How that Owlglass without money bought poultry at Quedlingburg, and for security gave unto the farmer's wife the cock.

In all things of old time were the people not so knavish as is now the case, especially they that are of the boors. On a time came Owlglass unto Quedlingburg, while that it was the weekly market day therein. And Owlglass had little provision; for when that it happened that he had money, in like manner that he wan it, it departed from him again. So he took counsel within himself, how that he might have good provision. And there sate upon the market a woman, and before her had she a large basket of live poultry, all hens; and among them was a cock. And Owlglass spake unto her saying: "How much wilt thou have for thy poultry?" And the woman made answer unto him, and said: "Truly mayest thou have them for a couple of St. Stephen's pennies." Then said Owlglass: "Wilt thou not give them cheaper?" But the woman said unto him: "Nay"; and then took Owlglass the basket, and departed therewith unto the town gate. Thereat ran the woman after him, and said unto him: "Merchant, how shall I understand thee? Wilt thou not pay me for the poultry?" Then said Owlglass: "Yea, most cheerily. I am the secretary of my lord's lady." "That ask I not," said the woman; "it brooks not me what noble people thou mayest serve. If that thou wilt have the poultry, then do thou pay me therefor, and with my lord or my lady have I nought to do. My father taught me that with noble folk should I nor buy nor sell, nor lend nor borrow. Therefore

75

pay thou me that which I demand from thee. Dost hear me?"
And Owlglass said unto the woman: "Woman, thou art of little
faith; if that all folk were like unto thee, the rich needy would not
long have their needs answered. But so that ye may, indeed, have
surety, give I ye the cock, the which will I fetch when that I bring
ye the money and the basket." Then took the good woman the
cock, and bethought her that of a truth was she rarely secured
to receive her money. But in all vain hopes can there be no happiness; for Owlglass returned not again, nor had she satisfaction
in any wise. And unto such as make themselves so greatly sure,
is it given to be disappointed, wherefore when that Owlglass
approacheth unto ye, do ye straightway deliver up unto him that
which he demandeth, lest with wily ways he doth beguile ye of
much more. And Owlglass thereafter departed thence, and the
good wife still kept her security.

The Forty and Third Adventure.

*How that Owlglass, with a knavish confession, did beguile
the priest at Riesenburg of his horse.*

Never was Owlglass unready to commit a vile piece of knavery,
when that there was opportunity thereunto. Now there abode
at Riesenburg the priest thereof, and he had a maid serving-
woman, who was of a comely countenance, and thereto also a
horse of much beauty, of the which he was greatly fond. And at
that time was the Duke of Brunswick at Riesenburg, and had, by
the agency of many persons, besought the priest that he should let
him have the horse, and for him would he pay many more times
than the value. But the priest at all times denied the prince the
favour, nor would in any wise grant him his desire, for he loved
his horse, and with violence might the horse not be taken.

And it came to pass, that this thing was told unto Owlglass, and he understood it well; and he went unto the duke, and said unto him: "Gracious lord, what wilt thou give unto me if that I bring unto thee the priest his horse?" "If that thou canst do it," answered the duke, "will I give unto thee the coat which now I wear." And the coat was of red satin, set and broidered with pearls. And Owlglass accepted this, and gat him away, and departed from Wolfenbüttel unto the village of Riesenburg, and there entered into the priest's house; for they were well known the twain each to each, for of old times had Owlglass abode with him and been welcome. And after that he had been there some three days, he did bear himself in such wise, that he seemed to be sick unto the death; and he laid himself down, and prepared for his end. And the priest and his serving-maid were greatly vexed thereat, and grieved over him. Thereafter grew Owlglass so ill, that the priest said unto him, that, in truth, for his soul's comfort, it was meet and fit that he should make confession. And Owlglass grew mightily inclined thereunto, but he begged the priest that he should make inquiry of him most acutely. Then said the priest unto him, that he should discover his soul unto him, and confess, for that in his lifetime had he wrought much evil. And Owlglass made answer, that in his lifetime had he only done one thing evil the which he regretted, and that would he not confess unto him; but if they brought unto him another priest, then would he confess, for he was afraid that the priest might be wroth with him.

Now when that the priest heard this thing, he thought that truly was there somewhat hidden under the words of Owlglass, the which he craved much to know; for priests are greatly more inquisitive than other men. Therefore he opened his mouth, and said unto Owlglass: "Dear Owlglass, the distance is great, and it would take me a long time to find another priest; and if that ye did give up the ghost while that I sought thee such an one, both thou and I would have a heavy sin to answer. Therefore be not afraid, and confess unto me thy sin; and so heavy also it be, will I absolve thee. An if I should grow angry thereover, what doth that matter unto thee, for thy confession may I not tell unto another?" Then answered Owlglass, and said unto him: "Verily, then will I confess unto thee, for the sin is not so heavy that I may not tell it; but only I feared thee, for it concerneth thyself." Thereat waxed the priest the more anxious to hear what Owlglass said, and he opened his ears to hear him, and said unto him, that if he had stolen aught from him, or wrought him any evil, let him only confess, and he would give him content, nor visit it upon him in any wise. Then said Owlglass unto him: "Alas! reverend sir, well know I that ye will be an angered with me. Yet I feel that soon shall I depart out of this world, and, therefore, must I relieve my soul of this confession. And of that which I did, most reverend sir, must ye shrive me. For I have in thy church kissed thy servant woman, the which I know to be an offence of much gravity against the Church, and against all dignity likewise." Thereat asked the priest of Owlglass, how often that it might have happened. And Owlglass answered, and said: "But five times." Then did the priest give unto Owlglass absolution; and he took a stick and departed unto the serving woman, and told her that which Owlglass said. But she answered that it was not so. But the priest said unto her, that Owlglass had confessed it unto him. Thereat said she: "Nay," and he: "Yea"; and with no more ado, took her and gave unto her a sound beating, until that she was black and blue all over. The while lay Owlglass in bed, and laughed, and thought: "Bravely doth thy purpose go forward, and ere long will thy harvest season approach."

And he lay still all that night, and when that it was morning he arose, and said: "Now am I whole, and well will it be if I depart unto another country. What have I to pay thee?" And the priest was right glad to be ridden of his guest, and he took his money, when that they reckoned. And the woman-servant was glad also.

Then said Owlglass unto the priest: "Wherefore hast thou revealed to another my confession? Truly will I now go unto Halberstadt before my lord the Bishop, and lay a complaint against thee, for that thou hast been unfaithful in thy office." Then did the priest tremble, and think how he might content Owlglass that he should not complain; and he entreated him and asked what he should give him to be silent thereupon, and would he have twenty pieces to say no word more? But Owlglass said: "An if ye gave unto me one hundred pieces, would I not do this, and verily will I straightway depart thither." And the priest humbly, and with tears, besought him to refrain, and that he would give him whatever he would have. Thereat said Owlglass: "Give then unto me thy horse, and I will say no more; but the horse will I have." But the priest loved his beast, and desired not to give it away, and he would rather have given unto Owlglass every penny that he had; but Owlglass demanded that he should have the horse, and would hear no word. So the priest gave unto Owlglass the horse, and he departed therewith, and he came unto Wolfenbüttel, and there upon the bridge stood the duke, and beheld the coming of Owlglass. Then took the duke the coat from off his back and gave it unto him, and received the horse. And the duke rejoiced greatly over Owlglass his cunning in beguiling the priest, and made pleasant sport with the tale; and he gave unto our noble Master Owlglass another horse; and the priest was wroth at losing his horse, and he often did comfort himself by beating the maid sorely, until that she departed from him. So lost the priest both horse and maid.

The Forty and Fourth Adventure.

How that Owlglass did hire him to a smith, and what he did while with him.

And it fortuned that on a time came Owlglass unto Rostock, in the land of Mechlenburg, and hired him unto a smith there. The smith had a favourite saying, when that he would have the bellows blown: "Ha! ho! follow ye with the bellows!" Then stood Owlglass and blew, and the smith spake unto him, saying: "Ha! ho! follow ye with the bellows!" And he gat him into the court thereafter. Then came Owlglass behind him with the bellows on his back, and laid it down beside him, and said: "Master, behold I have done thy bidding! Where would you have me to put it?" Then the master looked upon him and beheld what he had done, and said: "My good man! so did I not mean it. Go thou in again and put it back where it stood." And Owlglass did as his master bade him, and placed it again where it had been before. But the master thought within himself how he might pay him handsomely for this knavery; and he resolved that for five days he would rise every night at midnight to begin labour in the forge. And he wakened all his men, and they began to labour. Then said Owlglass his comrade unto him: "What is this thing that now we labour at midnight? Wherefore is it; of old did our master not this thing?" And Owlglass said: "Wilt thou that I shall ask of him wherefore it is?" And his fellow said: "Yea;" and then Owlglass asked him. And the smith made answer unto him, and said: "It is my rule that at first my men shall not, for eight days, lie on my bed more than half the night." And Owlglass held his peace, and his companion dared not to speak.

And it came to pass the next night that Owlglass and his fellow were again awakened by the master; and the other man went down and fell to work. Then took up Owlglass the bed, and, with cords, bound it upon his back, and when that the iron was hot, he cometh down unto the forge, and taketh a hammer, and beginneth to smite the iron, so that the sparks flew into the bed and burned holes therein. Thereat said the smith: "What is't thou dost? Why didst not thou leave the bed lying in that place where that it should lie?" Then answered Owlglass and spake unto the smith, saying: "Master, be not angry; my rule is it that half the night will I lie upon the bed, and the other half shall it lie upon me." Then the master waxed wroth, and said unto Owlglass: "Go thou lay the bed where thou tookest it from;" and furthermore said he: "Marry, thou knave, get thee up out of my house, and may I never see thee more, for evil is the day in which I beheld thee." And Owlglass said "Yea," unto the master's commands, and he went and laid back the bed upon its place. Then gat he a ladder, and climbed up into the garret, and he broke through the roof, and mounted up and drew the ladder after him, and so gat him up out of the house as his master told him, and thereafter descended he unto the street, and left the ladder, and so departed. And the smith heard the noise that he made, and ran up stairs, and lo! there was a great hole in the roof.

Then grew he yet more angry, and sought his pike, and departed in haste, and ran after Owlglass. But the other man held him, and said: "Nay, master, do not this thing, for behold, he did but that which thou didst command him. Thou didst say: 'Get thee *up* out of my house,' and that hath he done, for he hath departed through this hole in the roof." And the smith was persuaded; and was not that the best thing? What booted it unto him; he could not longer lay hands upon Owlglass, for he had departed thence. So he fell to mending his roof, and the fellow of Owlglass said: "With such comrades, can but little be won. And he that knoweth not Owlglass, let him only have to do with him, he shall surely know him well in no long time."

The Forty and Fifth Adventure.

*How that Owlglass did cause all the tools, hammers, and
tongs of a smith to be as one mass of iron.*

Now when that Owlglass departed away from the smith, it came near unto the winter season, and the weather was very cold. And it did freeze hard, and all things soever waxed very dear, and at great price could you alone get victual, so that serving-men went with scant lining to their stomachs. Like unto many others, Owlglass was without money in his pouch, and he came unto a village, where was another smith. Now Owlglass craved not again to become a smith's man; but great hunger and thirst and cold drave him thereto, and merciless masters be they. So went he unto the smith, but the smith would have none of him, by reason of little work which there was; yet did Owlglass beseech him, so that at last the smith took him. And Owlglass promised that he would eat whatever that the smith set before him. Now the smith was a knave, and thought in himself, he shall not eat me until that I am poor.

And it came to pass in the morning, that they fell to labour, and laboured very hard until that it was dinner time. Then took the smith Owlglass, and led him unto the court unto the lime-pit, and he said unto him: "Thou didst promise to eat that which I set before thee. Now take, eat, and make thee good cheer." But he departed into the house, and ate roast and boiled. Then Owlglass abode without, and thought within himself: "Unto many hast thou wrought great knaveries, thou art repaid in that coin which thou didst pass to others. Yet shall master smith dearly pay for this deceitful practise." And after the dinner hour did Owlglass return in silence unto his labour, and said nought at all, and so went it until supper time. Then had the smith pity for Owlglass, and gave unto him some supper, and said unto him: "Rise ye up early in the morning, and do ye begin in good time. Then shall ye knock together what ye shall find, and make me a round number of horse nails. The maid may stand at the bellows until that I come unto thee." Then did Owlglass go to rest, and when that it was morning he rose up early, and thought: "Now shall he pay for the dinner." So he took the tongs and hammers, fire-irons, sand-ladles, and everything that he could find, which was of iron, and hammered it into one mass in the fire. The same did he with the horse-nails; and when that he heard the master coming, departed he.

And when that the smith came in and found the pretty business, he waxed wroth, and asked the maid how it came that this was so, and where might his man be? And the maid answered and said: "He hath gone forth without the door." The smith said: "Like unto a knave hath he gone; and if that I wist whither that he went, I would beat him with heavy stripes." Then said the maid: "Before he departed, he wrote somewhat over the door." Then went the smith and beheld that Owlglass had, as his fashion was, painted over the door an owl and a glass, the which signified his name. Then knew the smith thereby who his man had been, and was glad that Owlglass had done him no worse knavery than that he had practised. But Owlglass returned not again unto that village, or that master. And the smith had heavy work to make his tools again as they should be.

The Forty and Sixth Adventure.

How that Owlglass did speak a word of truth unto a smith,
his wife, man, and maid, each one before the house.

Unto Wismar came Owlglass upon a holy day, and when he passed by over against the smithy, he then beheld before the smithy door a good wife standing dressed in her best clothes, and with her was her maid, and she was the smith's wife. And Owlglass went and lay at the inn opposite that night, and in the night time he brake from off his horse's feet all his shoes, and the next day went over unto the smithy. On this wise came he to know them. And when that he approached unto the smithy, lo! they perceived that he was Owlglass; and the good wife, and her maid, came forth before the house door, so that they might behold that which Owlglass said and did. And Owlglass lifted up his voice, and spake unto the smith saying: "Wilt thou now shoe these my horse's feet?" And the smith answered him "Yea"; and it pleased the smith that he should talk with so wonderful a man as was Owlglass. After that they had talked and conferred together awhile, the smith said unto him: "Behold now, if that thou canst unto me say a word of truth, then will I give unto thee a shoe therefor." And Owlglass answered: "Yea"; and thus spake unto him:

> "An if hammer and iron and coals have ye,
> And wind enow in the bellows free,
> Brave smith of might then can ye be."

Then said the smith: "That word is truth," and gave unto him a shoe. Then did the apprentice put the shoe on the horse's foot; and he spake unto Owlglass and said: "That an if Owlglass would say unto him also such a word of verity, he would likewise bestow upon him a shoe." Then answered Owlglass: "Yea"; and said unto him:

> "The master and the man they two,
> If that work they fain would do,
> Hard labour should they never rue."

"True is thy saying," answered the smith's man, and gave him a shoe. Thereat marvelled the good wife, and her maid; and they came unto him, and conferred with him, and the good wife said unto him: "That an if he said also to her words of true meaning, she would give unto him a shoe." And thereat answered Owlglass, and said: "Yea"; and spake thus:

> "Good wife, good wife, eye that's bright,
> Sparkling with such knavish light,
> Loves a trysting place at night."

Then said the good wife: "Marry but thou sayest truth," and therewith gave him a shoe. Then would the maid fain have a true word also spoken unto her; and if that Owlglass did it, she would give him a shoe. And he said:

> "When that thou dost dine on veal,
> Eat with care, or thou shalt feel
> Tooth-ache pangs thee over-steal."

And the maid said thereat: "O and alas! how true is that saying," and gave him a shoe. Then departed Owlglass from that place with his horse well shod. But if any of us, my masters, went unto a blacksmith, I fear me greatly we should have no satisfaction, or horseshoes, for telling truths unto him. This sheweth that of old time were the people wiser than now.

The Forty and Seventh Adventure.

How that Owlglass, at Frankfort-on-the-Main, did with guile delude two Jews of rings.

On a time came Owlglass unto the city of Frankfort-on-the-Main, and it was yearly market day when that he entered therein. And in that town dwelt many Jews, and those that dwelt not there, dwelt in other places; and some have come out thence, and go not thither again. Then did Owlglass send for two rich Jews, and he spake unto them, saying: "That he would have two pair of ear-rings of them, beset with precious stones; but they must all be of one pattern and size, nor one in the least larger or smaller than the other." And it was for a noble lady that he said he would have them. Then the Jews brought a great number of costly rings, and Owlglass dealt with each alone, and of each did he have a pair. But unto the first he gave back a ring, and said:

"That he should take it unto the goldsmith and have it made a little larger." And this the Jew agreed should be done, and departed with the ring, and promised that he would return ere long; but he left the other ring with Owlglass. And Owlglass did likewise with the second Jew, and kept one of the twain rings. And the Jews departed each alone. Then had Owlglass wan him a pair of ear-rings, and therewith did he go forth from Frankfort, and came not again. But the Jews were beguiled; yet cared not Owlglass a jot therefor.

The Forty and Eighth Adventure.

How that Owlglass served a shoemaker, and how that he inquired of him what shapes he should cut; and the master answered him, and said: "Great and small, as the herdsman driveth forth to field." Therefore cut he oxen, cows, calves, sheep, and pigs.

Now in a place where Owlglass sojourned on a time, was there a shoemaker, who loved rather to walk about in the market than to labour, and he hired Owlglass for his servant, and he bade Owlglass cut out the shapes himself. Then said Owlglass unto him: "Master, what would you have me to cut?" And the shoemaker answered him, and said: "Cut ye out great and small, as the herdsman driveth forth to field." And Owlglass spake unto him, and said: "Yea, master, that will I." And therewith departed the master unto the market. Then fell Owlglass to work, and began to cut out pigs, and oxen, and calves, and sheep, and goats, and all kind of cattle. When that it was night, the master returned him home again, and fain would see what his serving-man had done; then found he these animals cut out of the leather. Thereat grew he angry, and said unto Owlglass: "What is it that thou hast done, so to cut and destroy my leather?" And Owlglass said: "Dear master, I have done it as thou wouldst most desire it should be." The master answered, and said: "Nay, thou liest; I would not have thee to destroy the leather; that did I not command thee that thou shouldst do." Then answered Owlglass to him: "Master, wherefore be ye angry? Ye commanded me that I should cut the leather great and small, like as the herdsman driveth forth to field; and most truly to be seen is it that I have thus done." Then said the master: "Nay, but I meant ye should cut out shoes great and small." Thereupon said Owlglass: "Had ye said that unto me so that I understood it, then would I have done it with great joy; and yet would I do it." Then agreed Owlglass and his master, the one with the other; and he forgave him the leather he had cut up, for Owlglass promised him that he would do him content thereafter, and as he told him that would he do.

Then did the shoemaker cut a number of soles for shoes, and laid them before Owlglass, and said unto him: "Look ye, sew ye them little and great as they be altogether." And Owlglass said: "Yea" thereunto, and began to sew them. Then tarried the master awhile, and departed not forth, for he desired to see how Owlglass did sew. For well knew he that which he had told him, and he craved to behold how he would do according to his words. And Owlglass took a small shoe and a great shoe, and with his needle and thread he sewed them together. And thereat stole the master secretly up to him, and he perceived that which he did. Then said he unto Owlglass: "Thou art truly a man after mine own heart; thou doest that which I desire thee to do." And Owlglass answered, and said unto him: "He that doeth his master's bidding will receive no stripes." Then said the master: "Yea, my good servant, my words were so, but my meaning was other. What I meaned was, that thou shouldst first make a pair of small shoes, and then make a pair of large, or the great first and the small ones after; but thou sewest them altogether, according to my words and not my meaning." And then waxed he wroth, and took the leather which was cut up, and said: "Now take thee other leather, and cut me new shoes on one last."

Thereafter thought he no more about the matter, and departed forth to walk. And when that he had been out for more than an hour, he remembered him that he had told Owlglass to cut all on one last; and he hastened him home to see what was done. And Owlglass had sate him still the while, and taken a small last, and cut all the shoes thereunto. So that when the master came, he found he had cut it all according to the little last; and he said unto him: "What dost thou mean, that thou hast on the one last cut me all these shoes? How can the great sole belong to the little shoe?" And Owlglass said unto him: "That will I do after, and the other will I cut." Then said the master: "But thou takest only one last, and makest them all for one foot; what dost thou expect can I do with thy work?" Then answered Owlglass unto him: "Of a truth, master, thou didst bid me to cut them over one last only, and that have I done." Thereat said the master: "If that I had much to do with thee, should I have to run with thee to the hangman;" and he furthermore said unto him: "Pay thou me for the leather thou hast marred." Then said Owlglass: "If that I have marred thy leather, the currier can he not make more?" Then arose he, and stood in the door, and turning himself round unto the master, said: "If that I come not again, have I yet been with thee. Farewell." And he departed from that city.

The Forty and Ninth Adventure.

How that Owlglass bought eggs and had them tightly packed.

On a time Owlglass came into a village in Swabia, where abode a man very stupid, who with lard and eggs drave a trade. And Owlglass did become serving-man unto him, and much business did for his master, by the which he gained greatly. In this wise and after this manner was it that Owlglass did all that his master required. His master sent him unto the market, that he might cheaply buy and dearly sell; for according to such modes grow all merchants rich. And it came to pass on a day, that Owlglass had bought so much, that his baskets, panniers, and chests were all full of lard and butter and eggs, and yet craved he to buy much more. Then lifted he up his voice, and spake unto his master, saying: "Behold, master, between each egg is there a great room; might it not be, that we might get more in if that, like unto cabbages, we trod them closer together?" And the stupid egg-merchant perceived that to be most true; and then bid he the folk which helped him to tread the eggs close together. And so did they; but, lo! then were their feet all yellow, and the eggs were soon broken to pieces. Then did the master of Owlglass cry out upon his man, and despatched him hastily to do business elsewhere; for the egg-trade did he not understand. Yet was the story soon noised abroad; and thenceforward laughed the people, and called the Swabians yellow-feet, the which name remaineth even unto days of this chronicler.

The Fiftieth Adventure.

How that Owlglass made a soup for a boor, and put therein shoemaker's oil; for that, in his nobility, he thought it good enow for the boor.

Now after these knaveries came Owlglass unto Stade, and there he again hired him unto a shoemaker. And when that he began the first day to work, his master went unto market, and of a boor bought a load of wood, and then came home, and commanded that the boor should have a soup given unto him. But he found no one at home; for the goodwife and the maid had gone forth, and Owlglass was alone within the house; and he was sewing shoes. And the master was obliged again to go to the market. So spake he to Owlglass, and said, that he should make ready a soup for the boor; for that had he promised him into their bargain. And Owlglass answered: "Yea;" then the boor unloaded the wood, and came into the house. But when that Owlglass sought in the cupboard, and had made ready the soup, he found nothing to flavour it save shoemaker's oil; so he took the bottle, and poured therefrom a goodly measure into the soup, and a fine flavour was there then therein. And when that the boor began to eat, he tasted that it was very evil; but he was an hungered, and he soon ate up the soup. In no long time thereafter came the shoemaker home, and asked the boor how the soup tasted. And the boor answered him: "That it was good all but one thing, and that was, that it savoured woundily of new shoes." Then departed the boor. And the shoemaker laughed, and said unto Owlglass: "What didst thou put in the soup thou gavest to the boor?" And Owlglass answered, and said: "Thou commandest me that I should take that I found and put in the soup; and I found nought but the shoemaker's oil. Therefore put I that in." And the shoemaker said: "It is well, and quite good enough to give for a bargain to a boor." And so were the two knaves contented; but as two of a trade never can agree together, in no long time parted they, and Owlglass continued his journey.

The Fifty and First Adventure.

This chapter is a special chapter, telling how that a boot-maker sought to beguile Owlglass by greasing his boots, and how that Owlglass looked through the window, and brake it.

Christopher was the name of a bootmaker, who, in Brunswick, lived upon the Cabbage-market. Unto him on a time went Owlglass, that he might have his boots greased. And when that he came into the house, he opened his mouth, and said: "Master, an if ye will smear me these boots well and throughly, I will pay your demand, so that I have them by Monday." And the master answered, and said: "Yea, truly shall ye have them." Then departed Owlglass from the house, and thought no longer thereupon; for when wise men say things shall be done, it is the fool's fault if they be not. And after that he had gone his way, the bootmaker's man said: "Behold, master, have a care; for that is Owlglass, and to all men doth he work knavery. Do, therefore, that he said, or he will work ye a vile turn." Then answered the master, and said: "What would he have?" And the man said: "He said, smear me these boots and throughly. Therefore do ye according to his words, and smear ye them within and without."

Then answered the master unto him, and said: "That will I do." So did he, in truth.

And on the Monday cometh Owlglass, and he saith unto them: "Have ye my boots ready?" And the master had hung them upon a hook in his shop, and answered unto him, and said, as he pointed unto them: "Behold, there have ye your boots as they hang." And Owlglass looked, and saw that they were so smeared within and without; and he laughed, and said: "How good and pious a master bootmaker have I found, that he doth smear me my boots throughly. And what may ye desire to have for your pains?" Then spake the master: "An old penny will I have." Then did Owlglass give him an old penny he had by him, and departed from the house; and then laughed the master and his man, and said one to the other: "How may he take that? Surely now hath he been made a fool!" That heard our good Master Owlglass; and he put his head within the window so that it brake, and head and shoulders followed after, to the great wonderment of all thereby. And Owlglass said unto the bootmaker: "Master, what lard used ye? Tell me if it be lard from a sow or a boar?" Thereat was the master amazed with his man, and at last perceived that Owlglass lay in the window, and he had broken it. Then the bootmaker grew angry, and said: "The genius of evil take thee! What meanest thou? With this lapstone will I break thy head!" Then said Owlglass: "Honourable sir, be not angry. It is but a simple answer I would have. Which is it from which ye have taken the lard, from a sow or a boar?" And the master wished his window whole. But he answered never a word; and thereat said Owlglass: "If that ye will not tell me, I must depart to foreign lands to have it certified, and of another must I learn whether it be of a sow or a boar." Therewith departed Owlglass.

Then waxed the master wroth with his man, and said unto him: "That counsel gavest thou me; now give me other counsel how that my window may be whole." But the servant was dumb.

So said the master: "Which hath been the greatest fool among these, and who shall pay the damage?" But the comrade held his tongue; and the master continued: "Who is it that hath mocked the other? How shall my window be made whole? I have always heard it said: He that is heavy laden with a fool may soon rejoice to lose his pack from his shoulders; and if I had done that might I have kept my window, nor would I have cared an if it had been in that wise." Therefore departed the apprentice, and bootmaker Christopher paid for his broken window himself.

The Fifty and Second Adventure.

Telleth how that Owlglass at Einbeck became a brewer's man, and did seethe a dog which was called Hops.

Owlglass tarried not at any time in doing his evil knavery. And he came unto Einbeck after a time, and in that town did he hire him unto a brewer to be his man. Then came it to pass, that the brewer his master desired to go unto a wedding; and he spake unto Owlglass, and said unto him: "Do thou brew with the maid while I am away from hence, and to-morrow will I return to help thee in thy labour. Yet, above all, do ye not forget to put hops into the beer, so that it shall savour strongly thereof, and be a most desirable thing to buy." And Owlglass answered and said unto his master, that would he diligently perform unto his content. Then did the brewer with his wife depart out of the door to the wedding. Then began Owlglass to brew the beer; and the serving-woman taught him what he should do, forasmuch as she understood it better than he did. And when it came to be time that the hops should be put therein, the maid said unto him: "Lo! my dear fellow-servant, thou canst boil the hops alone as well as while I am with thee. Therefore do thou boil them, and

I will go for an hour unto the dance." And Owlglass said: "Yea;" and thought within himself: "When that she hath departed out of the way, then canst thou better do thy knavery. What shall it be that thou wilt do unto this brewer?"

Now the brewer had in his house a great dog, whose name was Hops; and when the water was hot, took Owlglass the poor beast, and threw him into the vat, and boiled him therein, so that the flesh was boiled from off the bones, and the skin and hair was sodden altogether. Thereafter thought the maid, that it was time she should return home unto Owlglass, for the hops must have been seethed enough. She entered in unto him, and spake unto him: "Lo! my brother, now have the hops seethed enough; draw off." Then took she a sieve and strained the beer, but found nought therein; then said she unto Owlglass: "Hast thou also put therein the hops, as I said unto ye? I find nought therein." But Owlglass said: "Thou wilt find all at the bottom." And the woman took a shovel, and found the bones of the dog at the bottom. Then cried she aloud: "What is this thing thou hast put therein? The evil one defend me from this beer!" And Owlglass answered: "What our master commanded me that did I. I seethed therein Hops our dog."

It fortuned that the brewer then entered in unto them, and he had drunken himself drunk at the wedding; and he said unto them: "Ha! ha! what is it that ye do, my children?" Then answered the maid, and said unto him: "Lo! I did but go for half an hour unto the dance, and bade this our new man to seethe the hops in the beer; and he hath taken our dog, and hath seethed him. Behold, ye may see his bones." Then spake Owlglass, and said: "Truly did I nothing more than ye enjoined me to do. Ye said that Hops should I seethe, and that have I done. But ye are ungrateful when that I am obedient. Had ye servants which ever did that which ye commanded as I have done, would ye surely have great content." Then departed he, and was wroth that they thanked him not.

HOW OWLGLASS BOILETH HOPS.

The Fifty and Third Adventure.

*How that Owlglass hired him unto a tailor, and sewed so
secretly that it was not seen of any one.*

And when that Owlglass approached unto Berlin, he there
hired him unto a tailor of that town. Then said his master
unto him, as he sate in the workshop: "If that thou sewest for
me, sew for me after that wise that it shall be seen of no one." To
him answered Owlglass: "Yea;" and with that took his work, and
crept him under the counter, and put his work across his knee,
and began there to sew. The tailor stood thereby, and looked upon
him, and said unto him: "What doest thou? Of a truth that is a
marvellous way to sew thy coat." And Owlglass answered: "Master, said ye not that I should sew in such wise as that it should be
seen of no one, and can any one behold me where I sew?" Then
said the tailor: "Nay; but, my dear serving-man, sew ye no longer
after that wise, but begin to sew that all may see."

So fared they on for a matter of three days; and it fortuned one
night, that a peasant's great over-coat, such as in that country is
called a wolf, lay unfinished in the shop. This took the tailor, and
gave it unto Owlglass, and said unto him: "Here, take the wolf and
make it ready, and thereafter mayest thou get thee to bed." Then
answered Owlglass: "Yea; and if ye go will I right quickly do it as
ye enjoin." Then departed the master; and Owlglass took the coat,
and he cut it up, and made first a wolf's head, and then legs and
body, and with sticks set it upright on the bench, so that it looked
like unto a wolf, and then gat he him unto bed. And when that
it was day, the master gat him up, and awakened Owlglass also,
and found the wolf standing in the shop. And he marvelled with

great wonderment at this doing of Owlglass; and he said unto him when that he came: "I' the prince of mischief's name, what is this thing thou hast done?" And Owlglass answered, and said: "A wolf have I made, as ye enjoined me." Then said the tailor: "Such a wolf would I not have; but a peasant's great coat. That called I a wolf." Thereat answered Owlglass, and spake unto the tailor, saying: "Dear master, that knew not I. An ye had said unto me, that ye would have a peasant's coat, then would I have made it; but ye said I should make a wolf, and, lo! have I not done it? And with greater content would I have made a coat than a wolf." And the tailor forgave him; for as it was ended, what should he do?

And after four days had passed, was the tailor fain again to sleep, and yet he judged that it was too soon for his man to get him to bed. And there lay a coat in the shop, the which had been finished, all save the arms, which should be sewed on. This took he, and gave it unto Owlglass, saying: "Whip me these arms to the coat, and then mayest thou sleep." And Owlglass answered: "Yea;" and therewith departed the tailor. Then did Owlglass light two candles, and he hung the coat on a hook, and made him a whip with whipcord, and 'gan to whip the sleeves, so that he might get them unto the coat. Yet stirred they not. And when that his candles were burned down, gat he two more, and lighted them, and burned candles through the whole night. At last arose the master, and came unto Owlglass into the shop, and said unto him: "What mystery play ye here?" And Owlglass answered gravely, and said: "No mystery is this, but hard labour; for the whole night through have I stood here, and whipped me these sleeves with whipcord, yet move they not unto the coat. Better had it been if that ye had bid me sleep; for ye surely knew that I must lose my labour." Then answered the tailor, and said: "Lay ye that to my charge? Am I ever to be finding ye brains to understand that which I say? Didst not see that I meant that ye should sew the sleeves on to the coat?" Answered straightway unto him Owlglass: "Nay; but, in the evil one's name, how can ye think that it be my fault, that when ye say one thing I should understand ye to mean another thing? If that I had known what ye would have done, would I not have sewn the sleeves on, and then slept an hour or twain? Now may ye sit ye down, for I will get me unto my bed." Thereat said the tailor: "Not so; I will not receive into my house folk that lazy be and sleep." Then did they strive together in anger; and the tailor would have payment of Owlglass for the candles he had burned, but this would not Owlglass give him; therefore took he that which belonged unto him, and departed.

The Fifty and Fourth Adventure.

How that Owlglass caused three tailors to fall from their board, and then would have persuaded the people that the wind had blown them down.

On the market at Brandenburg, Owlglass abode in an inn for a matter of fourteen days. And hard by there dwelt a tailor, and on his board had he three of his men sitting at work. And when that Owlglass passed by over against them, they did nothing but mock him, and throw rags after him. And all this time kept Owlglass silence; and one day when that it was a full market-day, did he secretly the night before saw through the posts which held up the board, and so left them standing. In the morning did the men put the board on the posts, and sate them down as usual, and sewed. At the time when that the swineherd blew his horn that every one might drive forth his swine, came the tailor's swine forth likewise, and ran under the window, and against the posts began to rub themselves; then came down the three tailors, and fell upon the ground, and sorely hurt themselves. And when Owl-glass marked that they fell, he cried with a loud voice: "Behold, ye people, of what light account are tailors, when that by the wind three are blown down from the board!" These words of Owlglass heard the whole market, and the people therein. Then ran all the market-place in great haste, and laughed, and mocked the tailors with great scorn; and then did the tailors abuse each one the other with much evil language, for they wist not how it had come to pass that they had fallen. At last did they behold that the posts were sawed through, and knew well that it was Owlglass. Then did they set new posts in the ground, but mocked him no longer.

The Fifty and Fifth Adventure.

How that Owlglass assembled all the tailors throughout the whole land of Saxony, by proclaiming that he would teach them a mighty useful thing, that would get bread both for them and their children.

On a time, Owlglass made proclamation in the whole of the Wendic Union, and in the land of Saxony, that is, in Holstein, Pommern, Stettin, and Mecklenburg, and likewise in Lübeck, Hamburg, in the Sound, and at Wismar; and in his letters said, that truly the tailors in those parts should come unto him, for tidings of great joy and content did he bring, and a cunning and rare art would he disclose unto them, by the which they should have great comfort and gain, and their children after them. And he said, that they should come unto him into the town of Rostock, and so should assemble together. Then did they all make answer unto Owlglass, that for so great an art would they willingly come, and learn that art of which he spake.

And so came they all together upon occasion to Rostock; and the folks were all amazed as to why so great a number of tailors came and abode in that town. When that Owlglass also heard that they had approached and entered into the town, he was right glad; and he let them grow in multitude until that among these tailors were a goodly number of men. Thereafter spake they unto Owlglass, and said unto him, that, according unto his word, they had come together, and that they would fain learn of him what that art was which they should be taught, and the which should benefit both them and their children. Then besought they him that he should soon teach them; and rarely would they recompence him therefor. And Owlglass answered, and said unto them: "Yea; do ye all together come into a field, so that all may hear." And according unto his saying did they.

Then gat him Owlglass up into a house, which overlooked the field, and there looked he forth from a window; and he lifted up his voice, and said unto them: "Honourable artificers in the tailoring trade, I bid ye mark and perceive, that when ye have by ye scissors, ellwand, thread, thimble, needle, and a smoothing-iron, the which ye call a goose, then have ye enough tools for your business; and to get them, therein is no art, for common is it, and cometh of itself. But do ye steadfastly learn of me this art, and bear ye me in mind when that ye do it. When that ye take a thread, forget ye not at the end thereof that is contrary unto that which ye thread in the needle to make a knot, or, in good sooth, ye will make many a stitch in vain." Thereat did one tailor look upon his neighbour; and they each one said unto the other: "Lo! was not this a thing well known unto all of us, and of old time a rule among us?" Then did they ask him whether he had anything further to tell them. "Verily! for phantasy's sake would not we have come twelve weary miles, or despatched from one to the other messengers of speed; and this art ye have told us have we known these thousand years." Then answered Owlglass unto the tailors, and said unto them: "That which hath been known these thousand years is marked of no man; and when that people are bidden to think upon it, do they not in any wise thank the speaker." Therefore might they depart again unto where they had come from. Then were the tailors who had come from afar very wroth with Owlglass, and would fain have come to him, and beaten him; but he was nimble and escaped them. Then conferred they one with the other, and laughed, and said: "Truly was it their own fault that they were thus befooled; for knew they not of old what a slippery fellow was this same Owlglass?"

The Fifty and Sixth Adventure.

How that Owlglass beat wool upon a saint's day, and that very high.

And when that Owlglass came unto Stendal, he gave it out, that he was a woolstapler, and hired himself unto a master in that town. Then upon a Sunday spake the master unto him, saying: "Mark ye, my good fellow, upon a Monday do ye commonly keep holiday, and that love I not in any man who cometh into my house; for here must all diligently labour." And Owlglass made answer: "That pleaseth me right well, master." So he gat him up early on the Monday, and laboured hard, and the same thing did he on Tuesday; and that pleased the master exceedingly. And on the Wednesday there fell a saint's day, the which was a holy day and should be kept; yet gat Owlglass to his labour again, and 'gan to work and beat his wool, so that ye might hear him right down the street. The master arose from his bed when that he heard the noise, and cried unto Owlglass with a loud voice: "Be ye still; be ye still; to-day is a holy day, and we may not labour." Then said Owlglass: "Dear master, said ye not on Sunday, that ye loved not that one should be idle on a holy day; but ye said, that I should work the whole week through." And the woolstapler answered him: "Nay; but I meant not that. Leave thy labour now, and that which thou wouldst have earned to-day will I pay thee." And this fitted Owlglass right well; and he kept the holy day, and at eventide he supped with his master. Then conferred they; and the master said unto him, that the wool contented him not, and he bade Owlglass, that he should beat it up a little higher. And Owlglass said: "Yea;" and in the morning he arose from his bed early, and fixed up the frame to the beam, and gat him a ladder, and mounted thereupon, and with his rod beat the wool, so that all the town could hear the noise. The while lay the master in bed, and he perceived right certainly that Owlglass was not beating the wool as he should do; therefore he gat up, and went, and looked upon him. And he spake unto him jestingly: "By my troth, and if ye stood upon the roof so would ye be yet higher; and little would it rede whether ye stood on the ladder or the roof." And therewith departed he unto the church. Thereupon did Owlglass take the frame, and climbed up on the roof, and there beat the wool. That saw his master from the street as he came along; and he cried aloud unto him, and came running: "Ha! ho! what do ye there upon the roof? Is that a thing ye should do, to beat the wool upon the roof?" And Owlglass said: "Truly did I according unto thy words. For thou didst say, that it would be better upon the roof than the ladder, for that the roof was higher than the beam." And the woolstapler said: "Play ye no more of your knaveries; get ye forth from my house, nor do ye again come hither." Thereat departed Owlglass, and lamented that he could never earn any thanks.

The Fifty and Seventh Adventure.

How that Owlglass was hired by a furrier, and did sleep among the skins.

On a time did Owlglass take service with a furrier, and when that it was night, he bade Owlglass get him to work and hang out the skins. But Owlglass loved not the labour, and would fain have escaped therefrom. And he spake unto his master, saying: "How is this that with so ill savour this smelleth. I' faith, I cannot bear it!" And the furrier answered him and said: "Verily, it seemeth unto me that of this trade knowest thou nought. For an if thou hadst slept only four nights among the furs, then wouldst thou no longer mark their ill savour." Then said Owlglass: "Four nights will I sleep among the skins, master, and then shall I not mark it." So the furrier gat him to bed. And behold, Owlglass took the skins which were prepared, and which hung upon the wall, and he took also the skins which were dry; and lastly, took he the wet skins; and he cast them together upon the floor of the loft, and crept in among them and slept until the morning. When that it was day, then rose up his master, and he beheld that the skins were taken from the wall; and he ran unto the loft, and spake unto Owlglass to inquire of him what it might fortune that he knew about the skins. And he perceived not Owlglass; but lo! his eyes fell upon the skins, which, wet and dry, lay together in a heap one with the other. Thereat was he strangely moved, and with a weeping voice called the maid and the women folk; and these cries did cause Owlglass to awake, and he looked forth from among the skins, and said: "Honoured master, what may it be that doth move ye so to cry out and to clamour?" Then did the furrier marvel greatly, and knew not what might be in the heap of skins.

And he opened his mouth, and said unto Owlglass: "Where art thou?" And Owlglass to him answered: "Behold, here am I." Then said the master: "That good fortune may never come unto thee! Hast taken me the dry furs from the wall, and the wet from the lime-pit, and cast me them together in this heap, so that they be spoiled. What wilt thou with this phantasy?" But the wise and prudent Master Owlglass answered him and said: "How, master, be ye not angry! for an if ye be angry for that I have slept one night amidst the skins, what will ye be when that I have slept the four nights ye enjoined me; for ye said that I knew nought of the labour." Then said the furrier: "Now liest thou like unto a false and ready knave! I bid thee not carry together the wet and the dry, and sleep amid them after this wise!" Then sought the furrier for a stick, and tried to beat Owlglass. But then went Owlglass towards the door to depart thence; and as he went he met the wife of the furrier, and the maid servant, and they would fain have held him. But he said unto them: "Peace be with ye, good friends, let me hasten for a chirurgeon, for my master hath fallen, and his leg hath broken!" Then they let him go, and ran up the stairs unto the master; but he came running down at a great pace, and overthrew the maid and his good wife, and they all stumbled and fell together. Yet our good master had speedily departed, and gotten him thence with all haste.

The Fifty and Eighth Adventure.

How that Owlglass on a time, at Berlin, did make wolves.

A cunning and wily mind are the Swabians, and where they come and find not victual, ye may approve it of a certainty that other folk will starve. Yet are they more lovers of the beer jug, and of drinking, than thoughtful of their labour, so comes it likewise that their business lieth but sadly. Now it happened on a time that at Berlin lived a furrier, and he was in Swabia born, and in his art was he most handy, and had much business, and thereto was rich, with a good workshop, by the which he had gained much, as he served those which held lands, and moneys, and houses, and goodly titles. And it came to pass that one winter season a great and noble prince, with all his court, desired to hunt; and they commanded the furrier to prepare for them not a few wolf skins to wear. Of this was Owlglass told, so he gat him unto the furrier, and besought him that he would give unto him work, that he might have money and food. At that time, also, did the master lack people, and was right glad that Owlglass had come unto him; and he spake unto him, and asked him, if that he would make such wolves. And Owlglass answered: "That he was of the land of Saxony, and knew well how to make them." Then said the furrier unto him: "Truly art thou well come unto me, and I bid thee stay. And touching the reward of thy pains will we agree, and thou shalt abide with me, and have a good time while that thou stayest." Owlglass answered and said unto the furrier: "Yea, master, I do bethink me that thou art right honest and true; and I crave nothing so much as that ye shall know me for what manner of man I am, when that ye behold my labour. But I work not in fellowship with other men; but ever alone in mine own company."

Then did the furrier allot unto Owlglass a small chamber wherein he abode; and he received from the furrier the metage of certain furs, and the wolves' skins. Then took Owlglass the wolves' skins as they were, and cut them, and made of them a number of wolves; and these he stuffed full of hay, and gat feet made of sticks, and they stood up in manner as if they lived. And when that he had thus cut up all the furs, and made an end of his labours, he cried aloud to his master: "Ho! master, come hither; truly have I ended my labour, and made the wolves." And the master answered and said: "Yea, my good man, verily have I yet much labour to do! Be thou diligent, and continue as thou art." Then turned he about to go thence, and he beheld the wolves standing in the chamber, and he lifted up his voice thereat, and cried aloud in great anger: "What is this that thou hast done! Thou bird of unhappy fortune! what evil hast thou wrought unto me? For this will I have thee cast into gaol, and thou shalt suffer therefor." Then answered Owlglass and said: "Master, call ye that my reward and my thanks. Ye commanded me that I should make wolves, and wolves have I also made. Had ye but said that I should make wolf furs, then had I understood ye, and also have done it with great joy. In the beginning should ye have explained carefully unto one that is a stranger that which ye would have. And, indeed, had it appeared unto me that I should have gained no greater thanks than that which hath been given me, then would I not have wrought thy work in any wise." Then departed Owlglass from Berlin, and gat him into the city of Leipzig.

The Fifty and Ninth Adventure.

How that Owlglass, being servant unto a great lord, did fetch for him wine and beer together in a most delectable manner.

Once again did Owlglass take service with a noble lord, and became unto him body servant. And it fortuned, that this master of his loved good cheer,—the which is a thing not rare among all manner of men,—and especially loved he a cup of generous wine, or a deep draught of good beer.

It came to pass, that on a time Owlglass and his master journeyed together, and lay at an inn. And the day was hot, and they twain were faint, for they had ridden hard. Then spake the lord unto his serving-man Owlglass, and said: "Go thou and find mine host the landlord of this inn, and fetch him unto me." That did Owlglass on that instant; for well knew he, that when the master drank the man was seldom dry. And his lord spake unto the host, and said unto him: "Lo! we have come far, and the sun hath burned us so that we be dry, and would have some drink." And the host answered him: "Verily, in all the wide world, and the Duchy of Mecklenburg to boot, is there no such liquor as in my cellar. Therefore have ye come unto the best place to slake your thirst." Then commanded the master, that

Owlglass should depart with the host; and he said unto him: "I know not the which is best, therefore do thou bring me good store of both wine and beer, and bring ye them together." And Owlglass said: "Yea;" and departed with the host. Then the host meted unto him both of wine and of beer; and Owlglass said unto himself: "If that I faint then loseth my master his good servant; therefore, that I may truly serve him, will I first drink, for peradventure I shall not have strength to bring the liquor unto my lord." Therefore drank he merrily the half of the wine and the half of the beer, and remembered his lord's words, that they should be together; therefore mingled he the wine and the beer in one measure, and gave unto his lord to drink. And when that the lord found how delectable was the mixture, he waxed very wroth, and said unto Owlglass: "What is this that thou hast done, and what vile liquor is this?" "Truly, my lord," quoth honest Owlglass, "it is wine and beer mingled together, as ye enjoined me to bring unto ye." But his master perceived it was a knavery, and bade Owlglass to depart from his sight; for, of a truth, was his beguiling most evilly done. But sorrowfully departed Owlglass, for he thought that he wrought no harm in doing the thing which was commanded unto him. Indeed, my masters, often times falleth the evil temper of the one upon the other; and for the too exact enactment of the commands of the master is the man chidden.

The Sixtieth Adventure.

How that Owlglass for a tanner prepared leather with stools and benches, at the good city of Brunswick on the Dam.

Now it fortuned that as Owlglass journeyed from Leipzig, he came unto Brunswick to a tanner there, who made ready the leather for the shoemaker. And it was winter time, and he said unto himself: "Now shalt thou stay the winter through with this tanner." Then agreed they together, and he hired himself unto him. And after that eight days had gone by, it came to pass that the tanner desired to depart unto a feast, and he commanded Owlglass the while that he should make ready some leather. For he said unto him: "The cauldron of leather prepare ye." And Owlglass asked him: "What shall I do it with? and where shall I find wood for the fire?" And the tanner answered and said unto him: "Wherefore ask ye such an idle question? If that I had no wood upon the wood-heap, have I yet store of stools and benches enough in the house, with the which thou mayest prepare the leather." And Owlglass answered: "Yea;" and then departed the tanner. Then did Owlglass take a cauldron, and hung it over the fire, and put one skin of leather after another therein, and boiled the leather until it was so soft that ye might, with two fingers, rend it in twain. And when that Owlglass found this he took a hatchet, and therewith hewed in pieces every stool and bench the which were in the house, and he put them in the fire under the cauldron, and boiled the leather yet more until that he looked therein again, and lo! these stools and benches were all burned up. Then took he the leather out of the cauldron, and put it in a heap, and departed out of the house and the city, and continued his journeying.

But the tanner thought not a jot upon the matter, but ate and drank, and gat him to bed, and slept. Next morning 'gan he to think it was time he should see what labour had been fulfilled of his man; therefore he arose, and went unto the workshop, and found the heap of leather so marred, and neither stool or bench in the place. Then grew he right angry, and went unto his wife, and said unto her: "Behold, I fear our man that we hired was Owlglass, that great knave, cheat, and beguiler; for it is his custom to do everything that is told according to the words spoken unto him. And now hath he departed, and marred me all the leather, and burned me up every stool and bench the which stood in our house." Then wept his wife, and spake unto him, saying: "Get ye after him with all speed, and bring him back hither." But the tanner said: "Nay, that will I not do. I have had of him enough." And perchance was this saying true.

The Sixty and First Adventure.

How that Owlglass was groom unto a noble lord, and what knavery he wrought unto his lord's horse, Rosimond.

On a time it fortuned, that with a lord of great wealth and much land, our noble Master Owlglass took service. Now this most noble gentleman, when that he entered into the lord his household, was made to be groom of the horses; and his lord commanded and enjoined him, that he should have a great care of the horses, and in especial he desired Owlglass to dress and tend a horse of a milk-white skin and gentle blood, named Rosimond. And this horse did his lord love better than any other steed; for that it was of a disposition most rare. Yet did Owlglass none the less bethink him of a knavery the which he might do unto this lord; for from a deceitful beguiling could he at no time refrain. But he answered his lord when that he charged him; and spake unto him, saying: "Yea, my good lord and master; all that ye bid me to do will I with great diligence perform." And therewith departed his lord from him, and rejoiced with great content that he had obtained for himself so excellent a groom.

In no long time thereafter were all the horses put forth into the fields, there to graze, and to exercise themselves after the manner of horses. Then gat Owlglass unto his lord, and stood before him, and said: "Of a truth, master, well know I that of thy horses there is not one that thou lovest so well as thou dost the milk-white steed Rosimond." And thereto said his master: "Yea." "Then of that steed," answered Owlglass, "have I had special care. Yet I fear me, master, that by thy answer unto me, he will not be long to live." Then said his master: "If that be so, and my beloved steed is not long to live, go thou, my trusty groom, and get ye me his skin, that I may have it." For Rosimond's skin was of a most rare beauty. Thereat answered Owlglass: "Yea;" and gat him to the field where Rosimond was grazing, and pursued him. But the horse was very fleet, and fled before Owlglass; and it was eventide ere Owlglass caught him. Then when he had thus caught him, he took a knife and killed Rosimond, and took his skin, and brought it unto his lord. And when that he brought it unto him, he said unto Owlglass: "How cometh this? Verily, the whole day hast thou been away, and surely in a less time than a whole day couldst thou have taken off the skin." And Owlglass excused himself, saying: "Lo! my good lord, most truly sayest thou that in less than a whole day could I have taken off the skin; yet had I great labour in the matter, for Rosimond fled before me, and was fleet of foot. Now have I brought the skin, as thou didst enjoin me." Then waxed the master of Owlglass very wroth, and cried aloud unto him: "Thou knave, was not my horse Rosimond dead then? Didst thou kill my horse?" To him quoth Owlglass: "Yea, truly killed I the horse; for so cruel am I not, that I should take the skin off a living horse. For in torture-chambers do they only such things, either unto man or unto beast." Then wept the lord greatly for his beloved horse; and he would have killed Owlglass, but that Owlglass fled, saying: "I did but according to the words of my master; for I said unto him, that I feared me that the horse would not live any long while; and then commanded he that I should take his skin, the which I have done, and my kind heart

hath injured me, in that I did not skin the horse ere I killed it."
Then departed Owlglass in great haste, and came not again into
that lord's house.

The Sixty and Second Adventure.

*How that Owlglass beguiled the drawer at the town-house
cellar of Lübeck, and did for a can of wine give him a can
of water.*

When that Owlglass came unto Lübeck, he took great heed
to commit no knavery; for in that town are the folk very
strict upon such as beguile or deceive. Therefore was our good
master sadly perplexed and unhappy, for that in no wise could
he gratify the feelings of his heart and content himself as he was
wont to do. And at that time there lived in the town of Lübeck a
drawer, named Lamprecht, who kept the cellar at the town house;
and he was a man very proud, who believed that no person in
Lübeck,—yea, no person in the whole world,—was so wise and
so important and so discerning as he. Nor did he at any time think
that he might not say it of himself; and when that he said it, he
used to add, that one that would beguile him must of a morning
rise very early. For this reason were the citizens very wroth with
him, and held him as an enemy.

Now when that Owlglass heard of the arrogance of this man,
he could no longer keep hidden the knave which he was; and he
thought within himself, that he would soon shew that he was
an even master in craft and cunning with him. Therefore took he
two cans of the same size and form; the one he carried openly in
his hand, and it was empty; but the other bare he secretly under

his cloak, and it was filled with water. Then departed he unto the wine-cellar, and there had a measure of wine meted unto him, and then deftly took forth the can with water and set it down, and put the wine-can within his cloak. And Owlglass lifted up his voice, and said unto the drawer: "Worshipful master drawer, what costeth this wine?" And he answered, and said unto him: "Truly, it is tenpence the measure." Then said Owlglass: "The wine is marvellous costly. I have no more than sixpence. Can I have it for that money?" Then waxed the drawer very wroth, and said: "Wilt thou dare to value the wine of my lords the town council? Here have we a fixed sum; and he that liketh not the price, may let the wine stay in the butt." Therewith taketh he in his wrath the can with the water in it; and Owlglass said unto him: "See thou, an if ye will not have the sixpence, therefore I am content ye shall pour it back." Then the drawer poured the water into the butt, for he thought that it was the wine; and he said unto him: "What a foolish knave art thou? Thou hast wine meted unto thee, but thou carest not to pay therefor." Then took Owlglass the empty can, and departed, and said: "Verily do I see that thou art a fool; and there is no one so cunning and wise in this world, that may not by a fool be beguiled. Aye, and that too if he were a drawer!" Then he returned forth from the cellar, and he thought himself safe.

The Sixty and Third Adventure.

How that Owlglass 'scaped hanging by his cunning, and would have hanged himself for a crown, yet did not.

hen that Owlglass came forth into day from the cellar, the drawer, Lamprecht, did bethink him of the words which Owlglass spake, and he ran hastily for a police officer, and they pursued Owlglass, and in no long time took him in the street as he went forward. The officer seized him, and they examined our noble Master Owlglass, and found upon him the two cans, and of them one contained the wine of the which he had beguiled the drawer, and the other was empty. And, O and alas! that the pen of this chronicler should write so sad a thing of the virtuous Master Owlglass!—they held him for a thief, and took him first and carried him and cast him into the city prison, and there lay he. And then assembled the council of the town, and they conferred together touching the offence of Master Owlglass, and it was agreed amongst them that he had committed a grave crime, for the doing and enactment of which it was fitting that he should be hanged up until that he was dead. Yet did some aver that it was nought else but a subtle device and knavery, and that the drawer should have, with more care, avoided the over-reaching with the which he had been visited; so that, indeed, the fault, in so much as it touched Master Owlglass, was but an impudent action. But the many who, with great hatred, hated Master Owlglass, carried it that it was flat robbery, so with their voices outweighed the rest, and he was decreed to die.

And when the day came on the which he should be hanged up, there was a great assembly of people in the city, for my good masters (as in this town of ours in the which this book is imprinted and published), there are ever lying in wait evil and cruel persons who, if it so chance, that they themselves be not in fear of the gallows' tree, will always hastily run and see another die the death they would not command should be done to their dogs. They came upon horses and on foot, and so great an uproar was there, that at last the council was greatly vexed that they had resolved to put him to death; for in good truth this deed was not sufficient to be worthy of the gallows. And some desired to look upon him to see how so marvellous a man would take his end. Others considered that he was a magician, and with the aid of evil demons would rescue and save himself, and of a truth did all hope that after some wise he would come off alive. But all this time, as he was led forth, remained Owlglass silent and still, and held his peace; and the multitude marvelled, for they thought he would have despaired greatly. And when that he was come unto the gallows' tree, he opened his mouth and spake, and besought the town council that as he was a dying man, and one that would never again speak, that they would grant unto him one grace, and he would not ask them for his life, nor for money, nor for anything the which should cost them a penny; nay, but that by it he might, in good sooth, save them a sum, and the charges of the town being heavy, it would relieve them.

And then stood the council altogether, and marvelled what this might be; and they conferred together, and agreed that, indeed, they would grant him that he desired, if that it proved not against the things he had himself said unto them. Then spake Owlglass unto the town council, and said: "Indeed, it shall be manifest unto ye that it runneth not counter unto my words. It is but a little matter the which can easily be told unto ye, and give me now your hands, that it may be granted." Thereat did they according to his words. Then said good Master Owlglass, the prisoner: "Noble and worshipful councillors of Lübeck! I have said unto ye, that for as much as ye have condemned me to death, I should truly suffer death as ye have decreed. But a grievous and heavy debt lieth upon the city, the which every man should strive to lighten according unto his means; and to do this will I also aid as best I may. This day have ye brought me out to be hanged up; but see ye the halter wherewith ye would hang me is a new one, and ye must be at charges therefor unto two crowns. Now, if I say unto ye that I will, an if ye give me a crown, go and fetch an old rope, and therewith hang myself, will ye make no little profit; for my good friend the hangman, will not be at the pains to hang me, and ye will save his fee, and all these men with the which ye guard me, may freely depart unto their homes. Therefore I pray ye that ye will give unto me the money, and at mine ease, when that I have nought else to do, will I hang myself, in good faith, with an old rope." Then said the chief magistrate: "Of a truth the knave is right, and we would do well to let him do this as he saith." And they granted his wish, and he departed thence; but in all his life was he never at his ease sufficient to fulfil his saying. But oft he meditated thereupon, intending to do it; yet the best intents are oft not to be discharged.

The Sixty and Fourth Adventure.

*How that Owlglass, at Helmstadt, caused a great pocket
to be made.*

A knavery did once Owlglass perform with a pocket. For in the town of Helmstadt there lived a pocket-maker, and unto him came Owlglass, and spake unto him, saying: "Wilt thou make for me a great pocket?" Then answered the pocket-maker: "Yea, that will I. How great will thou have it to be?" And Owlglass said unto him: "So that it be great enough I shall be content therewith." And at that time was it the set fashion to wear great pockets of hair, broad and deep. Then did the pocket-maker make for Owlglass such a great pocket as he would have him to do. And when Owlglass came and looked upon it, he said: "Lo! this pocket is not great enough. This is but a pocket-kin. Make for me one the which shall be large enough. Of a truth will I pay thee well all thy labour." Then took the pocket-maker the skin of an ox, and made the pocket so great that one might have put a calf of one year old within it, and it would tax one man's strength to lift it. Thereafter came Owlglass again unto the house of the pocket-maker, and looked upon it, but it liked him not, and again said he: "This pocket is not great enough. If that thou wilt make me a pocket great enough, will I now give thee two crowns on the business." And the pocket-maker answered him: "Yea;" and took the two crowns, and made another pocket; and thereunto took he three ox-hides, and it was so heavy that two men would have had to bear it upon a frame, and within might ye have put great store of corn. But when Owlglass looked again upon the work of the master, he spake unto him, saying: "Lo! my good master, this pocket is great enough, but the pocket I would crave is not this one; therefore will I not have it. But an if ye would fashion for me such a pocket that when I take from it one penny I shall ever leave therein twain, I would most willingly pay thee for thy labour." And therewith departed Owlglass, and left the man with his three pockets and the two crowns. Yet in leather had the work cost hard upon ten crowns.

The Sixty and Fifth Adventure.

How that Owlglass, at Erfurt, beguiled a butcher.

When that Owlglass came unto the town of Erfurt, he forgat not to work some piece of knavery. And soon was he well-known of the students and townsfolk. One day he was going through the market-place, over against a butcher's shop, and the butcher cried aloud unto him that he should buy somewhat of him that he might carry it home. Then answered Owlglass unto the butcher, and said unto him: "What wilt thou that I shall take with me?" And the butcher said: "What shalt thou take, sayest thou? Why, truly, a good piece of beef!" Then said Owlglass: "Yea," and took such a piece and departed. Then ran the butcher, and pursued him, and said unto him: "Nay; but do thou now pay me for this meat!" Thereat spake Owlglass unto him, saying: "Of money didst thou say nothing at all unto me. Thou didst say unto me with great kindness and courtesy, that I should take something, and when I asked thee what it should be, thou didst single out the beef; and that took I. And I can, by thy neighbours, prove that it was after that wise that thou gavest unto me the beef." Then came the other butchers, neighbours of the one who had controversy with Owlglass, and they confirmed

our noble master from hatred of their neighbour, and said: "Yea, that it was as the butcher had said unto the young man." For when that folk came to buy in the shambles, this butcher would always cry aloud unto the customers that they should buy always of him. Therefore did the neighbours help good Master Owlglass unto his piece of beef. And while that the butcher was arguing and contending with anger and strife on this matter, Owlglass put the beef within his cloak and departed; thus left he them to contend together as long as it delighted them.

The Sixty and Sixth Adventure.

Telleth how that good Master Owlglass again beguiled the butcher at Erfurt, by pleasing him with a most grateful jingle.

In less than a week after, came Owlglass again unto the shambles. And the same butcher spake once more to Owlglass, and mocked him, and said: "Come hither again, and for thyself get a piece of beef." And unto such comforting words answered Owlglass: "Yea;" and would have taken a good piece of meat; but the butcher in haste took hold of his meat, and kept it. Then said Owlglass unto him: "Bide a while, and let the meat lie; I will pay thee for it." And the butcher laid the meat again upon the bench. Then said Owlglass unto him: "Hear me what I say. If that I speak such a word unto thee as shall content thee, will that be payment for this meat, and I will not touch it in any wise?" And the butcher said: "Lo! thou mightest say words unto me that would content me most greatly, or words that would not agree; yet if thou sayest such words as shall be pleasant, then canst thou take the meat." Then spoke Owlglass after this wise:

> "Be merry this day, and drink good wine;
> Thy meat will be paid for,—the money thine."

"Truly this is a brave saying," said the butcher; "but I would rather have the doing. This likes me not. Say on." Thereat spake Owlglass once more:

> "The good wife scolds nor prates to-day;

Be happy therefore whilst thou may."

"Nay, nay," said the butcher; "how can that be when that I have no wife. Thy saying likes me not. Say on." Then laughed Owlglass, and said:

"The butcher best likes to be paid,
So money-bag be now my aid."

Then cried the butcher: "Such words are brave and true words. Behold, thou speakest sensibly, and the saying like I well." Thereat said Owlglass: "Behold, then, the meat is mine. Good friends that stand around, is it not true that I have now fulfilled my part?" And with much clamour said they: "Yea;" and Owlglass took the meat, and departed. But the butcher stood still, and knew not what to say unto them; for the neighbours mocked him, and turned him to scorn. And if thereat he was vexed, truly was it no great wonder.

The Sixty and Seventh Adventure.

Touching the faults of the which our noble Master Owlglass had a few; for he was human, and in all human things is imperfection.

My worthy masters, truly must ye have seen how virtuous, how wise, how kind, how excellent a man was our noble Master Owlglass; so that as a mirror of honesty and simplicity ye mote admire him. But, alas! this present chronicler hath, with grief and sorrow, to confess, that even in this great man was there error; and it behoveth a true historian justly to set forth the imperfections of men as much as their marvellous excellencies. And thus, with scrupulous care, say I now, that Master Owlglass

had, with his many noble qualities, the error of a short memory.
Most strange is this defect in so great a person: yet is it true, that
if he received money to pay to another, he forgat it; if he owed
money to another, he forgat it; and in eating and drinking most
of all was his memory treacherous and failing.

He sate at meat once in a noble house, where the folk were
making excellent cheer, and where, for more than six hours, sate
they eating and drinking; and Owlglass was with them, for he
marked not the time. Yet, at last, it was meet they should rise
up from the table, and depart each to his home. Then departed
Owlglass also; and as he went, he passed by a house where they
sate at supper, and the master of that house entreated him, that
he should enter in unto them and eat. And so did he; for he had
forgotten altogether, that for six hours he had dined. Then most
excellently played he the guest at the table; and one that knew he
had come from the feast spake unto him, saying: "Lo! my beloved
Master Owlglass, how cometh it that ye eat so well now, having
lately at the banquet so lustily eaten?" And Owlglass answered:
"Did I so? That have I forgotten; for I have the misfortune to carry
with me a belly that lacketh memory in every wise."

The Sixty and Eighth Adventure.

How that Owlglass at Dresden became a carpenter, and
for his pains earned little thanks.

Soon departed Owlglass, and came unto Dresden, near unto the
Bohemian forest, upon the Elbe water, and there proclaimed
that he was a carpenter. And it fortuned, that a master carpenter
in the town heard of him, and hired him to be his journeyman;
for his man had departed from him, and he lacked some one to
be man unto him. And as in this world of ours, my masters, there

be pleasure and gadding about and weddings as well as woe and buryings, so fortuned it, that at that time there was in the town such a wedding, and thereunto was the master carpenter bidden. And he spake unto Owlglass, saying: "Good fellow of mine, unto this wedding must I go, and to-day shall I not return home again. Do thou, therefore, labour diligently, and bind me these four table boards most cunningly together with glue." And Owlglass answered, and said unto him: "Yea; but which of these belong together?" Then laid the master the table boards together as he would have them joined, and gat him forth with his wife unto the wedding.

Then did our Owlglass, that pious man, diligently go to work, and, after his manner of doing all things wrong, took the four table boards, and bored holes in them, and laid them one upon the other. Then set he the glue-pot on the fire, and heated it, and with the brush glued all the boards together, and carried them up stairs unto the top of the house, and put them forth out of the window to dry, and then kept he holiday all the eventide. And at night cometh the master home, and well had he drunken at the festival. Then spake he unto Owlglass, and said unto him: "How hast thou laboured during the day?" And Owlglass answered, and said: "Lo! my good master, verily have I done that which thou didst bid me to do, and joined the boards together with glue, and then made I an early holiday at eventide." And therewith was his master right well pleased and content; and he said unto his wife: "In good sooth is this a most excellent serving-man, and he doth with great diligence fulfil that which I have commanded him. Therefore must we hold him in great honour and esteem." These words spoken, he gat him to bed.

And when that it was day he arose, and so did also Owlglass; and the master bade Owlglass that he should bring unto him the table that he had made. Then went Owlglass unto the loft, and brought down the boards all glued together and marred. And when that the master saw how the work was spoiled, he said unto Owlglass: "Where didst thou learn the art of carpenter's work?" And Owlglass answered, and said: "Wherefore ask ye me this thing?" Then said the master: "Forasmuch as thou hast marred me much costly wood in thy labour." When that Owlglass heard this he was greatly moved, and said: "Nay; but, master, I did only that which ye commanded, and if that I marred the wood, it is thy fault, not mine." Then was the master right wroth, and said unto him: "Thou knave, get ye forth from my house, and be gone from my workshop; for of thy work have I no profit." Thus departed Owlglass, and very little thanks earned he for his labour.

The Sixty and Ninth Adventure.

How that Owlglass did hire himself unto the master of a saw mill.

Owlglass journeyed on from place to place, it fortuned that he passed hard by a saw-mill, at a time when the men were diverting themselves, and eating their suppers, the which a maiden servant had brought unto them. Owlglass then conferred with the men, and told them of his many marvellous adventures, the which he was not unmindful of extolling. Thereat came the master, and listened with an attentive ear. Now, it happened, that the manners of Owlglass pleased the master of the saw-mills much, and he took great delight in his merry jests. Then Owlglass told him he was a carpenter, and had also worked in saw-pits, which caused the master to move him to tarry, for he might have as much work there as it pleased him to do. Thereat did Owlglass consent unto him; and in order that the bargain might at once be shewn of effect, he sate himself down, and did eat of the supper; nor did he seem after that in any wise strange at that house, but did eat with so much appetite, that in truth it appeared unto all as if he had eaten of that fare all his life.

Thereafter did they depart unto their work again, and Owlglass had to carry heavy oaken stems up unto the saw-mill, the which did not agree with him in the wise that meat and drink always did. Soon, therefore, was he aweary of this labour, and he cast about in his mind how cunningly he might become quit thereof. So when it came to pass that his work-fellows set a huge block of oak over the pit, and began to saw it, drawing the saw each way, Owlglass spake unto them, saying: "What is that I see ye do? Wherefore pull ye the saw so as if each would have it alone. In my country, every man hath his own labour; but ye labour not to do any good purpose in pulling away the saw each from the other. But I will shew unto you a simple way by which ye can profitably labour." Therewith took he the axe in his hand and brake the saw in two pieces, and said unto them: "Now can ye each labour in comfort without getting into anger." Then ran the workmen unto the master to tell him how Owlglass brake the saws; and when the master came to demand money for his saws, had Owlglass departed thence.

The Seventieth Adventure.

How that Owlglass became a maker of spectacles, and perceived that trade was very bad.

Ngry and contentious were the monarchs and electors, and there was no Roman Cæsar or king all this while. And it came to pass, that the Count of Supplenburg was chosen to be Roman king; yet were there others who with might desired to enter into the empire. Therefore was it, that the newly chosen Roman king had to sit down before Frankfort with a large army for the space of six months, and there lie in wait for some one to beat him off. And as with him abode there much folk, both foot and horse, Owlglass bethought him within himself: "Lo! now among the king's people shall thy affairs be most profitably advanced; and now will I get me up, and among the many strange lords which be there, will I make happy fortune; for of money will these gentles bestow not a little upon me." Then did he according to his words, and gat him up, and departed on his way. And all the great folk of all countries came together there. And in the Wetterau by Friedberg it came to pass, that the Bishop of Trier, with his folk, encountered our noble Master Owlglass by the way, as he journeyed on toward Frankfort. Now Owlglass was curiously apparelled; and the bishop—who, like unto most meddling priests, delighted much in prying into all matters—asked of Owlglass what manner of man he was, and in what way he earned his living.

Then opened Owlglass his mouth, and spake unto the bishop, and said unto him: "Most reverend lord and father, a maker of spectacles am I, and from Brabant do I fare. And in that country do people so clearly see, that I can by my trade win nothing. Therefore do I journey in search of work, the which I might do because trade is bad." Then said the bishop: "Of a truth believe I not that which thou sayest unto me. For thy trade should wax greater and greater every day, for as much as people now grow more shortsighted, and see less and less that which is before them. Thus do folk require many spectacles." To him replied our noble master after this wise: "Yea, my noble lord; but there is one thing that destroyeth our handicraft, and that would I tell you, but that you would with great scorn reject my saying, and with anger visit me."

And the bishop answered, saying: "Nay, to the crying out of the people are we well used. Say freely on that which thou wouldst say." Then said Owlglass: "Noble and reverend lord, one thing is there the which doth mar our handicraft altogether, and I fear me greatly, that, with all obeisance unto thee, it will utterly ruin and destroy it. For that ye and other great lords, popes, cardinals, bishops, Cæsars, kings, princes, counsellors, governors, and judges, now look rather through your fingers, than after any other wise. And thus think ye your sight long and true, and therefore buy ye not of such poor artizans as we be. And of old time read we, that men which are reputed learned did with much diligence read, study, and explore the mysteries of wisdom, so that their eyes grew faint and weak, in order that thereby no evil might arise unto the people; and at that time was our trade yet good. In the like manner did the parsons most carefully read and study; but now is every one so learned, that, without looking upon any book, doth he know everything, and by his inward wisdom perceiveth he all that he would know. Thus is our trade marred. Now run I from one land unto another, and nowhere can I find any work; for even hath this reached so far into the hearts of men, that the very boors do ape and imitate their betters, and would be so wondrous wise." Without gloss perceived the bishop good Master Owlglass his text, and spake unto him fair words, and said: "Behold now, come thou with us unto Frankfort, and there will we mend thy trade, and recompence thee richly for thy pains, and to thee shall be given our dress and arms; for truly art thou worthy to be with us."

Thus did the bishop reward Owlglass, and chose the vagabond for his fellow, and in right fellowship were they the twain; and from the Church, the which Owlglass despised, gat he at last great comfort. For that which now with great contempt we put away, may anon be of great worth and advantage. So he abode with the bishop until the count was confirmed emperor, and then departed again into Saxony.

The Seventy and First Adventure.

How that Owlglass of a boor at the fair of Gerau took leather.

In the town of Gerau was there a fair, and from all the country side and parts both far and near, came folk in great multitude exceeding many, to buy and to sell and to chaffer. All manner of ware might ye behold there; but (O good fortune!) in especial was there no lack of leather, and almost every boor which came

unto that place bought of leather a roll or twain. But the crowd of folk pushing hither and thither, each contending and striving with each, was so great, that it was hard to tell which owned any special roll of the good leather they had bought.

And among the good folk which came unto that place was our worthy and trusty Master Owlglass, and he came with the crowd, and was greatly contented therewith. And, behold, there came before him a boor with a roll of leather; and Owlglass perceived what an excellent knavery could be practised. So took he a needle and thread with speed, and deftly sewed a corner of the leathern roll unto his own doublet. In no short space of time did he with his hands pluck by force the piece of leather from the boor, and turned him about, and departed another way among the folk.

Thereat marvelled the boor with great marvel, and stood still; but in a little while thereafter departed he after Owlglass, and took him, and said: "Thou knave, thou hast from me stolen my leather." But Owlglass answered, and said unto him gently: "Nay, friend, thou art unjust towards me. Seest thou not that the leather is mine, for it is sewed unto my coat, so that none may steal it. And hadst thou done so likewise, then couldst thou not have lost thy leather." And the boor believed the words of Owlglass, and departed elsewhere to seek the leather he had lost.

The Seventy and Second Adventure.

How that at Hildesheim Owlglass did hire himself unto merchant to be his cook, and what tricks he played unto him.

As thou goest down that street at Hildesheim which leadeth from the Haymarket, dwelt, on a time, a rich merchant, and he did come forth unto the gate, and would have entered into his garden. And he passed along, and behold, he found Owlglass lying in a green field, and he greeted him and spake unto him, and would have known of him what manner of man he was, and in what wise he earned his bread. Then with hidden knavery answered Owlglass unto him, and said: "I am a cook, yet have I now no service." And the merchant said unto him: "If that thou would be pious and diligent, would I myself hire thee, and give unto thee new clothes; for my wife doth every day most bitterly cry out touching the cooking." Then did Owlglass, with great sincerity, promise and vow unto him obedience. Thereafter hired him the merchant, and asked him what his name might be? And Owlglass answered, and said: "Pan-cra-ti-us." The merchant said:

"Of a truth is this name very long; behold, one cannot with brief time speak it. Thy name shall be Crazy." And Owlglass answered: "Yea, most excellent master, so mote it be, for it is all one to me, what I am called." Then did the merchant approve him, and said to him: "Behold, thou art a servant in whom I can have pleasure. Follow me, therefore, and we will get unto my garden before the town, and there gather herbs, and carry home with us young chickens, for on the next Sunday have I guests coming, and I would fain give unto them good cheer." Owlglass followed him unto the garden, and there cut they rosemary, to make a stuffing for the chickens, after the Italian mode; and they took of onions, and of other herbs good store, and thereto of eggs, and departed, and came home again.

And when the good wife looked upon the strangely apparelled Owlglass, she said unto her husband, and asked him: "What manner of man have ye here? Would ye waste our bread on such a fellow?" And the merchant straightway answered and said: "Be content good wife; to thee shall he be obedient. Lo! he is a good cook." And the wife replied unto him: "Yea, good man, I am content, and goodly messes shall he cook for us." Then said the merchant: "To-morrow shall ye see how bravely he can cook." And he called Owlglass, and said unto him: "Crazy!" Then spake Owlglass: "Master!" "Go thou and take the meat sack, and follow me unto the shambles, for I would buy meat for the dinner." Then followed Owlglass his master, and the meat was bought accordingly. Then the merchant enjoined Owlglass, and said unto him: "Behold, take thou the meat and set it me down where it may slowly become cooked, in a cool place, so that it be not burned. And the other meat set me down likewise." Owlglass answered: "Yea," and rose up early the next morning, and some of the meat put he unto the fire to roast; but the other put he upon the spit, and laid it in the cellar between two butts of Einbeck beer, so that it could not be burned.

And when the friends of the merchant entered, among them was the town clerk, and many other worthy folk; and the merchant went unto Owlglass, and said unto him: "How doth the meat fare? Hast thou done as I told thee." "Yea," said Owlglass, "that have I. For no cooler place in all thy house could I find than the cellar, and there lieth the meat upon a spit between two casks of Einbeck beer." "But is it not ready then?" asked the merchant. "Nay," said Owlglass, "I wist not that ye would have it."

And then came the guests, and the merchant told them how Owlglass had put the meat in the cellar; and thereat laughed they greatly at the merry jest, and so was Owlglass excused. But the good wife was not content therewith by reason of the guests, and besought her husband that he would let him go, for well saw she that he was a knave. Then said the merchant: "Dear wife, behold! I fain would have his services to assist me when that I go unto the town of Goslar; be patient, and when that I return thence will I bid him depart in God's name." And they sate and made good cheer, and drank good wine, and had much comfort; and at eventide the merchant called for Owlglass, and said unto him: "Toll, prepare thou the coach and smear it right well, for to-morrow will we depart unto Goslar, and with us doth ride that good priest, Master Henry Hamenstede, for there abideth he, and will go with us." Then said Owlglass unto his master: "Yea, he would do his bidding." And he inquired of him, saying: "What manner of unction shall I use to smear the coach withal?" The merchant cast down a shilling for him to take, and said unto him: "Go ye straightway and buy ye cart grease, and that unction will serve thee as well as any other." And the obedient Owlglass did, therefore, according unto the words of his master.

When that all men had gat them to bed, stood our Master Owlglass and smeared the coach within and without with the cart grease the which he had bought, and on that spot where his master sate smeared he the most. In the morning arose his master, and came with the priest unto the coach, and commanded that he should put the horses unto the coach; and that also did Owlglass. And then departed they in the coach; and as they went forward, the grease with the which Owlglass had greased the seat began to smell with no sweet savour, and the priest opened his mouth, and spake unto the merchant, saying: "Lo! what is this? There is a savour in this coach which savoureth not of a goodly savour. And when that I would hold me unto the sides of the coach, for as much as it jolteth and jarreth me, then are my hands covered over with grease, the which love I not." Then commanded they Owlglass that he should stop, and then told they him that of a truth were they smeared all over with grease, and with grievous anger visited they our good master.

Then cometh by a peasant with a load of straw, going unto the market; of him bought they sundry bundles, and they wiped the coach, and all their clothes, and again gat them in. And the merchant spake with great anger unto Owlglass, and said unto him: "Thou evil and most beguiling knave, what is this thing which thou hast done? Get ye unto the town gallows with all speed." And Owlglass did as he was commanded, and when that he came unto the gallows tree, he stayed the coach, and unharnessed the horses thereof. Then cried the merchant unto Owlglass, with a loud voice: "What is this other thing which thou hast done, thou knave?" And Owlglass said: "Of a truth bid ye me drive unto the town gallows, and there stand we. I thought that here would ye rest." Then looked the merchant and perceived the place where they stood, and the gallows thereby. What could these worthy men do? Was it not the best to laugh thereat as they might. So laughed they; but the merchant said unto Owlglass: "Now do thou drive straight forward, and look not round in any wise." Then drew Owlglass the pole from out of the carriage, and drave the horses forward.

And it came to pass, when that they had driven some small distance, that the fore-part of the coach was from the hinder part loosened, and the merchant and the priest sate within, and abode standing on the road. They cried aloud unto Owlglass, but he would not look round, but departed with the fore-part of the coach and the horse, and cast not his eyes behind to see what had happened. And though they pursued him, was it a long time ere they came up with him. Then would the merchant have killed him, but the priest would not have this done. And when that the journey was ended, said the merchant's wife unto him: "What manner of voyage hast thou had?" And the merchant answered unto her: "Marvellous strange hath it been; yet have we returned back again with safety." Then called he Owlglass, and said unto him: "Hear me what I say, fellow voyager. This night mayest thou yet remain here with me, and thou mayest also bravely eat and drink. To-morrow morn do thou rise up and clear me the house that I may be quit of thee and of thy company. For a knave art thou wheresoever thou wert born." Then said the poor and worthy Master Owlglass: "Dear heart of me! all that is required of me that do I, but no one giveth me thanks therefor. Yet my service contenteth me not, then according as thou commandest will I in the morning clear the house and get me hence." "Yea, so do thou," said the merchant.

The next day arose the merchant, and said unto Owlglass: "Do thou eat and drink until thy stomach is contented, and then get forth from this house, so that I look not upon thy face again, when that I come from the church." But Owlglass held his peace. And when that the merchant had departed from the house, he began to clear the house, and stools, benches, tables, and all that he could drag forth took he and cast it in the street. The wares of the merchant likewise cast he forth, and the neighbours marvelled greatly what it should signify that all the goods were thus brought out from the house. And one that was a friend of the merchant departed and told him, so with great wrath ran he unto his house, and sware more than in the church he had prayed. And then said he unto Owlglass: "How cometh it that yet ye are here? Did I not command thee to go hence?" "Yea, master," quoth honest Master Owlglass, "I would fain only have fulfilled your command, for ye enjoined me that I should clear the house, the which am I not performing? And truly am I glad ye are returned, for some matters are too heavy for me, and I would crave your help." "Let all things lie," said the master, "I have been at more charges for them than that they should be cast into the mire. And thou, get thee unto the evil one, and let me not see thee more." And Owlglass lamented and said: "Alas! is it not a marvellous strange thing that everywhere do I what I am told; yet am I ever chidden for my pains? In an unfortunate hour must I have come into the world." Then departed he, and left the merchant to carry back into his house his chattels and merchandise. Thereat laughed the neighbours with great content.

The Seventy and Third Adventure.

How that at Greifswald good Master Owlglass came unto the Rector of the University, and proclaimed himself to be a master in all languages, save in one only, to wit, the Spanish tongue.

Now unto the good town of Greifswald, on that stormy sea which is called the Baltic, came Owlglass on a time. And when that he arrived set he upon the church doors letters, and upon the University gates also, proclaiming therein, that of all languages, save one only was he the master, and he could understand every tongue save one, to wit, the Spanish. Thereat marvelled the people with great marvel.

When that the Rector saw the letters which Owlglass had set upon the university gate, he called together his masters, and they conferred together; and then was it agreed amongst them, that Owlglass should be bidden to come before them, and that if he could do that which he said, then would they do him high honour, and entertain, and endue him with all the dignities of their venerable college; but if that he might be a deceiver, then would they with great indignity visit him, and command him to depart out of their town. So appointed they a day for this to be done. And Owlglass accepted the challenge which the rector and masters sent him; and the town was busy all the time with gossips here and gossips there, talking of the marvellous professor which had come. And, after the manner of gossips, did they make two where before was one; and of the foreign master was great conference and noise.

When that the day had come for this wonderful disputation and examination, there assembled together the rector and the masters, the chief councillors of the town and the most considerable citizens; and then entered to them Owlglass, who was attired in like manner unto them, with gown and grave look. And the rector bade him, that he should sit on a stool in the midst of the assembly, over against him. And Owlglass signified unto him, that now would he fain be examined. Then arose the rector, and, with much gravity, spake unto him, and addressed him in the Latin tongue. And Owlglass said to him: "Most noble rector, but one language in the world have I not learned, the which language is Spanish; and now that thou speakest unto me, it appeareth unto me that thy words savour of that tongue." Then the rector said unto him, that truly was Latin like unto Spanish, yet was it not Spanish, and, therefore, should he have known. But Owlglass said: "Nay; but if any tongue were like unto Spanish, then shut he his ears; for that it was great shame unto the Christian world, that yet should in Spain such vile unbelievers be as the Moors and their black king." So by reason of his fervour excused they Owlglass. Then stood up the rector, and spake unto him in the Greek language. And Owlglass answered, that unto him it sounded like Spanish. And the rector said unto him: "If that thou knowest all languages, then must thou truly also know the Greek tongue." "That," quoth Owlglass, "is the reason why unto me it sounded like unto Spanish. For of old time were the Greek nations idol worshippers, and bowed down unto senseless stocks and stones; and shame were it that Christian man should speak such a tongue." Then did the assembly praise Owlglass with great praise.

A third time arose the learned rector, and spake unto Owlglass; and this time spake he Italian. And Owlglass said unto him: "Behold, that too is like Spanish, and I must hold my peace." And the rector told unto him that it was Italian. "Shame should it be," said Owlglass, "that I should speak the language of brigands and robbers." And again praised the assembly the wisdom of the new professor. And the rector spake unto him in the French. "Marvellous like unto Spanish," cried Owlglass. "Nay, but it is the French," said the rector. "Then marvel I no longer," said Owlglass; "for the French would everywhere continually have more land; and the mountains which lie betwixt France, Navarre, and Spain, would they fain have cast into the sea." Then spake the rector to him in English. "That tongue likes me not; I fear me it is Spanish," quoth Master Owlglass. The rector told him that it was English. "Let me hear no more on't," answered he; "for in England is mist and fog and snow, so that there be no marvel if that it sound like Spanish or any other. Give me," he said unto the rector, "the honest German tongue, for that must for ever be a noble tongue and a useful." And the assembly had great content with Owlglass; for they perceived, that truly he was a master of languages, and understood not the words so much as the intent, and that he judged of the lands by the tongues used by the inhabitants thereof. For truly, my masters, all languages are like each unto the other; for in every one will ye find liars, cozeners, knaves, cutpurses, deceivers, and beguilers, in number a great multitude. So with honour departed Owlglass.

The Seventy and Fourth Adventure.

*How that Owlglass did at Wismar become a horse-dealer,
and beguiled a merchant.*

By the water at Wismar most knavishly did Owlglass beguile a horse-dealer. For unto that place came a horse-dealer, and he bought no horse unless by a certain thing he learned whether the horse was long to live. And thus did he: when that he had bargained and the price was fixed, he seized the horse by the tail, and marked, by the plucking of the tail, whether he would long live or no. For if the horse had a long tail, and he plucked him thereby, and the hair was weak, then judged he the horse would not long live. Then bought he not that horse. An if the tail were firm in the horse, then did he buy it, and believed truly that it would long live and had a hardy body. For this was a common saying at Wismar, and in it believed all people which abode there. Of this saying heard Owlglass, and upon it meditated he a great knavery; for he held it to be a thing most grave, that all error should from the folk be taken, for Owlglass would have no beguiler of the people but himself; and, my masters, was not this our good master an exemplar unto many which even unto this day have followed in his footsteps?

In the black art was our master also well grounded; therefore with rosin and blood made he a tail unto a horse, the which had no tail, and therewith gat he him to market, and there did he bid to the folk dear enough so that none would buy it. And the merchant, which plucked the horses by the tail, after that came by, and Owlglass offered it unto him at cheap rate, in all good

conscience. Then the merchant looked upon the horse that it was fair, and in truth worth the money which Owlglass demanded therefor. So he came thither, and desired to pluck it by the tail. Now Owlglass had so wrought the tail, that if peradventure the dealer so plucked, the tail would therewith stay within his hand, and it should seem as if he had plucked it forth. And so also it came to pass. Then stood the merchant with the tail, and was abashed; and Owlglass cried with a loud voice: "Behold the knave, he hath plucked my horse by the tail, and lo! he hath plucked it out, and my horse hath he marred." Then ran the townsfolk, and held the merchant, and would not let him depart until that he had satisfied Owlglass with ten crowns for the damage unto the horse. Then Owlglass went on his way rejoicing.

The Seventy and Fifth Adventure.

How that Owlglass wrought a great knavery upon a pipemaker at Lüneburg.

At Lüneburg abode a pipemaker, and he once had been a pedlar, and, with a pack, had trudged many a league; and this man fortuned to sit drinking his beer. And to him entered Owlglass, and much company found he there. And in jest did the pipemaker bid Owlglass to dine with him, and said unto him: "To-morrow do thou come unto meat with me, and eat that which thou wouldst have, an thou art able." And Owlglass answered: "Yea;" and took his words to be serious, and the next day came unto the pipemaker's house, and would have entered in and eaten at his table. But there found he that above and below was the door bolted and the windows shut. Then Owlglass walked up and down before the house a few times, until that the dinner-hour came; but the door was fast shut all this time, and he perceived that he had been beguiled of the pipemaker. So he departed from that place, and said not a word, but held his peace. And it came to pass, that on the next day Owlglass beheld the pipemaker in the market-place, and he stood before him, and spake unto him, saying: "Thou dost bid guests unto the feast, and when that they come, find they the door fast closed, so that they cannot enter therein." Then answered the pipemaker unto Owlglass, and said unto him: "Behold, I bid thee to be my guest, but with certain words; for I said unto thee that thou shouldst eat with me, an thou wert able; but that couldst thou not, for when that thou camest were the doors shut, and thou mightst not enter therein." "Truly," quoth Master Owlglass, "we live and learn. That wist not I before, so have thou my thanks." And the pipemaker laughed, and said: "Yet shalt thou not fast this day. Go thou unto my house, and, behold, there wilt thou find boiled and roast, and the doors are open. Enter therein and eat, and in no long time will I follow thee; and thou shalt be alone, and no other guest but thee will I have." And Owlglass meditated within himself, and said, privily: "Bravely goeth this forward." Then gat he him unto the pipemaker's house, and findeth it as the master said unto him. And the pipemaker's wife stood cooking by the fire. Then said Owlglass unto her: "Behold, thy good man is at the market, and hath received a great fish as a gift, and he desireth that thou shouldst depart unto him, and help him to carry it home. Meanwhile will I turn the spit for thee." The good wife answered Owlglass, and said: "Alas! good Master Owlglass, that will I do; and with my maid will I get me quickly unto him, and soon return." And Owlglass said: "Peace go with thee." Then departed the good wife and her maid unto the market, and as they went forward met they the pipemaker coming towards his house; and he said unto them: "What do ye here?" And they answered, and said: "Owlglass came unto us, and bade us hasten unto thee upon the market, for thou hast had a large fish given unto thee, and thou wouldst have help to carry it home. And Owlglass hath remained in the house, and turneth the spit." And the pipemaker waxed very wroth, and said unto his wife: "Here is a knavery. Why didst thou not stay within; for he hath not done this without thereby signifying some deceitful work. Behold, I have no fish." Then turned they, and altogether came unto the house; and while they were conferring together, Owlglass had shut both door and windows, and that found they when that they came unto the house. Then spake the pipemaker unto his wife: "Now seest thou what manner of fish thou shouldest fetch?"

Then beat they upon the door. Thereat came Owlglass behind the door, and said: "Beat ye the door no longer, for to no one will I open it. The host said unto me, that I should be alone within the house, and no other guest would he have but myself. Therefore depart ye, and after dinner come hither again." The pipemaker said: "It is true, I said according unto thy words, but I meant not that it should be thus." And the pipemaker said unto his wife: "I' good faith, let him now eat and drink, for I have in my pate that which shall reward him for his knavery."

So the three departed, and abode in a neighbour's house until that Owlglass had made an end of eating and drinking. Then set Owlglass to his labour, and boiled the meat, and roasted the roast, and set it upon a dish, and brought a stool unto the table, and with great content ate and drank and made good cheer; and he drank health unto his worthy host, the pipemaker. And when he had filled himself, then arose he and opened the door, and set the dishes unto the fire again. Then entered in the pipemaker, his wife and maid; and he said unto Owlglass: "After this wise, the which thou hast done, do not honest folk." But Owlglass answered and said: "How might it be that I should do otherwise? For, behold, thou didst say I should be alone and the only guest; and if that I had let more guests in, shame would it have been to me, for my host would have brooked it not." And therewith departed he. Then looked the pipemaker upon him as he went, and said: "Be not afraid, this matter will I richly repay unto thee, thou knave!" Thereat said Owlglass: "He is the best man who is ever the master." Then in that same hour went the pipemaker unto the hangman, who also gat money by carting dead horses; and he said unto him: "At the inn lieth a pious man, named Owlglass, and this night hath his horse died. This would he have carted away." And the pipemaker showed the hangman the house where lodged Owlglass. And the hangman perceived that it was the pipemaker, and agreed with him that he would do it, and took his cart and went unto the house. Then said Owlglass unto him: "What wouldst thou have?" And the hang-man answered Owlglass, and said unto him: "Lo! the pipemaker hath been with me, and said unto me that thy horse was dead and should be carried away. Is it truly so?" But Owlglass mocked him, and bade him carry the pipemaker unto the gallows. Then was the hangman wroth, and departed unto the pipemaker's house, and made complaint, and with six shillings did the pipemaker satisfy him. But Owlglass saddled his horse and rode forth from the town.

The Seventy and Sixth Adventure.

How that an old woman mocked the good Master Owlglass when that at Gerdau he lost his pocket.

Of old time lived there at Gerdau, in the Lüneburg country, an aged and venerable couple, who for fifty years lived there together, being good man and wife; and had goodly sons and daughters, the which had grown to ripe age. And it came to pass, that the priest of the town was a merry good-humoured wight, who loved jolly company; and wherever there was a cup of wine to be quaffed, there would he fain be. With his parishioners had he so fitted it, that every boor in the country side did at least receive him and his cook once in each year; and then stayed he some day or twain, and made excellent cheer. Now, the two old people had for many a year kept neither dedication, nor christening, or any feast at which the priest could have content for his fair round belly; and thereat was he greatly moved and vexed. Therefore he meditated much within himself, how that he might bring it about that they should give a feast.

Then sendeth he unto the boor a messenger, and asketh how long that it had been since he had by Holy Church been married unto his good wife? To him answered the boor: "Reverend father, so long is it ago, that I have forgotten how many years it hath been." And the priest rejoined unto him: "That such forgetfulness was an evil thing for the salvation of his soul, and he should strive to remember that thing." Then did the boor confer with his wife, and considered the matter; yet could they not find the true time to tell it unto the priest. Therefore came they both unto the priest, and were greatly troubled, and entreated of him that he should give unto them some wholesome counsel wherewithal they might comfort themselves. Then said the priest unto them: "Forasmuch as ye know not the time at the which ye were married, will it be best that next Sunday I marry you again, and then will ye be comforted. Therefore do ye prepare a feast, and kill an ox, and a sheep, and a pig, and bid your children and good friends to rejoice with ye on that day, and with all favour give unto them good cheer; and I promise ye that I also will be with ye." Then said the boor: "In good sooth, reverend father, is thy counsel most comforting unto the spirit. It shall go hard, but I will have a feast which shall be fitting unto the day; for it would not be well that after fifty years we should be put forth from the marriage state." These words spoken, he departed unto his house, and failed not to do as the priest had advised him.

And the priest bid unto the feast several of his own friends, other priests and dignitaries of the most Holy Church. Among these was the Dean of Epsdorf, who in his stables had always a horse or twain, the which were not to be despised; and, like unto other priests, he loved good cheer. And with him had Owlglass served some time. And the dean said unto him: "Sit ye upon my young horse and ride with me, and to that are ye right welcome." To that agreed Owlglass. And when that they were right merry, and did eat and drink with marvellous content, the old woman, the which was the bride, sat at the head of the table. And after so much labour was she tired; so she gat up and departed out of her house, at the back, down to the river Gerdau, and therein bathed she her feet. By this time did the Dean of Epsdorf and Owlglass set forth to ride home; and when that they approached unto her, Owlglass caused his horse to prance and curvet, that the

bride might have content thereof; and so lustily did he this, that his girdle came unfastened, and his side-pocket fell down upon the ground. And when that the woman beheld this, she rose up and took the pocket, and sat down thereupon by the water. So it came to pass, that when Owlglass had got about a field's length from the place where the woman sate, he found that he had lost his pocket, and therefore turneth he about and cometh again unto Gerdau, and he saith unto the woman: "Hast thou seen an old pocket anywhere upon the ground?" And the woman said: "Aye, upon my wedding-day did I find an old rusty pocket, and that have I yet unto this hour." And Owlglass said unto her: "Thy wedding-day? Oho! long since was it that thou wast a bride! truly must it be an old rusty pocket, such an one will not I have!" Then said the woman: "Is it this?" but would not give it unto him; and so cunning might he be, yet gat he not his pocket, and he was fain to leave it behind him; and at Gerdau it is unto this day, and thither mayest thou travel if that thou desirest to look upon it.

The Seventy and Seventh Adventure.

How that Owlglass gained money by a horse.

On a time was Owlglass very poor; and of all his possessions there remained unto him nought but his horse; and he was sorely troubled in his mind, how it might be that he should get him food, lodging, and raiment. Then came he unto a village where there was a fair, and he gat him unto the chief inn, and in the stable lodged he the horse, and he bade the host bring him food to eat, and good cheer of wine. And according unto his words was it done.

And when he had eaten and drunk, and was no longer hungry, he bethought him how that he might get him some money. Therefore went he into the market-place, and there cried with a loud voice, that he had brought with him the most marvellous horse which had ever been seen, and that its tail was where its head should be, and in the place of its tail was its head. And this horse would he for little money show unto the village folk. Then came they unto him in great multitude, and each gave unto him some money according to his wealth; and he let them into the stable, and required of them that they should not in any wise betray him, and this promised they unto him. Then did he display unto them the horse, and lo! his tail was tied unto the manger, and his head looked forth the other way. Then laughed the village folk at the merry jest of Owlglass, and forgave him the money he had taken from them. Thus gat he store of money, and departed on his way with great content.

The Seventy and Eighth Adventure.

How that at Oltzen Owlglass did beguile a boor of a piece of green cloth, and caused him to confess that it was blue.

Of roast and boiled was Owlglass most woundily fond at all times, seasons, and occasions; and for that hunger pinched and griped him, by reason that honest bread he would never eat, it so befel, that to eat he must seek diligently for what he would have. Now it came to pass, that while the fairing was going forward in the good little town of Oltzen, whither from the Wend country came many, and also from divers other towns, it came to pass, I say, that the great and beloved Master Owlglass bent thitherward his steps, with intent to sell of his ware, which be fool-making and coney-catching, like any other honest merchant of them all. And truly do ye know, that all goods be most difficult to sell, and such ware as Master Owlglass possessed not less than other kind; so it behoved him to walk hither and thither, that he might have occasions to display that wit and honesty, for the which he was so famous.

Thereafter as he was, with weary steps—believing that honest trade had departed clean out of this mad and strange world in which we be—purposing to turn away, he beheld a country boor, of loutish mien, chaffering and cheapening with a peddling huckster vagabond, for a piece of green cloth, the which the boor gat, and therewith set forth toward home. "Fine work be this," thought Owlglass unto himself, "that loutish boors should thus chaffer and cheapen cloth, the which for their betters was woven! Here be thou arbiter, and of wrongs redresser." And within himself took he counsel how that cloth he might himself have, for, as being the compeer of princes and bishops, it would the better grace his good and fair personage and trappings. Therefore he sought out the name of the village unto which the boor was departed, and went and took unto him a hedge parson, and one other, a loose fellow, and gat him with them forth from the city, on that road whereby the boor should go; and bidding the twain to swear in faith and by'r lady to all he might say unto the country boor, set them in order upon the road, removed some little space the one from the other, and in such wise lay in wait for the coming of good master green-cloth boor.

In no long time came that worthy trudging along the road, with great rejoicing within his heart; for it seemed unto him most brave, that in good green cloth he should attire himself, like unto such as did with reviling and hard words take service from him; and he was, in very truth, right merry at heart, for he loved the colour green, as do all country wights. Unto him approached Owlglass, and opened his mouth, and spake unto him, saying: "Lo! what a fine blue cloth hast thou there. Of a truth it is azure, like the darkening sky which hangeth above our heads in marvellous mystery. Nay, but such a blue cloth is rarely woven. Prithee, whence didst thou get it?" And the boor answered, and said unto Owlglass: "Ne'er a blue cloth be this at all, but a swart green, the which I bought in the fair of Oltzen." Then said Owlglass: "Nay, but it is blue; and thereon will I set twenty silver marks, and let the first man that cometh by between us twain determine and end the contention." Thereat said the boor: "Nay, if that thou be beside thyself and wilt lose thy money, have with thee. I am content." So they agreed thereupon.

With a good swinging trot cometh the first of Owlglass's fellows trudging along the road, for he spied that the boor had made agreement with Owlglass. And the boor said unto the voyager: "Hold thou an instant; we have here a contention betwixt us upon the colour of this cloth. Say thou the truth if that it be blue or green, and we will therewith be content." Then the man spake unto them, saying: "It is, of a truth, as fine blue cloth as ever eyes of mine beheld." But the boor would not agree thereunto, and said: "Nay, but ye are two beguilers, cheats, and cozeners; green it is, but ye have agreed to deceive me." But unto him quoth the wily Owlglass: "Lo! now that it may be perceived of me, that in this matter I am as innocent as any spotless lamb of the flock unto which I pertain, and that right and truth is on my side, let us make fresh agreement. See, hither, with measured steps, cometh a most reverend priest, who in pious meditation beguileth the weariness of travel. Let him be judge betwixt us, and by his word be we bound; for if Holy Church bind us not, then will no ties constrain us within virtuous paths." And with such speech was the boor content.

Then when the priest (right good exemplar of all his tribe!) drew nigh unto them, Owlglass spake unto him, and said: "Reverend father, upon thy devout thoughts may we for a brief space intrude the base matters of this outer world; and we beseech thee, determine between this boor and myself what be the colour of this cloth." "Nay, son," quoth the reverend man, "but that can ye for yourselves most easily behold." Thereat said the boor: "Yea, reverend father; but here have we two that would with knavery constrain me to believe a thing the which is contrary to reason and justice." And unto him answered the priest, and said: "What have I to do with your contentions? So many things there be in this world which, contrary to reason and justice, find hot believers, men heated and molten in the furnace of vanity and self-conceit; and would ye contend over the hue and dye of a cloth? What care I if it be black or white? That with your own eyes can ye see." "But, reverend sir," quoth Master Bumpkin, "do ye, in the plenitude of your kindness, judge betwixt us, and say what be the colour of this cloth." Then the priest said: "That ye twain may be at peace, and have no grief or ill-will at heart, or vain rejoicing one above the other, will I say that which ye may so easily see. The cloth is a deep blue." And the boor marvelled thereat; but Owlglass turned round unto him, and said: "Lo! hearest thou what the good priest sayeth? O Holy and Excellent Church, in the which such true and faithful men be! O noble and worthy cause, which is upheld by such instruments of acute and keen temper! Behold, boor, the cloth is mine; and unto the Church must I pay somewhat of its value, as by decree of ecclesiastic it hath been awarded me." Then the boor looked upon the three with much amazement, and said these words: "O' my halidom! an if this man were not an ordained and sanctified priest, I would fain believe that ye were all liars, intending to cozen me of my cloth with conspiration and deceit, being three thorough-going knaves; but as I perceive that ye be a priest, I must put faith in ye whether ye be knave or no."

Then he gave the cloth unto Owlglass; but if that he had known jack-priests as well as thou and I, he had not left it. Yet such is the world's way; when the parson doeth justice, the boor must trudge home in ragged frock.

The Seventy and Ninth Adventure.

How that Owlglass most strangely gat a potful of money.

Nay but wiles and deceits be many in this world! Nor can it grow better, or wiser, or nobler, unless the sayings which men, in the fulness of their hearts and their wine-cups, publish abroad, be regarded and reflected in the deeds they do the next morning. It fortuned that Owlglass had been carousing with companions, who, indeed, were neither worse nor better than was he himself in proper person; but who, for that he discharged the expenses of the tippling, was extolled to the skies by ruined gamesters, cunning and lying boon companions,—noble pothouse friends, whose faces, marred and scored like the table whereon, in grimy circlets, pot and glass lovingly stand together, would, in after days, look grimly forth from the tablets of memory, and brand the soul of any man but such a philosopher as was Owlglass. And elated and ennobled, besmouched and bemired, by their commendation, he descended from the throne of the wine-chamber, and set forth to come homeward, where he lay that night. Philosophy was in his heart beaming with placid face upon the world; from his countenance looked forth universal love of brother to brother, in bond, apparently as firm as that of Church, in truth, as rotten at the core, and Owlglass, in such thoughts as fumy wine bestoweth, was for a while no longer the roving knave, cheat, and cozener, but a true man filled full of impotent benevolence, clasping the world in drunken joy.

Therefore, master mine, marvel not if that in mazy glory, our good friend and brother journeyed on, and forgat what place it was where he should lie. And while that the stars 'gan to blink down upon him, he found that he had departed clean forth from the village, and was nigh unto another. "Nay," quoth he, "but here must I find me a lodging, for I am aweary, and my steps be short and leaden." So he shook away from himself the loathly praise and glorifyings of reeling brethren of the wine-pot, and diligently sought in that village for some house where he might sleep. But of a truth it was late, and no friendly door stood wide to let him enter. Coming at last unto the village end, he beheld a twinkling light, and he took counsel within him what he should do. Then crept he up privily unto the casement, and lay in wait thereby, and looked in and beheld how a boor did count the money, the which he had taken at the mart for a lusty yoke of oxen he had sold. "Nay," thought Owlglass, "here be we close by the threshold of avarice, for i' faith why should a man sit in the midst of the night to count and finger the greasy coin, the which by chaffering he hath obtained? Could he not i' the morning's light full as happily have set forth the gain?"

Money waxeth neither with counting nor with handling; and yet men tire not in the reckoning thereof. Better bid farewell unto a shiny Edward shovel-groat, say I, and let it work its office in many and divers pouches, than mar its silver beauty with the hot hands of a miser. For if that money be a great instrument of wicked wills; yet on its course it encourageth much and great good, and the evil that it doth is weighed down in the balance by a hundredfold of happiness. Put ye but a penny forth, my masters, in a faithful device, it will bud, and blossom, and fructify, and ripen, to the harvest of a thousand pound; but an if ye bestow it in evil design, it dieth in the hands where ye laid it, nor enricheth any, save the unsated innkeeper or the lurking thief. And that avarice is punished by its own miserly griping after gain, shall ye presently perceive set forth in the true chronicle of Master Owlglass, his doings and life. For hard by the boor sate his little son; and in children, mark me, with all their innocence, there be the seeds of greed; nay, the seeds of every vice and virtue under heaven.

Now he beheld how that his father, with trembling hands, and by a farthing candle, did count the moneys he had received, and the child lusted to become possessed of a penny, and besought that he should bestow it upon him. "Nay," quoth the other roughly, "this must never be. What can a child like thee desire to have money for? Hast not food, and lodging, and raiment, bestowed on thee, and wouldst thou have money beside. Go to!" And he refused the child the gift which he beseeched of him. Yet the child would not be discouraged, but again besought his father, who denied him, and waxed wroth, and spake unto him saying: "If that thou dost seek to obtain of me aught of this, I will give it unto the black man without the casement, and put it forth to interest after that wise." Yet he wist not that in the darkness of the night lay Owlglass hidden. Yet did the child, with speech and gesture, entreat a penny of his father. So, with violent hand, the father swept from the table all the fair marks he had received, and in an earthen pot bestowed them and held it forth through the casement, and said: "Here, black man, do thou take the money." For he would affright the child. And Owlglass put forth his hand and took the pot of money; and like an evil doer fled forth unto the fields therewith rejoicing with an aching heart at the fortune which had thus come unto him.

The Eightieth Adventure.

How that Owlglass ran great peril of his neck for receiving the pot of money, yet gat fifteen shillings in stead of a hanging.

When that Owlglass had, with nimble legs, gat forth with the pot of money into the fields, and looked about, lo! there was not any man which followed after him, and thus guilt was its own constable, lashing the trembling culprit, and driving him forth to seek a bed in the fields, with stubble for a pillow. Marvel not that none did with hue and cry pursue good Master Owlglass; for it came to pass that when the boor had found his pot of money taken, he cried aloud with a great voice, and spake unto such as from their drowsy pillows would with sleepy head give heed unto his speech. But for as much as it was well-known to the worthies which abode in that village, that good master peasant was a miserly hunks, they cared not at all when that he cried aloud that a thief had taken his treasure, and fled with it into the night.

Thus did none follow Owlglass until the day dawned, and

then search was diligently made, for in truth men's hearts, lacking charity in the night season, do sometimes become strangely moved in the face of morning,—and search being made, they encompassed Master Owlglass, and set upon him, and took him and carried him before my good justice of that village, who was a right worthy and true judge. Then the miserly boor stood forth, and said: "Last night while that I sate in my chamber and counted my moneys, this knave lay in wait under the casement thereof, and when that to fright my child, I put forth my pot of money, he with rascally guile took it from me, and fled away therewith. And that he had the money that can he not deny, for when that we took him, he had it in his pouch." Then the judge said unto Owlglass: "What hast thou to answer unto this man? Dost thou confess and make restitution unto him, for this be a hanging matter, and thou art like to be food for the crows?" Thereat Owlglass answered and said: "Nay, but I entreat ye that of this boor I may have some answers touching this matter." The judge said: "Speak on." Then said Owlglass: "Lo! didst thou not open the window and say aloud: 'Here black man, do thou take the money?'" "Yea," quoth the boor. "And was not the night dark?" "In good sooth it was," answered the boor. "And in dark night are not all men black?" "I' faith that is true," said the boor. "Then I being a black man, may it content your worship's reverence, was bidden to take this boor's pot of money, the which I graciously received, and for the which I bestow the thanks of a poor man upon him." "Of a truth, thou speakest wisely," observed the judge, "and for such deed can I not hang thee; and for as much as thou art a proper man and of a quick wit, do I free thee, and bestow upon thee these fifteen shillings; but be thou very heedful to depart forth from this our village, and come not again by day or by night." Then the boor departed homeward and thought it had been better to have bestowed a penny upon his little lad, than lose the goodly marks by such a rare coney-catcher as was Owlglass. Yet for this cared Owlglass not a whit; but set forth with full pouch and merry mood to the next country; and praised the judge for the just and true judgment he had given.

The Eighty and First Adventure.

How with good luck Owlglass told many that he had lost his money-girdle, and thereby came unto a warm fire.

Now the winter season came, and with white mantle hid the earth, and it was bitter cold. Yet it fortuned that Owlglass had urgent reason to travel, for his occasions never happened to keep him in one place or city for any time. And as the night drew near, Owlglass came unto a village, and there entered into the inn and the chamber where the guests and village gossips sate talking around the fire. Our noble master was covered over with sleet and snow, and the frost had bitten him sore and his garments held within them icy proofs of the wintry season; yet for as much as the boors concealed the fire he could not warm himself. Thereat he cried out lustily for good master host that he should bring him some wine, the which was readily done. And Owlglass opened his mouth and spake unto the host after this wise: "Good mine host, I beseech thee do thou allot unto me a candle in a lanthorn, and one which should go forth with me unto the road, for there lieth by the way, a money-girdle, the which I have lost; and though I sought it diligently, yet by reason of the darkness of the night, could I not discover it." But the host answered: "Nay, but this night seek not after it, for where it lieth shall we find it to-morrow at sun-rise, and there will be no harm come thereunto." And he said this, for that he was wily, and would have sought it himself, and taken it. And the boors which were talking about the fire, pricked me up their ears, and one by one departed out of the inn that they might seek the money-girdle, so that at last the chimney nook was empty, and Master Owlglass might, with comfort, drink his wine in the warmth, while the others delved and digged in the snow abroad. When that they were all departed thence, Owlglass discovered the pleasant jest unto the host, and they laughed hugely, and drank in the ingle a most joyous cup thereupon.

The Eighty and Second Adventure.

How that Owlglass did at Bremen of the market-women buy milk, and cause it to be poured altogether into one tun.

A pleasant jest wrought Owlglass at Bremen. At one season when that he came thither, he stood on the market, and he beheld that the boors' women brought great store of milk thereto; and therewith he 'gan to think what a merry piece of knavery he might perform. Therefore he tarried awhile until a day on which the market was very full, and much milk was brought thither, and he fetched him a great tun, the which he set upon the market-place, and cried aloud unto the boors' women that they should turn unto him, for he would buy their milk, and they should pour it into the tun. And every good wife of the which he took milk he bade write the measure and price therefor, upon a paper, and then sit down, for he would pay the money when that the tun was filled.

So the boors' wives sat in a circle around Owlglass, and waited for their money, and rejoiced greatly at such a noble milk merchant (for they knew him not); and it came to pass, that after a while there was not any other good wife who had milk to sell. Then Owlglass opened his mouth and spake unto the women, and said unto them these words: "To-day have I not any money in pouch.

And such of ye as cannot abide and give me credit for a matter of fourteen days, would do best to take forth her milk again:" and having thus maliciously ended his speech, he hasted to go away from the market-place. Thereafter contended the boors' wives with much anger, and each would fain take her milk out of the tun first, and in their quarrelings the milk was spilled on the ground and on their clothes, and in their eyes; and it did most certainly appear as if milk from the clouds had been rained down. And all the townspeople beheld the merry conceit, and they were greatly contented with the wit of Master Owlglass.

The Eighty and Third Adventure.

How that Owlglass spake unto twelve blind men, and persuaded them that he had unto them given twelve shillings; and how that they spent the money and came evilly off thereafter.

And, it came to pass, that as Owlglass journeyed hither and thither up and down in the land, like an uneasy spirit as he was, he came again unto Hanover, and there he wrought not a few strange things. Therefore one day as he sate upon his horse beyond the city gate and rode a good way, there came along the road twelve blind men, the which he encountered. When that he beheld them he cried aloud unto them: "God give ye grace, blind men, whence come ye?" Then the company of blind men stood still and perceived that he sate upon a horse, and by that they judged him to be an honest gentleman—for respect is always due to one who is a cavalier; and who rides must needs be honest—so they took off their hats and saluted him, and spake unto him, saying: "Lo! noble and worshipful sir, good kind Christian gentleman, we have been within this city of Hanover; there had a rich man given up the ghost, and at his funeral feast were alms and baked meats bestowed upon us and other poor men, as be we. Yet for as much as frost and snow be on the ground, we were right sorely pinched with the cold." Then answered Owlglass, and said unto them: "Ye say truly that it is cold; I fear me that of frost ye will utterly perish. Now look you, here be twelve shillings, enter ye again into the city, and get ye unto such an inn, [and he told them what inn they should seek], and spend ye these twelve shillings for God his grace and my sake, until that the winter be gone by, and ye be able to again set forth in comfort upon your voyage."

Then the blind men stood in great honour and worship of the noble gentleman's person, and bowed themselves before him, and gave him their thanks for his guerdon. For each blind man believed that his neighbour had received the money, to wit, in the manner that the first thought the second had it, and the second the third, and the third the fourth; and after this wise were they all hoodwinked, for not one stiver had Owlglass bestowed upon them. Thereafter they turned back, and gat them unto the hostel of the which Owlglass had told them; and when they had entered in, they spake unto the host, and told him how that it had come to pass that a good charitable gentleman had encountered them by the way, and had bestowed upon them twelve shillings, that they might eat and rejoice during the hard winter, until that spring should come again.

Now the host was a man greedy of gain, and he thought no more upon that saying, but how he might get the money; and he received them, and never did he dream within his stupid sconce to ask which had the money in pouch of them all. But he spake unto them, saying: "Dear and beloved brethren, ye shall here receive satisfaction, and your afflictions shall be comforted." And he made haste to kill and hew down oxen and calves; and he made ready meats boiled and roast, and set them before the blind men, who fell to right gladly; and this feasting went forward every day, until he thought that they had eaten the value of the twelve shillings.

Then he spake unto them, and said: "Dear brethren, ye have eaten the value of the twelve shillings, methinks, let us therefore reckon." And the blind men answered: "Yea;" and spake each unto his fellow, that he should take forth the twelve shillings, that good master host should be rewarded. But the one had it not, neither had the other; moreover they found that not a penny had any man of their company. And the blind folk sate still and scratched their pates, but found not the twelve shillings anywhere behind their ears; and they perceived that they had been beguiled. Then the host saw likewise that he had been cozened of his charges, and he sate there, and pondered what he should do. For he thought within himself: "Here be a company of blind rascals, and if that thou permittest them to depart, then dost thou lose thy charges; and if that thou keepest them will they eat yet more, and then thou wilt be at double cost." So with no more ado he claps me the blind company of dear brethren into the pig-stye, and there may they make fine cheer with hay and straw.

At this time, Owlglass 'gan to think,—for with all his malice he had a good heart:—"Nay, but thy blind men must very nigh have eaten up the provision thou madest for them, and therefore go thou and seek news of them." And he saddled his horse and disguised himself, and rode unto Hanover, and came unto the inn where the blind men lay. Thereupon, as he came into the court, and would have bound his horse up in the stable, he looked, and behold the blind men lay in the pig-stye. Thereat he gat him into the house, and spake unto the host, and said unto him: "What is this thing which thou hast done unto these blind men? Wherefore be they amidst the dirt and mire of the pig-stye? Have ye no bowels of mercy when ye see the vile fare they eat?" And the host answered him: "Nay, but I wish that in the water they lay all perished, if only my charges were paid." Therewith telleth he unto Owlglass the whole story of the matter. Owlglass said unto him: "How, sir host, could ye not have a surety for this debt?" "Alas!" quoth the host, "right gladly would I have a surety if that it could be—and if that a certain surety be found, I would set free these poor men forthwith." Thereat said Owlglass unto him: "See now, I will go and in this city make quest, if that I can find some charitable man that will do this thing for thee."

So Owlglass gat him forth, and came unto the priest of the parish, and said unto him: "Most reverend and learned sir, hast thou a will to do a Christian kindness? For lo! I must expound unto thee, that mine host of the inn where I lie is possessed of an evil spirit within the past night, and he beggeth hard that ye would exorcise him, and cast out the evil demon." The priest answered, and said: "Yea, that I will most cheerfully; for is it not mine office? Yet must we tarry a day or two; for with such things is haste greatly to be avoided." Then quoth Owlglass: "I will go fetch his wife, that ye may repeat this thing unto her." The priest replied: "Yea, bring her unto me, I warrant she shall be content." Then departed Owlglass, and gat him to the host, and said: "I have found for thee a surety in good master parson of the parish. Give me now thy wife to bear me company unto him; for he will give her satisfaction." Thereat was the host right glad, and bade his wife immediately resort with Owlglass unto the priest; and when they came thither, Owlglass said: "Behold, reverend sir, here is the woman, wife unto the host of the which I spake anon. Assure her now as before thou didst assure me." And the priest said: "Yea, my good woman; be thou content. For is it not mine office to do deeds of charity? That which thy husband seeketh shall be in a short time performed within these few days." And the woman was content, and returned again unto her husband, and said unto him, that the priest would perform the payment duly; and then was the host glad, and let the blind men depart, and rewarded Owlglass for his pains; and this last set forth on his journey, and tarried no longer in Hanover.

The third day after this, the woman went again to master parson, and demanded of him, that he should pay the twelve shillings. And he asked her, if her husband had said this thing unto her; and she said: "Yea." Thereat he observed, "that such was the way with evil spirits; they would always have money." But the woman said: "There be no evil spirits here; pay ye the charges, and therewith are we ended." The priest quoth thereat: "I was admonished that your good man was possessed of an evil spirit, the which he would fain have cast forth; now this will I do, but of money know I nothing." To him straightway answered the goodwife: "Nay, but this is the fashion with liars and shufflers; when that money is to be paid, they would with knavery escape. If that my husband be of an evil spirit beset, ye shall surely be advised thereof," and therewith ran speedily unto her husband, and told him what the parson said.

After this took the host halberts and pikes, and ran with a company unto the parsonage. And when the parson beheld it, he cried aloud, and assembled his neighbours, and said unto them: "Do you, I charge ye, help me against this madman, who of an evil demon is sore possessed." And the host said unto him: "Priest, remember thy surety, and do now pay me." But the priest stood and blessed himself, and payed not at all. Then would the host have with a goodly staff stricken the priest, but that the boors came and parted the twain with great difficulty. But, so long as the host lived, he was ever seeking payment from the priest; and the priest affirmed that he had an evil spirit, and of that would he free him, but of money owed he unto him not a doit.

Thus fell out the end of the excellent adventure of Owlglass with the blind men, the host, and the parson.

The Eighty and Fourth Adventure.

How that in a city of Saxony Owlglass sowed knaves.

Knaves abound in many places; there be knaves of every degree: there be black knaves, white knaves, copper-coloured knaves, red knaves, and yellow knaves. There be knaves which ride in coaches and waggons; there be knaves on horseback; there be knaves on foot. There be knaves of high degree; there be knaves of low estate. There be knaves in Holy Church, devout knaves, which cheat heaven in their prayers, and earth in their tithes; there be knaves out of Holy Church, which, for wise reasons, do simulate a contempt thereof; there be knaves which buy, and there be knaves which sell; there be knaves which, with honest mien, declare themselves no better than they be, for thou in thy vanity condemnest them not, but thinkest them better than their speech declareth, and yet be these very knaves, sorry knaves, and shallow knaves. There be knaves which bear rule, and there be knaves over which rule is borne; there be knaves which bow the knee to knavish kings, princes, and lords; and there be knaves which set foot forth against all rulers, princes, and governors. There be knaves which help ye with seeming good fellowship, and there be knaves which, by opposing ye, do ye true service; there be knaves which amuse ye; there be knaves which laugh in turn at that which ye do: lo! indeed, not in this world can ye find any place which is devoid of knaves, creeping like caterpillars through your gardens, and destroying your fairest flowers, to fatten and batten, and crawl and die like other things.

Knaves sit smiling by your own hearthstone, deluding ye

with love and fair service—your children be knaves, your fathers were knaves;—for in this world are secrets hidden—and, indeed, are we unto ourselves not true, but knaves altogether, excusing, palliating, concealing, hugging, with not a little fear and trembling, our favourite vices, or our evil desires. O what a discourse of knavery would a history of our mad world be, what quaking terrors of evil doings, what fierce self-destructions, what insane flight from self-condemning would be unfolded! Let us rejoice, my masters, that a little spice of honesty leaveneth the whole lump and maketh life endurable, our meat not poison, our porridge not altogether rat's-bane. And truly this chronicle affirmeth, averreth, and with loud voice saith, that an if such words as these had been set down in courteous phrase, and not hurled from the priest's pulpit or babbled from the fool's booth, ye had not received, but had denied utterly the gracious assent which I do perceive sitteth upon your heart; thus, therefore, like all other things, is this chronicle but a knavish matter.

Of a truth, it may be most certainly believed, that to such a world it was necessary and fit, that a pitying eye and brain should see, and purpose despatch, from highest heaven to insulted earth a Prince of peace and justice. But in this chronicle, as in this world, is all honesty discarded; for the world is so turned topside t' other way, that it may not be that we should distinguish gentle from simple, wise from foolish, honest man from knave. "Yet be of good cheer," saith One who is higher than any of us; "I have overcome the world."

Yet in one little town of Saxony espied Owlglass, when that he was therein, that not within its walls there could be a knave; yet might this be, for that he was strange unto the devices and nature of the folk which dwelt therein; and he fell into a deep contemplation and musing upon such a marvellous matter. And he took his way beside of the river Weser, the more at ease to reflect thereover. For while that he abode in that city, beheld he all that was done by the folk therein; and so strangely honest appeared their dealings, that he was tired and sick at heart with folk among whom he could not have any profit. And as he took his way along the bank of the Weser, he looked, and, behold! of pebbles shiny and clear, rolled in mass by the stream, was there a goodly heap; and he bethought how that of old some wondrous one did, by casting stones over his shoulders, produce men and women, the which in knavery excelled greatly. "Nay," quoth he thereat; "why should not in this place a like marvel happen?" and with no more ado, he catcheth me up a sackful of these so shining stones, and entereth with great joy and content into the city.

Then in that street which is hard by over against the town-house, he beginneth to sow his crop of marvellous nature; but the people came running unto him and inquired of him, and fain would know what it might be that he was doing. "Why," quoth noble Master Owlglass, "in this town here be ye so woundily honest, that for fear ye should be altogether without praise for your virtue, I sow ye a crop of knaves." With that, my masters, ye should have heard the outcry and hallabaloo which the burghers did make. "Nay, nay!" they cried, "this city be, indeed, so crammed with an abundance of knaves that an if ye sow not honest folk, we shall surely perish." But Owlglass said: "That may not be, for in this town have grown virtues so long that ye must change the crop, or let the ground be for awhile fallow." Then they laid hands upon him and took him, and bade him answer his deeds before the town council. And the town council admonished him, and would have none of his crop, and bade him therewith carry his seed-sack out of their bounds. So Owlglass gat him forth, and entered into another city; but the fame of what he bare had been noised abroad, and so entirely did they detest knavery, and loathe cheats, that neither to eat nor to drink nor to tarry for rest would they permit Owlglass. Aweary of such ware, at last he entered into a ship, and would have departed by water, but the seed brake the bottom through, and he was nigh drowned; so into the River Weser returned the stones he had taken; and unto this day, whenever that any man is seized of great virtue, they give unto him water of the Weser to drink, the which strangely promoteth chousing, coney-catching, and gulling.

Thus endeth a great feat of our modern Deucalion.

The Eighty and Fifth Adventure.

How that in the good city of Hamburg Owlglass hired him unto a barber and went through the casement unto his service.

On a time came Owlglass unto Hamburg and there stood upon the Hop-market, and gazed hither and thither as he was wont to do. And unto him came up a barber, and spake unto him and said: "Lo! what seekest thou, and whence comest thou?" Then Owlglass said: "Of a truth, I come now straightway from the last place in the which I abode." Upon this saith the barber: "What art thou for a workman?" And Owlglass said: "I am a barber, an it please ye." Thereat the master hired him, and spake unto him saying: "Mark me, dost thou see yon house over against us with the casement down unto the ground." "Yea," quoth the man. "Then do thou straightway enter in there, and soon will I follow," said the master. "Most truly," said our worthy Owlglass. Then he gat him unto the house, and brake the casement all in pieces, and entered in thereby, and saluted the barber's wife, who sate spinning within, and spake courteous words and said: "God bless this handiwork." But the barber's wife was afeared, and cried: "What labour and handiwork be this that thou dost, breaking me the casement after this wise? The foul fiend seize thee, loon!" "Nay," quoth Owlglass, "impute not the marring of the casement unto me, except as diligent service, for your good man bade me enter in thereby, and I ever perform that which is enjoined me." Then the woman said: "Truly, a faithful servant is he who marreth his master's substance!" But Owlglass said: "Should not a servant perform his master's bidding?" With that, during such conference betwixt the twain, cometh the master, and looked upon the broken casement. And he said unto Owlglass: "What is this? Couldst thou not enter by my house door, and leave me the casement whole? What be the cause that thou shouldst thus enter by a window." "Nay," answered Owlglass, "beloved master, ye bade me look upon the tall window and there enter in; and I did but according to thy words." Thereat was the master content, for he considered within himself: "I can but from the money of his hiring take what will pay the charges of making my casement whole."

Thereafter they went forward in comfort for some days. Then did the barber enjoin Owlglass that he should take a razor, and he instructed him, and said: "Now do thus evenly with the edge grind me the back, so that no notches be." And Owlglass answered: "Yea, most willingly." And after a season had gone past, the barber cometh privily behind Owlglass to see after what manner he was performing his labour, and Owlglass had ground the back as sharp as the edge, and marred the work altogether. So the master spake unto him saying: "What vile thing is this that thou dost?" And the other to him answered: "I do not any vile thing? But only according to thy words; didst not bid me to grind the back evenly with the edge? And so do I." Then did the master wax very wroth, and said unto him: "Lo! get thee forth hence, and return in manner that thou didst come." Owlglass answered him: "Yea," and taking his bundle, springeth me forth through the casement again, and breaketh it, and so departeth. And though the barber was lithe and active, as be the fashion with barbers, yet could he never seize Owlglass, who, indeed, was a match for a good fleet runner.

<h1 style="text-align:center">The Eighty and Sixth Adventure.</h1>

How that Owlglass did cause the host of the inn at Eisleben to be beset with great terror, by showing unto him a wolf, of the which he professed no fear.

Eisleben there dwelt an innkeeper who was mocker of others, and who thought that of all great hosts he was the exemplar and flower. Unto him came Owlglass in the winter time; and he abode in the inn with him while that the snow was on the ground. And while that the night was dark, there came three merchants from Saxony unto the inn, who would fain come unto Nürnberg. The host, who was swift of speech, spake unto them, and, with ready words, said: "Whence come ye folk so late, and why have ye tarried so long by the way?"

And the merchants answered him, and said: "Behold, master host! be not wroth with us by reason of our lateness; a wolf did lie in wait for us by the way and attacked us, and with him had we to contend and beat him off; from that cause is it that we be so late with thee." And when that the host heard their words, he mocked them, and said unto them: "Great shame is it that ye do let yourselves be stayed by a wolf—for if that I met two wolves in the field, I would alone contend with them and slay them; little account would I make of such a pair! And there were of ye folk three people, and by a single wolf were ye affrighted." And thus continued the host to mock them the whole even through until that they gat them to bed.

All this while sate Owlglass by the fire, and heard what was said. And when that the night was far spent, in the which this host so despised the merchants, they gat them to bed and Owlglass lay with them in one chamber; and then conferred the merchants one with the other, as to how it might be brought about that the host should be rightly recompenced for his mockery and scorn, so that they might make him to hold his peace, for that afterwards they might take their ease in the inn. Then did Owlglass open his mouth, and spake unto them, saying: "Lo! an it please ye, beloved friends, truly do I mark that our host is nought but a vain speaker. Now, if that ye are content to hear me what I would say unto ye, I will so do that never more shall he speak unto ye of the wolf." Thereat rejoiced the merchants with great content, and did promise him money, the which should be given unto him; and his reckoning, likewise would they pay. Then he bade them depart freely unto their business; but as they returned, he would have them lie at that same inn, and he would then also be there present, and he would cause the host to hold his peace, thereafter in the matter of the wolf. To that agreed they, and gat them ready for their voyage on the next day, and paid their charges and those of Owlglass likewise, and they all rode away therefrom, and the host called after them with mockery: "Be ye sure, ye merchants, that no wolf doth beset ye by the way." But they answered, and said unto him: "Great thanks do we give unto thee; and if the wolves devour us, then come we not hither again."

Then did Owlglass ride unto the hunt, and chased the wolves, and by God his grace killed he one, and this one did he put in the ice until that it froze hard. And when that it was about the season that the merchants should again come unto Eisleben unto the inn, Owlglass took the dead wolf within a sack, and gat him unto the inn according unto his promise, and there found he the three merchants. At supper time did the host yet mock the three merchants about the wolf; but they said that of a truth it had so happened unto them as they had said unto him. But the host continued to speak words of vain import, and declared unto them, that if he did meet two wolves in the field, he would shake the one by the head until that he died, and then would cut the other in pieces.

Thus went all conversation forward, until that they departed unto bed. Yet kept Owlglass silence, and spake no word until they had entered into their chamber and shut the door. Then he opened his mouth, and said unto them: "Lo! gentlemen and good friends, do ye still keep watch for a space, and put ye not out the light." And when the host had gat him to bed with all his folk, Owlglass crept privily from the chamber, and bare with him the dead wolf, the which was frozen hard, and carried it into the kitchen, and with sticks supported it that it stood upright; then did he open its mouth wide, and therein set two children's shoes, and thereafter gat he him unto the chamber where he abode with the merchants. In no long time thereafter cried he aloud for the host. Then did the host hear him, for yet was he not asleep; and he called unto him and demanded what he would have. Then they cried aloud unto him: "Alas! worthy master host, send unto us the maid or the man, for of thirst shall we else die!"

When that the merchants cried aloud after this manner, the host waxed very wroth, and said: "Even thus is it ever with the folk from Saxony, for by day and by night are they always bibbing." Then he called the maid, and bade her that she should arise and give them drink in their chamber. So the maid arose and went unto the fire, and would have taken a light; then beheld she the wolf, and looked straight into his jaws, and she was affrighted, and let the light which she had taken fall, and fled away into the court; for she believed nought else but that the wolf had devoured the children. But with a loud voice did Owlglass and the merchants yet cry for drink. Then thought the host that the maid had gone to sleep, and called the man, and he arose and would have taken a light; then beheld he the wolf, and he believed at once that the wolf had devoured the maid, and he fled and gat him unto the cellar. Thereat said Owlglass unto the merchants: "Be ye but patient! soon will ye have rare sport withal." And he called the third time to know where the maid and man might be, for that they perished of thirst; therefore besought they the host that he should take a light and bring them to drink with his own hand, for that they could not come forth from their chamber.

The host was thereat very wroth, and believed in his heart that the man had slept as he went, and he said: "Of a truth these Saxons, with their continual drinking, cause me to have much labour!" Yet he arose and lighted a candle in the kitchen, and with that beheld he the wolf as he stood by the hearth, bearing the shoes between his jaws. Then fled he unto the merchants in the chamber, and cried aloud with fear: "Come hither to help me, beloved friends! By the hearth here standeth a terrible raging beast, the which hath eaten me the children, and maid, and man." Then went the merchants and Owlglass with him; and the man came forth from the cellar, and the maid returned from the court, and his wife brought the children out of the chamber, and lo! they were all alive. Thereupon went Owlglass unto the wolf, and with his foot cast it down, and it lay quite still.

Then spake Owlglass unto the host, and said: "Behold! this wolf is a dead beast, and dost thou thereat cry out so lustily? What a craven man are ye? Think ye that a dead wolf will bite ye, and cause your people to flee into corners? Yet last night were ye so brave, that one wolf, the which was alive, would not have contented ye to strive withal? and with two such beasts would ye have fought in the field. But with thee is it in words, what with most others lieth only in the mind." And the host heard these words of Owlglass, and perceived that he had been beguiled, and crept into his chamber, and was ashamed that he should by a dead wolf have been so cozened. But the merchants laughed hugely at the excellent wit and merry conceit of our prince of good fellows, honest Master Owlglass, and right willingly paid for his provisions with their own, and rode with him upon their way. Since that time, however, hath not the landlord extolled his own bravery in like manner.

The Eighty and Seventh Adventure.

How that Owlglass paid his host with the ring of his money.

One day Owlglass entered at Cologne into an inn, and it came to pass, that the provision was put unto the fire to cook when that it was very late, and the time for dinner came soon thereupon. And Owlglass loved good cheer, and therefore was he wroth thereat, for he loved fasting no more than a pious friar. This perceived the host, and spake unto him, saying: "He that cannot bide until that dinner be ready, may eat that he hath." Then gat Owlglass a small loaf, and that did he eat; and thereafter sate down by the hearth at the fire, and he smelled the savour of the meat upon the spit, and it satisfied him. And when dinner-time came, the table was set and the meat brought up, and the host sate with the guests at the table, but Owlglass abode in the kitchen by the fire. Then said the host unto him: "Wilt thou not sit at meat with us?" "Nay," quoth Owlglass, "I care not to eat; with the savour of the roast am I filled."

Then the host held his peace, and continued to eat with the guests, and after dinner they paid him and departed this way and that way; yet abode Owlglass by the fire. To him entered the host with his pay-table, and would have of him two Cologne pence for his dinner. And Owlglass said unto him: "Sir host, are ye that kind of man which demandeth pay of one who hath not eaten?" Then was the host angry, and said "he should pay, for an if he had not eaten of the meat, had not he confessed himself filled with the savour thereof?" Then took Owlglass forth a Cologne penny and threw it on the table, and said unto the host: "Hearest thou the sound of that penny?" "Yea," quoth the host. And Owlglass quickly took up his penny again, and put it into his pouch, and said: "As much reward the sound of my penny is unto thee, even so much have I profited of the savour of thy meat." And when the landlord would have received the penny of him, Owlglass denied it unto him, and mocked him with much scorn, and departed thence over the Rhine water, and gat him back again into Saxony.

The Eighty and Eighth Adventure.

How that Owlglass at Lübeck did escape from a house when that the watch would have taken him for his debts.

Master Owlglass, like unto most other great and glorious personages, esteemed money but lightly; and he could not bear to look upon the same piece of coin oftener than twice—once when that he received it and put it in his pouch, and again when that he took it forth to spend it in joyous company. Therefore marvel ye not when that I say unto ye, that Master Owlglass did oftentimes make debts, the which he could not pay. And it fortuned, that on a time when that he was abiding in that good town of Lübeck, that he had not a penny, and the officers of the watch did go about to catch him, and cast him into gaol until that he paid every person to whom he owed aught. But he kept within his house, and went not forth but at eventide, when that darkness had with its black mantle covered the town. Yet on one evening he perceived that they had surrounded the house where he lay, and would have entered and have taken him. And he beheld, that for him was only one thing possible to be done—that he should in a church find sanctuary. Now, in that same house lay an old woman who was sick unto death, and sorely afflicted. Unto her went Owlglass, and took her hand, and did, with a most grave countenance, say unto her: "Behold, is it not time that thou shouldst think of thy soul, and make thee ready to depart; for near unto death dost thou lie." And therewith sent he unto the priest of the parish, that he should come, that she might confess unto him, and receive extreme unction from his holy hands. Then when the host entered in at the door, did the watch arrive from the guardhouse, and beheld it, and they prostrated themselves before it; and then Owlglass, while that they saw him not, departed out of that house, and thereafter gat him unto the church, where he lay until even, and then departed he out of the town.

The Eighty and Ninth Adventure.

*How that Owlglass at Stassfurt of a dog took the skin, the
which he gave unto his hostess for her charges.*

On a time it came to pass, that Owlglass entered into an inn,
and there found the hostess quite alone. And this hostess
had a little dog, of the which she was greatly enamoured; and
ever mote it be, that, when she had nought to do, this dog must
lie in her lap. And Owlglass stood by the fire, and drank from the
beer-can. Now it was the custom with that hostess, that when
she drank beer, she did always, in a small dish, give thereof unto
the dog. So when that Owlglass drank, the dog arose, and came
unto him, and would, by leaps and look, have entreated him for
some beer. That saw the hostess, and she said unto Owlglass:
"Behold, beloved guest, do thou give him to drink in the dish of
thy beer for so would he signify unto thee." And Owlglass said
unto her: "That will I do cheerfully." Then departed the hostess
to perform whatever business she had about the house; and
Owlglass gave him to drink in the dish, and therein put likewise
a little piece of meat; and when that the dog had eaten thereof,
goeth he to the fire and lieth sleeping thereby. Then said Owlglass
unto the hostess: "Let us now reckon our charges." And he asked
her: "Good, my hostess, if that a guest eat of thy meat and drink
of thy beer, yet hath not any coin, would ye also unto such an
one give credit?" Then thought the woman not of the dog, but
had great suspicion of his own worthy person (the which, as ye
know, my masters, was most unjust!); therefore she answered
quickly unto him: "Master traveller, here must I have money, or

a pledge in place thereof." And Owlglass said unto her: "Truly am I right content therewith for mine own part; let the other look to it for his."

Then departed the hostess again, and Owlglass took the dog beneath his cloak, and went into the stable, and there took he his skin off, and entered again into the house, carrying it privily beneath his coat. Then called he the hostess again, and took out his money, and said: "Lo! let us now reckon." And the hostess reckoned up the charges. Then did Owlglass lay down half the reckoning upon the table, and said: "There have ye my part." And the hostess asked of him: "Who then shall pay the rest? Have ye not eaten and drank alone in my house?" But he said unto her: "Nay, but I had another with me, who ate of thy meat and drank of thy beer. Yet hath he no money, but a pledge can he give thee, the which is his coat; and therewith will he pay the other half." And the hostess said: "What guest mean ye?" Then Owlglass drew forth the dog's skin, and spake unto her saying: "Behold, mine hostess, here have ye the best coat that he hath." Then was the hostess moved, and saw that it was the skin of her dog; and she waxed wroth, and said unto Owlglass: "May the evil thing be upon ye ever! Wherefore didst thou take the skin from off my dog?" And Owlglass answered her, and said: "Woman, this is thine own fault, for thou didst demand either money or a pledge. And thou thyself didst desire that thy dog should drink, and I said unto ye the guest had no money; and thus, as he had nought else to give ye, take ye now his skin for the beer the which he drank." Then waxed the hostess yet more wroth, and commanded and enjoined him to go out of her house. "Nay," quoth Owlglass, "out of thy house will I not go, but ride." And therewith did he saddle his horse, and rode forth, and said unto her: "Hostess, do thou keep the pledge until that thou dost receive the money; and once again will I visit thee, to see if that thou hast had it redeemed. Farewell."

The Ninetieth Adventure.

*How that our noble master gave assurance unto the same
hostess, that Owlglass lay upon the wheel.*

Hear ye now that which Owlglass did on another day at Stassfurt. It fortuned, that thither he came again to lie in the same
inn; and he took other clothes, and so disguised himself, and came
thither, and entered in unto the court there, and lo! he perceived in
that place a great wheel. Now did a knavery enter into his sconce
therewith, and he lay down upon it, and gave the hostess a good
day. And he inquired of her, if that she had heard aught said of
the famous Master Owlglass? And she straightway answered him,
and said: "Why should I desire to hear tidings of the knave? Truly,
his name hath an ill savour in my nostrils!" And he said unto
her: "Woman, what hath he done unto ye that ye should speak
so bitterly concerning him?" And she answered, and said: "Truly
should I speak bitterly of him. Came he not hither, and stripped
me the skin of my dog from off his back, and gave me the skin for
the beer, the which he drank; for, of a truth, should he have had
shame to consort with a dog as a guest, and thereafter take off his
skin in such wise?" And Owlglass spake unto her, saying: "Hostess,
that was not well done." And the hostess said: "Aye, and unto a
knave's death will he also come." Then said Owlglass to her: "It
goes not well with him even now, for he lieth upon the wheel."
And thereat said she: "As the labour so the hire. God be praised
for all good things." And Owlglass stood up, and said unto her:
"I am Owlglass; have ye forgotten me? Farewell, I depart hence."

The Ninety and First Adventure.

How that Owlglass caused a Hollander from a plate to take an apple, the which evilly ended for the eater.

Honest and true was the payment the which Owlglass gave unto a Hollander at the village of Andorf, in an inn at that place, where that they abode, and whither many merchants of Holland did resort. Now Owlglass was somewhat sick, and did

not care to eat meat, and in place thereof did seethe him soft eggs. Now when that the guests sate at table, came Owlglass and brought the eggs with him, and the Hollander looked upon him as a boor, and said: "How is this, boor; dost not like the fare the which our host giveth unto us, and must eggs be seethed for thee?" Therewith taketh he the twain eggs, and breaketh them, and the one after the other doth he swallow; thereafter layeth he the shells before Owlglass, and saith unto him: "Lo! do thou lick the vessel, forth have I taken the yolk." And at this merry jest of the Hollander laughed the guests, and Owlglass with them.

But the same evening went Owlglass forth, and bought him a handsome apple, of the which did he scoop out the inside, and filled the same with flies and gnats. Then set he the apple to the fire to roast, and thereafter peeled it, and with sweet honey did cover the outside. And at night, when that all the guests once again sat at table to supper, came Owlglass with the apple on the plate, and turned his back upon the table as if he would have fetched some other thing. And when the Hollander saw it, he put forth his hand, and plucked the plate unto him, and took the apple, and swallowed it. Thereupon was he grievously sick, and did vomit forth the apple and all that in his stomach was beside, so that the host and all the guests thought that Owlglass had put poison therein. Then said Owlglass: "Nay, therein is no poison; it is but an apple to cleanse the stomach; an he had but said unto me that he would have eaten the apple, would I have warned him; for in the eggs which I seethed were there not any flies or gnats, but within the apple lay there a goodly company." Thereafter was the Hollander well enough again, and he opened his mouth, and spake unto Owlglass, saying: "Of a truth do thou eat roast or boiled, whatever thou wilt; even if thou hadst quails like unto those the which ate the children of Israel in the wilderness, would I not eat with thee."

The Ninety and Second Adventure.

How that Owlglass caused a woman to break in pieces the whole of her wares in the market-place at Bremen.

Now that so happily had Owlglass, unto his great comfort and content, brought to pass this knavery, departed he again, and journeyed unto the Bishop at Bremen, who loved Owlglass much; and by reason of his great wit and continual jests, did hold him in great honour. And he caused the bishop oftentimes to laugh right merrily, so that he gave unto Owlglass a house, in the which he had free provisions granted unto him by the bishop. When that he arrived there, Owlglass did as if he were tired, and desired to give up his knaveries, and was fain to enter unto the church there to pray. At that mocked the bishop—as bishops have done before that time and since—at the resolve of Owlglass—yet would he not be persuaded, but gat him unto the church, and prayed until that time that he could not any longer bear the quips and quiddities, the which were put upon him by the bishop. And privily had Owlglass with a market woman agreed, and she was the wife of a potter, and in the market-place sat she with pots and pans to sell: then did Owlglass pay unto the woman the price of all her ware, and enjoined her what she should do when that he gave unto her a sign.

Thereafter departed Owlglass, and came unto the bishop, as if he had come from the church, and the bishop reviled and mocked Master Owlglass, in that he was so pious and not any longer the same man. At last Owlglass said unto the bishop: "Gracious prince and reverend father! do ye now grant me to come unto the market-place, and there sitteth a potter's wife, and a wager will I set with you, that without my speaking unto her, or making a sign unto her with mine eye I will cause, by magical words, the which I will mutter, that she shall arise up and take a stick and herself break in pieces all her ware." Then said the bishop unto Owlglass: "Such a thing would I fain behold." Therefore with him made the bishop a wager of thirty pieces of gold that the woman did it not. And Owlglass did accept the wager, and with the bishop gat him unto the market-place. Then did Owlglass shew unto the bishop the woman where she sate, and they departed, and sate upon the house of the town council hard by. Then 'gan Owlglass to make incantation and conjuration, at the which stirred the potter's wife not a whit, and in good sooth the bishop rejoiced that he had most truly won his wager. At last gave Owlglass the sign unto the woman, the which they had agreed, thereupon arose she up and taking a stick, doth soundly belabour the ware, and breaketh it all in pieces very small. And with much content laughed the bishop; yet was vexed in the matter of the thirty pieces of gold, the which he had manifestly lost unto Master Owlglass. And when that they came again unto the bishop's court, did he confer privily with Owlglass, and said unto him: "If that he would discover unto him after what manner he had so brought it to pass that the woman should, after that wise, have broken her wares in pieces, then would he pay unto him the thirty pieces of gold." Then answered Owlglass unto the bishop, and said unto him: "Yea, gracious lord, that will I most cheerfully do." And therewith said unto him: "Most simple was this matter in every particular, for I paid unto the woman the price of her wares before that she brake them, and I made agreement with her beside."

Then laughed the bishop right merrily, and paid unto him the thirty pieces of gold, requiring of him that he should not disclose unto any one that which had come to pass. And if he kept his counsel, the bishop promised him that he would help him to a good fat ox thereto. "Yea," quoth Master Owlglass, and thereafter departed thence. Now when that the bishop sate at meat with his knights and gentlefolk, he opened his mouth and said unto them: "That he had learned an art whereby he might cause the potter's wife to break in sunder all her ware." Then the knights and gentlefolk craved much to know how this was done, and desired much to see the same performed; and this sheweth that in all times are men rather desirous to know how a mystery may be unfolded than patiently to follow it and wait until it doth itself give unto them the explication they would have. Then said the bishop: "Lo! an if ye will each of ye give unto me a good fat ox for my kitchen, will I teach ye all this art."

And it came to pass that it was the autumn season when the oxen were at the best. Then thought each noble knight and gentleman: "This will not be a great charge unto me, truly then will I do it for in this art to become learned." Thus did the bishop have of them sixteen fat oxen, and such was their price, that thereby was the bishop recompenced some three-fold for the thirty pieces of gold which he had paid unto Owlglass. And at this time came Owlglass riding thither upon his horse, and he said unto the bishop: "Of this booty is the half mine." And the bishop answered, and said unto him: "If that thou dost hold thy promise unto me, will I faithfully perform unto thee our contract; do thou leave me that which I have won." Then gave the bishop unto Owlglass a good fat ox, the which, with great reverence, did Owlglass receive from him. Thereupon did the bishop, discover unto his knights and gentlefolk in what manner they could perform the same marvellous thing, according to that wise by which he had learned it himself; for that Owlglass had paid unto the woman the price of her wares ere she brake them.

Then sate the noble knights and gentlemen silently upon their stools, and perceived that with cunning they had been beguiled; nor could they in any wise murmur thereat. So one scratched his head, and his neighbour sought for comfort in his neck, and they were sorely troubled for the loss of their oxen. But it could not be otherwise answered, and therefore comforted they themselves in that unto their gracious lord the profit had fallen; yet grieved they for their foolishness. But Owlglass rejoiced thereat, and departed with his booty. Thus may ye see, my masters, that when a wise man like unto Owlglass, with a bishop sitteth under one cap, ye may expect not a little knavery to come thereof! Therefore take heed and let not knaves approach near unto holy bishops of the Church, lest they be defiled, and much mischief come unto the commonwealth thereafter.

The Ninety and Third Adventure.

How that Owlglass sold a horse, the which would not go over trees.

On a time had Owlglass a horse, the which he would fain sell, and one came unto him, and looked upon it, and desired to buy it. And this buyer spake unto Owlglass saying: "Hath this horse any fault with him, the which thou oughtest to reveal unto me; and if that he hath shall it be no break to the bargain, I will yet buy him of thee, and in good money pay thee the price therefor." And Owlglass answered and said unto him: "Verily I say unto you, that I find no scathe in him, but this one, the which I confess openly, over the trees will he not go." And the merchant said: "I crave not that he should go over the trees, and therefore will I pay thee the price, if thou wilt let me have him for an easy penny." Then answered Owlglass and said: "Of a truth for a penny canst thou not have him; but for five pieces of gold mayest thou receive him from me," and they twain agreed the purchase. And when that he would have ridden the horse forth from the town,

came he unto the town bridge, over the which would the horse not go, for it was a wooden bridge, and built of trees. And he returned again unto Owlglass, and would have his money back; but Owlglass said unto him: "That most clearly had he told him the fault the which was in the horse." And the merchant gat him unto the judge, who said: "Most certainly should Owlglass give back unto him the money." Then summoned they Owlglass, but he came not; neither at any time would he make restitution for that he had said the horse would not go over trees.

The Ninety and Fourth Adventure.

How that of a horse-dealer Owlglass bought a horse, and only paid half of the money therefor.

When that Owlglass came unto the town of Hildesheim he encountered there a horse-dealer, who, for twenty-five pieces of silver, did offer him a good horse. And they marketed together for twenty-four pieces; and Owlglass said unto him: "Lo! the half of it will I pay thee straightway, and the rest shall I remain indebted unto thee. Thus will I now give unto thee twelve pieces of silver." And the horse-dealer (for he knew him not) said unto him: "Agreed; take thou the horse." And Owlglass took him.

And some three months fled by; then came the horse-dealer unto him, and demanded the twelve pieces of silver. Then said Owlglass unto him: "Behold, did we not agree that I should remain indebted unto thee for these twelve pieces of silver?" Thereat the other answered him, and they strove together, and came unto the house where the judge sate, and entered in, and would therewith have it appointed how the matter should stand. And then did Owlglass say he would remain faithful unto his bargain, according as he had bought the horse; and said unto the judge: "For twenty and four pieces of silver bought I the horse, and I paid him twelve thereof in good money; the other twelve agreed we that I should remain indebted unto him. If now that I do give him the money shall I falsify my word; and that have I never yet done, but always performed the thing which was commanded unto or required of me. And so let it be." Then was the suit before the judge withdrawn; and so stands the business, as if it were in the Chancery Court, unto this day.

The Ninety and Fifth Adventure.

How that in the land of Brunswick Owlglass turned shepherd.

Owlglass was a man that, with all his endeavours, could never grow rich, the which is a marvel, considering how it is that so many knaves prosper right well; and here was one that in honesty could never be approached, and yet was poor. Now he took counsel within himself, and said: "I have heard it said, that peradventure if one turneth shepherd, by the cunning of the patriarch Jacob one may grow rich." And he also had heard it said, that in the Duke of Brunswick's service all men grew rich in no long season. So he gat him unto the duke; and when that he had come unto him he spake unto him, saying: "Most gracious duke, do thou, with thy marvellous goodness, appoint me that I shall be a shepherd in thy service for some years; for I would fain have money, that in mine old age I may live; and for my service I desire no other recompence." And the duke did grant the post unto him for ten years. Then was Owlglass an excellent shepherd; and when that he heard that in any part of the duke's country there was good grazing land, then wrote he straightway letters unto that land, and told the people thereof that he would bring thither his master's cattle to graze. And in great terror did the farmer boors assemble, and did, for fear that the cattle should eat up all their substance, make collection, and send unto him five and twenty pieces of gold to go elsewhere. Then thought Owlglass: "A most fair thing is this;" and wrote unto another city, and thence also came money unto him; and this went forward

so long, until the duke himself asked Owlglass how that his post prospered. "Truly," quoth he, "I have a fair inheritance thereby, and a coat of delicate workmanship; for there is no office so little, that by it one may not have profit." "Nay," answered the duke; "I must unto this see myself." Hence comes it that dukes, princes, kings, emperors, and all their lackeys, do continually take into their own hands the work and labour of lesser men; for the duke said unto Owlglass, he himself would do this thing; and Owlglass answered him, saying: "No office is so little, that the hangman may not from it draw an inheritance. For the great be in marvellous peril alway."

The Ninety and Sixth Adventure.

How that without money Owlglass bought a pair of shoes.

Now it fortuned, that on a time Owlglass was at Erfurt, and there went through the Shoemaker's street; and a woman called loudly unto him, that he should come unto her and buy a good pair of shoes. Then came he straightway unto her, and took a shoe, and put it on his foot; then took he up its fellow, and put it upon the other foot, and said unto her: "Lo! they do suit me marvellous well," and therewith ran off. Then made the woman a great outcry, and said: "Stop me yonder thief, ye good folk!" And they would have held him. "Nay," said he, "good people, now do we run for a wager; therefore let me go, and then shall I win a pair of shoes." Thus came he off with the pair of shoes; but so ill made were they, that he gave them unto the servant at the inn where that he lay.

The Ninety and Seventh Adventure.

How that Owlglass sold unto the furriers at Leipzig a live cat, the which was sewed into the skin of a hare; and how rare sport came thereof.

In no long space of time was Owlglass ever ready with a knavish device. This proved he to be a great truth when that he was at Leipzig, among the furriers on Easter Even when altogether they held their feast. And it came to pass that most willingly would they have had some kind of game to make them a hunt therewith. Of this heard Owlglass, and in his knavery he bethought him: "The furrier at Berlin gave thee nought for thy labour, therefore shall these men pay thee thy pains." With that departed he into his inn, where he lay, and there found he that the host had a fine fat cat. This took Owlglass, and under his frock he carried it off; and then gat he him to the cook and besought him that he should give unto him the skin of a hare. For therewith would he play off a knavery of great and merry conceit. The cook gave unto him the skin which he demanded of him; and then he took needle and thread and sewed up the cat therewith in the skin. After did our master put on a boor's frock, and gat him to the town-house, and stood over against it. But his hare held he concealed under his coat until that a furrier came by. Then said Owlglass to the furrier: "Would his honour buy a good hare?" and then shewed it unto him, where that he held it under his frock. And the furrier and Owlglass conferred together; and they agreed that he should give unto him four silver bits for the hare, and six pennies for the old sack, in the which Owlglass had put the hare. Then the furrier carried the hare into the house of their alderman, and they rejoiced with great merriment, and were content in that they had got such a good live hare, for the furrier was right proud of getting such an one. Then did all the furriers feel and punch the hare to see how fat he was; and not that year, did they all agree had they seen such an one—the which was very true! And at the time they would hold their games, they fetched dogs and let the hare run in the garden, for they would have a hunt.

Now when that the hare could run no more, it leaped up into a tree, and cried out *Miaow*, for most willingly would it again have been at home. And when that the furriers beheld this, they cried aloud: "Brethren, brethren, come let us pursue the wicked knave, which hath beguiled us, and strike him dead!" And so would it

HOW OWLGLASS SOLD PUSS.

have been if Owlglass had not put on other clothes, so that they
knew him not. But now, my worshipful masters, hence came
the proverb: "The cat hath leaped up into the tree." Yet were the
furriers beguiled, and so remained.

The Ninety and Eighth Adventure.

How that Owlglass hired himself unto a boor.

It came to pass on a time that Owlglass served a boor; and the
boor did desire that they twain should, with a horse and cart,
get them unto the forest to cut wood. And Owlglass sate upon the
horse's back, while his master sate behind him upon the shafts of
the cart. Then ran a hare across the road whither they journeyed;
and the master, when that he beheld it, said: "Lo! my man, turn
we back again upon this day; for it is a most evil fortune when
that a hare doth run across the way. To-day will we do some other
thing." So they gat themselves home again.

On the next day departed they as before unto the forest; and
Owlglass spake unto his master, and said unto him: "A wolf hath
run across the road, master; what shall we do?" "Ha! sayest thou
so?" quoth the boor. "Drive forth, drive forth; great good fortune
is it when that a wolf doth cross thy road." So Owlglass drave the
horse into the forest; and when that they gat thither, they took
the horse out of the traces, and left the cart standing, while they
gat them to their labour. And when that they had done, the boor
despatched Owlglass, and bade him fetch the horse and cart, that
they might load and get them home once more.

Now when that the excellent Owlglass came before the forest,
he beheld the horse lying dead, and the wolf was inside thereof
devouring him with great appetite. And at this sight was Owlglass secretly glad, and ran back and said unto the boor: "Come

hither, boor come hither! the good fortune is within the horse!"
Thereat said the boor unto him: "What dost thou mean?" Yet
Owlglass hastened him, and said: "Do thou lose no time; but
get thee forward, or thou wilt have lost the good fortune." When
that they came thither, lo! the wolf lay within the carcase of the
horse, and eagerly tore and devoured him. Then said Owlglass:
"Boor! an if ye had gone into the forest yesterday, when that the
hare crossed our path, would your horse have been whole! But I
crave not to abide with one that on signs and omens setteth his
trust. Farewell!" And so departed.

The Ninety and Ninth Adventure.

How that Owlglass gat him to the High School of Paris.

Once Owlglass gat him as far as Paris, that learned city, at a
season when the examination for licentiate was going forward. And he went in and stood over against the one who on the
stool sate and looked upon him. Then the learned doctor said
unto him: "What wouldst thou have! Dost thou desire to say
aught unto me?" Then Owlglass took counsel within himself, and
said: "Yea, most learned, I have a most difficult question I would
desire resolved. Thus: Is it better for a man to do that which he
knoweth, or to learn that which he knoweth not? Make the doctors the books, or the books the doctors?" And at this question
marvelled everyone, and disputed thereupon; and the greater
number thought that it was better that a man should do that
which he knoweth, than that he should first learn that which he
knoweth not. Then said Owlglass: "Then what fools must all of
ye here be, in that ye ever crave to learn that which ye know not,
and what ye know, that do none of ye." Then departed he with
great scorn of pedants and scholars.

The Hundredth Adventure.

How Owlglass would fain have been an innkeeper at Rouen, but was beguiled by a one-eyed man, and again, in turn, cozened him.

In the town of Rouen, it fortuned that there was a certain tax to be taken from those who desired to keep an inn, which was named the Sign-tax, for to set up a sign you must give a crown, and of this tax a one-eyed man was the receiver. Owlglass thought to keep an inn, but could never have permission from this man to put up a sign unless he would give him a piece of gold, for that they had had a quarrel at some time before. But at last he was obliged to give a piece of gold, and he set his mind to make the receiver sorry for having taken it. So soon, therefore, as he might set up a sign, Owlglass had a one-eyed man painted, to whom another man was giving a piece of gold, and underneath he had written, *"Au Borgne qui prend."*[10] Those who beheld that sign, and who knew the story, laughed much thereat; and when it came unto the ears of the tax-receiver, he was very angry, and went and laid his complaint before the judge. Owlglass was cited to come to answer the complaint, the which he did at once, and confessed that he had set up the sign in shame of the man who had so cheated him; upon which the judge commanded the other to be sworn, who then said it was true he had taken so much money, and offered to return it. This he was ordered to do; and Owlglass was commanded to alter his sign, but all that he did was to paint out the p in the writing, which thus read: *"Au*

10   To the one-eyed man who takes.

Borgne qui rend;"[11] for in sooth it was not easy to discover in the painting whether the man was giving or taking the gold-piece. Thus Owlglass satisfied justice, and the judge would not hear the second complaint.

The Hundred and First Adventure.

How in Berlin Owlglass was an officer, and collected taxes of the boors.

When, unto his shame, Owlglass forgat his noble and virtuous estate, and became a tax-officer, he was on a time sent forth unto a village, to demand money of a boor, who either loved not to pay money, or was poor and could not. And as Owlglass with his little lance went forth, the following matter came to pass. For as an evil and wicked office bringeth shame unto the mind, so also leadeth it every man into bad company; therefore marvel ye not when that I say unto ye that the Devil, that prince of evil and darkness, encountered Owlglass as he ran. And his high estate had the devil put off, and appeared in the likeness of a boor, yet did Master Owlglass perceive right well who it was. Then 'gan they to confer together, and walked together on the way. The boor said unto him: "Thou goest about to receive money, let us now make fellowship; for I go to find a concealed treasure, and of that will I give thee half, and do thou the same with me."

Now Owlglass had heard it said of old time, that the devil knoweth full well of many a hidden treasure, so he agreed with him, and they departed together. And it came to pass, that as they went through a village, they heard a child crying and screaming. Then came its mother by, and said unto it: "Hold thy peace, wilt

11 To the one-eyed man who returns.

thou? May the foul fiend take thee!" Thereat said Owlglass unto the devil: "Lo! hearest thou, there hast thou a child given unto thee?" The devil said: "My good friend, the mother meaneth not that she saith; I dare not take it, for it is but spoken in choler." Then went they forward unto the field, and came unto a herd of swine; and lo! a great fat sow had departed from the herd, and the swineherd pursued it, and cried aloud, as he ran: "May the devil take thee!" That heard Owlglass, and for as much as he loved bacon, would fain have received his share, and said unto the devil: "Lo! dost thou not hear? Now hast thou a fat sow given unto thee. Put forth thine hand and take it, for it is thine. With thee will I have no further fellowship." Then said the devil: "Worthy Master Owlglass, what could I do with a sow? Nor hath he any grave intent to give it unto me; and if that I took it, the poor swineherd would have to pay for it. Nay, I will await something better than this." For the devil was tenderhearted; but Owlglass thought upon the treasure.

Thereafter came they unto the court-yard of the boor of whom Owlglass was to receive the money; and he stood in the barn and thrashed the corn. When that he looked up and beheld Owlglass, he opened his mouth, and spake unto him, saying: "Art thou there again? The devil take thee, for I would fain never see thee again." Thereat said the devil unto Owlglass: "Now dost thou see? He meaneth this thing most devoutly; do thou, therefore, come with me, for of a truth have I found my treasure, the which was hidden." But Owlglass answered, and said unto the devil: "Nay, but now will we reckon with each other; for I said unto thee that I would no longer have fellowship with thee, and now do I fulfil my saying; therefore do thou nothing contrary to law." Therewith cited he the devil before the judge, and bade him hold his hand not to touch him, for was he not a government officer? I know not, my good masters, whether the devil,—who is contrary unto all law, and existeth contrary thereunto,—had no great love for judges, or whether they were so steeped in evil-doing that even the foul fiend held them in contempt; yet most true it is, that he came not unto Owlglass his citation. Thereafter grew Owlglass greater in virtue, and left off his evil ways, and laid down his office.

The Hundred and Second Adventure.

How that in his latter days Owlglass became a pious monk, and what came thereof.

Unto all men is there appointed a time when that their manifold and heavy sins sit upon their remorse-laden souls, and they groan for mercy, and writhe under the pangs of repentance. And though Owlglass had, throughout his life, been a virtuous man (as I have clearly manifested unto ye, my masters!) yet after he had journeyed hither and thither in all lands, there came unto him a gallows-repentance; and he bethought him how that he unto a convent might depart, taking the vows of poverty, and there end his days, and cast forth all that old leaven of his evil-doings, and be a pious and a good man henceforth, so that his soul should not be lost. Therefore he gat him unto the Abbot of the convent at Marienthal, and entreated of him that he would receive him as a brother, and unto the convent would he in his testament give all that he had. Now, the which was not a most marvellous thing, the abbot with such fools was greatly contented, and therefore spake he unto Owlglass, and said: "For that thou hast yet some gear of valuable treasure, art thou welcome unto me. But, seest thou, some office must thou have, for among our fraternity is no one without somewhat to do; every one among us hath an employment, and therefore must thou too labour." And Owlglass answered, and said: "Yea, reverend father, that would I cheerfully do." Thereat said the abbot: "Then, with God's grace, as thou lovest not much labour, do I receive thee, and be thou our gatekeeper. So wilt thou stay within thy chamber, and wilt have neither sorrow nor great work, only to fetch thy provision and beer from the cellar, and to lock and unlock the gate." And the pious Owlglass said: "Reverend father abbot! God give you guerdon therefore, that ye do so kindly consider the infirmities of a poor old man, borne down with the weight of his sins and broken with sickness, of a truth will I perform everything that ye do enjoin me." Then said the abbot: "Behold, do ye now receive of me the keys, but let not every one enter herein, or will the convent soon grow poor, for the robbers will waste our substance, and eat up all our provision; therefore do thou let but few in, scarcely more than the third or fourth." And Owlglass answered, and said: "Yea, reverend sir, I will do your bidding as ye command me." Then did he never let more than the fourth person enter into the convent, it recked not whether they belonged unto the convent or no.

And a complaint came unto the abbot of this action of Owlglass, and he called him and spake unto him after this wise: "What a vile and doubly condemned knave art thou, that thou wilt not let such enter in that unto the convent do belong." "Reverend Lord Abbot," answered Owlglass, "lo! unto the fourth have I let them enter, according as thou didst signify unto me. Thy words have I fulfilled with great diligence." "Like unto a knave hast thou fulfilled those words of mine," said the abbot, and would fain have again been free of him. Then the abbot appointed another door-keeper, for he marked well that Owlglass would not hold from his ancient beguilings. And he gave unto him another office, and bade him count the monks in order as they gat them down unto matins, and he spake unto him, saying: "And behold, if thou dost overlook one of them then must thou get thee hence." Then said Owlglass to the abbot: "Verily is this a heavy business; yet an if none other hath command to do it, must I fulfil it as well as may be."

Thereafter brake he privily by night some boards from the staircase, by the which the monks came down unto the chapel. Now the Prior of that convent was an old man and a pious, and ever was he the first the which entered into the chapel to be at matins. And he came unto the stairs and sought the steps the which by Owlglass had been broken away, and found them not, but fell through and brake his leg. Then cried he out with a loud voice, so that all the other monks ran with great haste unto that place to see what had come to pass, and fell one after the other over the prior. Then did Owlglass get him unto the abbot, and said unto him: "Most reverend sir! I have fulfilled mine office as thou wouldst have from me." Therewith gave Owlglass unto the abbot the piece of wood, the tally on the which he had nicked down the number of the monks as he stood thereby. And the abbot said unto him: "Like unto a most vile knave hast thou fulfilled my command; get thee now straightway forth from this place." So Owlglass departed, and put from him his monk's frock, and came unto Möllen, where he thereafter lay sick and died.

The Hundred and Third Adventure.

How that when at Möllen Owlglass lay sick, his mother came unto him.

In sickness and in health hath a man but one ever kind friend, who in him can see no fault, whose good counsel abideth within his heart, and bitter sore is it when he followeth not the words spake unto him with such noble and truthful intent; yet such was the action of Owlglass. For when that in his youth his mother would have restrained him from his knavery, would he not be persuaded. Now at Möllen lay he grievously sick, and not one of his noble friends, unto the which he had caused such great laughter, cared to come nigh unto him; yet came his mother, who with fear and trembling had, in her solitude and desolate home, marked the courses of our noble master; and she besought him, saying: "Soon wilt thou depart unto the land of darkness and shadow, the which men traverse with shuddering, quaking with fear for the evil they have done, for of a truth is no man good, no man worthy of grace! Therefore do thou, I pray of thee, bequeath unto me of thy substance, that in my old age and decrepitude I may have some comfort; for I perish of sadness and sorrow, the which killeth more than an empty stomach, and destroyeth more than the bitterness of winter frost."

And, as he lay sick before her, did his evil youth rise up against him, and proclaim him a cunning and deceitful knave. Then took he his mother's hand between his twain, and opened his mouth and said unto her: "Lo! evil gotten riches reward not any man, neither canst thou on them place thy comfort. Now in this world is it a rule, the which none doth, that of him which hath anything should you take of his substance, and to him that hath not allot ye a part. Yet is my good fortune so great that my treasure is hidden where no man can find it. If that thou canst discover aught that is mine take it and use it freely. But an if thou findest it not, be not grieved, for my treasure is subtle and lieth most privily concealed." Then understood his mother the words which he spake unto her, and cared not any more to receive from him aught that by guile and cunning he had received of others. Yet may we perceive, in another place, what that treasure was, and how eagerly men strove thereafter.

The Hundred and Fourth Adventure.

How that when Owlglass was sick unto death, he made confession of three things, the which it sorely troubled him he had not done.

Sorrow and trouble had Owlglass for his manifold wickedness; but the mood in which he spake unto his mother, remained not upon him any while. For as the tree falleth so doth it lie, and in so much joyous company hath Master Owlglass spent his life, that now at the end of it can he not send forth the remembrance of it, and a smack of his ancient knavery cometh back unto him. When those which were around him perceived that he was near unto his end, they besought and moved him to confess his transgressions unto the priest. And that would he not do until an old nun of marvellous wisdom came and entreated him. Then he opened his mouth and spake unto her, saying: "Nay, but I die not sweetly, for death is bitter indeed, and unto me cometh with a face of woe; and why should I confess unto any man in

HOW OWLGLASS REBUKED THE PRIEST'S COVETOUSNESS.

secret? For what I have done,—knowing that in my manhood I have perfected many and divers things,—is perceived by me to be noised abroad over many lands and countries, and unto not a few is it well known, and of me converse they continually; and unto the end of time shall the inheritance of my life come unto others that arise after me. Of a truth do I not think so scurvily of the world. But an if I have done therein any good, it shall not be remembered; and if man receive it not, then will the Almighty Lord record it within the glorious book he hath of his creatures. And yet of my evil doings will there be constant report, so that without confession shall they be multiplied. Three sorrows have I, the which I have not done and performed, and the which could have been accomplished by me."

And the holy nun answered him, and said: "Dear heart! be ye content; for an if it might be an evil thing that ye would do, have ye in the thought concerning it wrought more than half thereof. But what be these things, evil or good?" And Owlglass answered, and said: "The first of these things is, that when I beheld a man walking in the street, and his coat hung below his mantle, I fol-lowed after him, and I thought that the coat would have fallen from off him; then would I fain have rolled it up, and did I not do it. For when that I approached unto him, I was grievously vexed that I could not cut off his coat as far as it hung down beneath the mantle. And this thing, the which I did not, troubled me most sorely. Unto this add I the second thing, the which is, that when I behold a man who sitteth, and with a knife thrust between his jaws, doth pick his teeth, then would I gladly jerk the knife into his wizen, for that thereby he might not again mar his teeth. And the last thing that I have not done is, that when a pack of old women sate conferring together, and gossiping away the character, conduct, and interests of those which be fools enow to look upon them with awe and reverence, I could not sew their mouths up, hath troubled me sorely." Then said the old nun unto him: "Meanest thou that, and wouldst thou do it unto me?" "Yea," quoth the dying knave. "Then would I give unto thee thy viaticum, and assoilzie thee,—and that thou shouldst get thee unto the foul fiend, the which owneth thee, and all like unto thee!" "Nay," answered Owlglass, "an if thou dost this, thou dost condemn the whole human race, for be we not every one of us fools or knaves?" But she tarried no longer with him, the which he deemed not civil, for with others, until that he was bidden to depart, remained he always.

The Hundred and Fifth Adventure.

Saith, How that to a greedy priest Owlglass confessed his sins, and paid him handsomely for his pains.

And it came to pass, that when the nun had departed from him, he still thought that with this world he would leave not a moment without profit; therefore when that they brought a priest unto him, lost he not any time in rehearsing unto him his sins, and likewise giving unto him such a lesson as in this true and veracious chronicle will now be set forth. For the greed of priests be very great, and ever delight they in clutching from the poor such money as would otherwise fill their ill-lined bodies with good meat and drink, and cover their pinched limbs with a fair doublet. So when that this priest came unto Owlglass, perceived he that an adventurous man had our master been, and in his time had made not a little provision for his purse, and could, therefore, pay unto his confessor a goodly sum. And unto him did he therefore speak, beseeching him to think of the peace of his soul, and that he should pay money for masses, the which should be said and sung for him. Thereunto answered Owlglass, that it was well said of him, and he bade him to come again that afternoon, and he would make provision therefor.

Then departed the priest, and came not again until even; and our good master made preparation, and gat a large vessel and filled it with pitch; and on the top of the pitch laid he some crown-pieces, and ducats, and other money, so as to hide the pitch from the eyes of the priest. Then confessed Owlglass his sins, and the priest gave him absolution, and then would have received the money of him. And Owlglass said unto him: "Lo! in yonder vessel lieth store of treasure, put in thine hand and pluck forth a handful; but do thou see that thou dip not too deep." Yet was the priest greedy, and hearkened not unto the words of Owlglass, but dipped his hand deep into the vessel, and behold! when he brought it forth again was it with pitch all defiled. Thereat was Master Owlglass greatly benefited, so that strength returned unto him, and he rose up from his bed and said unto him: "Dost thou not see! I required of thee that thou shouldst not dip too deep into the vessel; but thou wouldst not hearken unto my words, for on the top lay the treasure, the which was thine." And he laughed and made sport of the priest's greed. Then was the priest wroth, and departed, and would with such a knave have no more to do.

The Hundred and Sixth Adventure.

How that Owlglass in three parts did divide all that belonged unto him; and the one part gave he freely unto his friends, and another thereof humbly to the town council of Möllen, and the third part unto the priest there.

Now when that Owlglass lay sick, every day grew he weaker, and knew that his death was approaching; therefore he made his will, and in three parts did he divide his wealth,—the one part gave he unto his friends, and the other unto the town council of Möllen, to pay the debts which lay upon the town, and the third part unto the priest of that place. But he made one stipulation, and caused them to promise that they would bury him in the holy earth of the churchyard, and after a Christian wise sing and say a mass and vigil for his sinful soul; and then, after four weeks, should they open the chest in the which lay his treasure, and the which chest was with three most excellent locks shut, and unto each gave Owlglass one key, and they accepted the trust of him, and then bidding them all farewell and enjoyment of the wealth he left unto them, he gently gave up the ghost, and so from this world departed one of the best and noblest men the which Germany had ever seen; nor since that time hath there been any like unto him in rarity of wit or subtlety of heart. And though there be no lack of fools and knaves who chouse and cozen, yet do none of them perform such chousing and cozening to the glory and advantage of true wisdom, in manner and form as did Owlglass.

And after the four weeks were gone by, and all things had been duly accomplished according to the promise made unto him, came the council and the priest and the friends of Owlglass to open the treasure, and enter upon the enjoyment thereof. And, behold! when they opened the chest, found they nought but stones. Then grew they angry, and strove together; and each believed that the other had from the chest taken the treasure. But it was not so; for of a truth understood they not until afterward, that all treasure is indeed of no greater account than stones. For a lusty frame and a cheerful heart be the best of riches.

The Hundred and Seventh Adventure.

How that at Möllen Owlglass died, and the swine did cast down the coffin when that the good priests sang the vigil.

Now after that time that Owlglass had given up the ghost, the people entered in unto the hospital where he lay, and took him, and put him in a coffin, and set it upon tressels. Then came the good priests to sing a vigil round his coffin, and they lifted up their voices and sang. But as they sang came the swine of the master of that hospital, and entered in unto the room where lay Owlglass, and they ran underneath the coffin, and cast it down. Then came the nuns and monks, and much folk likewise, and would have driven forth the swine, but that could they not do; and the swine leaped and ran, and upset the nuns and monks, so that it was a most lamentable sight to look upon. Afterwards gat the swine forth into the street, and the nuns entered in, and laid Owlglass within his coffin again; and they bare him forth unto the graveyard to bury him.

The Hundred and Eighth Adventure.

How that our for ever prized Master Owlglass was buried.

And at the burying of Owlglass was there a most wondrous strange thing. For when that they all stood in the graveyard round the coffin in the which he lay, they took ropes to let it down into the grave, and, of these twain ropes, brake the one which was under his feet, and the coffin fell down, and stood on end. Thus stood Owlglass in his grave. And the folks around marvelled greatly thereat, and said: "Nay, let him stand an if he will; for in his life wrought he many great marvels, and he will be strange in death likewise." Then they filled the grave with earth, and above his head set a stone, and on it did they cunningly hew the likeness of an owl, who within his claws bare a glass, and upon the stone set the words which stand written in the chapter which here followeth.

The Hundred and Ninth Adventure.

Telleth what stood upon his gravestone.[12]

EPITAPHIUM.
This stone dare none to overthrow,
For Owlglass upright stands below.

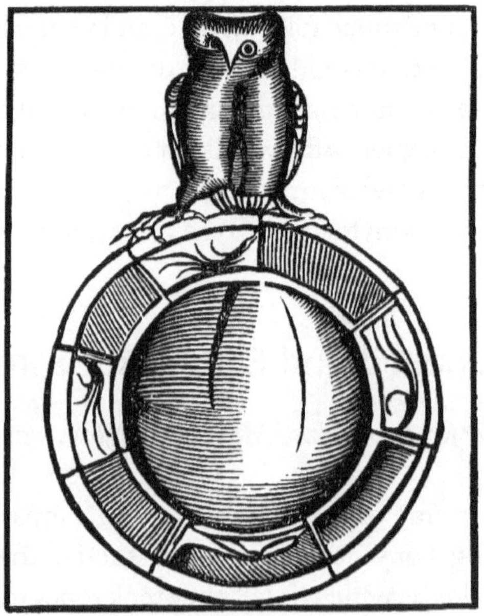

Anno MCCCL.

12   This device is faithfully copied from that in the edition of 1519.

The Hundred and Tenth Adventure.

*How in after time our most excellent Owlglass was esteemed
so worthy that he was made a holy Saint; and on the day
of All Fools in April do the folk alway keep his memory, as
also when they do a foolish thing, the which maketh him
continually esteemed of great and small.*

That which is accomplished of a great man must at some season
bring him honour and glory; therefore be not astonished at
the matter which came to pass when that Cardinal Raymundus
lay at Möllen great number of years after. For in those parts did
many bear in mind the virtues of the illustrious Owlglass; and
the cardinal himself went and looked upon the gravestone of
Owlglass, and had report made unto him of his doings and sayings. And, for as much as the people of Möllen gave great glory
unto his memory, the good cardinal wrote unto the Holy Father
at Rome; and unto the great content and delight of the townsfolk
of Möllen, Master Owlglass was made a Saint, and beareth rule
over all manner of chousings, beguilings, cozenings, cheatings,
and knaveries having fellowship with Saint Nicholas; and when
that a man goeth about to do a foolish thing, remembereth he that
holy man, Saint Owlglass, and doth call upon his name—and of
a verity is Saint Owlglass, of all the saints that be in the calendar,
that one which hath the government of the greatest number of
devout folks here on earth. For fools be there many; and upon the
first day of that fair month of April, the weather of which is as
various as were the adventures of the holy saint—upon the first
of April, I say, do all men honour him, and indeed every day; for

in that hour in the which they accomplish any idle vain work, do they increase his glory. So that Saint Owlglass doth receive the continual esteem of both great and small.

The Hundred and Eleventh, and Last, Adventure.

Reciteth a few grave reflections of this present chronicler.

That thing which a man maketh his own, and causeth aye to be his beloved work, be it evil or good, will beset him for ever, nor, save in the prickings and movings of his trembling conscience, and timorous spirit, will he acknowledge his own desperate courses, the which seemed fair to enjoy, but turn unto the apples of Sodom and Gomorrah i' the mouth; and like unto the red-hot ploughshare, over the which the hardened criminal walketh, doth the sin all done in life sear the aspen soul, which quivereth in terror at evil doing. And verily when that I look me back over the book, my good master, which now I present unto thee, do I perceive right well that deep meaning and truthful lesson which can be gathered by the careful reading of such a life as that one of good Master Owlglass. It hath been said unto us, that we should not do evil that good may arise therefrom; yet from such actions and enactments as those of our master came forth good, for we are taught therein to know the wisdom of the saying of Solon unto that ancient King Crœsus, that until the end be perceived ye should esteem no man happy. And what profit had Master Owlglass of his knaveries? A life of continual change and hurrying to and fro upon the face of the earth—of carking care, and, oftentimes, pinching hunger and parching thirst. For whatsoever he wrought was a thing spoiled thereafter, and his knavery and wickedness at not any season brought him content. Lo! do we not live in other times; but yet those very same things which lay so heavy upon Owlglass, sit yet openly among us, in defiance of the judgment which the voice of the righteous man pronounceth against them. O that folly, knavery, and injustice, could be rooted up from the fair soil of this world, and cast forth unto the burning! This book was brought forth with not a little travail, for while it should cause the merry laugh upon the cheek of old and young, peradventure it may enter into the hearts of some, and they may read that lesson which we do all merit. If that Master Owlglass had not been a knave and a beguiler, might he not, with his rare wit and ingenious brain, have waxed strong in good and noble things? Therefore strive we to understand the intent of his life, and use those talents with the which God hath endowed us, to the greater glory and honour of the Giver; for truly hath it been here clearly set forth how the fool's cap doth extinguish all light of use, beauty, or excellency.

APPENDIX A.

Bibliographical Notes for the Literary History of Eulenspiegel.

In the foregoing volume, as has been announced in the preface, the edition followed in chief has been the oldest Low German quarto, printed at Strasburg in the year 1519. This is the one with which the Franciscan Friar, Doctor Thomas Murner, has been identified; and, as all reasonable surmise and possible evidence indicate him to be the author of the original Eulenspiegel, we have no reason to believe that any older edition will ever be discovered, although there is a rumour of a Low German edition of 1483. The title page is as follows:—"Ein kurtzweilig lesen von Dil Ulen | -spiegel geboren, vsz. dē land zū Brunszwick. Wie er | seī lebē volbracht hat. & evt (?) seiner geschichten." Underneath Owlglass on horseback with owl and glass. It consists of one hundred and thirty paged leaves in small quarto, and contains twenty-five sheets, marked A–Z, and *a–b* iiii; but the number of pages in a sheet varies from four to six and eight. The number of stories contained in the edition is ninety-six, and, with the exception of nine stories, each is provided with a rudely-executed woodcut, in all of which Eulenspiegel is represented in the ordinary dress of the period, his head uncovered, and without the fool's dress which it has been the custom since to bestow upon him. Panzer was only acquainted with one copy of this edition mentioned in Wenker's Catalogue, Strasburg, 1783, p. 215, No. 3175. This is preserved in the Ducal Library of Gotha, and no other is known to exist. It is now readily accessible to the student, being reprinted by

Dr. Lappenberg (Dr. Thomas Murner's Ulenspiegel. Leipzig, T. O. Weigel, 1854).

2. In 1520–30, we meet with another edition, the title of which we here transcribe: "Ayn Kurtz Wylich | lesen van Tyel Ulen-spiegel: geboren | vyss dem land Brunzwyck. Wat he seltzamer boitzen be | dreuen hait syn dage, lüstich tzo lesen." Printed by Servais Kruffter, in quarto, in old Gothic letters; thirteen sheets, A-N, with 104 unnumbered pages. This edition is known from two imperfect copies, which, however, restore, when collated, the whole. The first twelve sheets are in the Imperial Library of Vienna, and the Royal Library of Berlin has the last eleven. This edition differs from all others by possessing no preface. There are seventy-eight stories; and the one which appears second in this edition (which has been taken from the English Black Letter) first makes its appearance as an Eulenspiegel, as do Adventures 93 and 95.

3. A Dutch edition is first found about this time (1520–30), printed at Antwerp by Michiel Van Hoochstraten. The following is the title page:

<table>
<tr><td>(Picture of the</td><td>"Vlenspieghel.</td><td>(Picture of the</td></tr>
<tr><td>Owl.)</td><td>Van Vlēspieghels leuen.</td><td>Mirror.)</td></tr>
</table>

Eñ schimpelicke werckē, eñ wōderlijcke auontueren die | hi hadde want he en liet hem gheen boeuerie verdrieten."

The sheets run to K ij., and forty leaves in small quarto. The only known copy is at Copenhagen, in the Royal Library, and wants two leaves. Forty-six, perhaps forty-eight, stories (counting two for the missing leaves) are contained in this edition, but they are not numbered.

4. 1528–1530. The two editions now to be described are perhaps more interesting to English readers than any others, and deserve careful examination. Of the English "Howleglas" two copies only remain, of different editions and presumed years. At the time when Dr. Lappenberg, in 1854, completed his bibliographical list, one

of these copies only had reached the British Museum. They are both imperfect; but, fortunately, what is wanting in one copy is completed in the other. The title is as follows:

"Here beginneth a merrye Jest of a man that was called Howleglas, and of many marueylous thinges and Jestes that he dyd in his lyfe, in Eastlande and in many other places."

Occupying nearly the whole of the remainder of the quarto page is a rude woodcut of a king upon his throne with two people standing before, alluding evidently to the story of the King of Poland's Jester and Eulenspiegel.[13] The colophon of the earliest edition, which has no date, but to which 1528 is assigned by the British Museum Catalogue (Dr. Lappenberg dates it at 1540–1556), is as follows: "Imprynted at London in Tame Street at the Vintre on the thre Craned wharfe by Wyllyam Copland (':')."

The book begins immediately at the back of the title with the following preface:

"For the great desyryng and praying of my good frandes. And I yᵉ first writer of this boke might not denye thē. Thus haue I compled & gathered much knauyshnes & falsnes of one Howleglas made and done within his lyfe, whiche Howleglas dyed yᵉ yeare of our lorde God.M.CCCC. &.L.[14] Nowe I desyre to be pardoned both before ghostly & worldly, afore highe & lowe afore noble and unnoble. And right lowly I requyre all those yᵗ shall reade or heare this presēte Jeste (my ignoraūce to excuse). This fable is not but only to renewe yᵉ mindes of men or women, of all degrees frō yᵉ use of sadnesse to passe the tyme, with laughter or myrthe. And for because yᵉ simple knowyng persons shuld beware if folkes can see. Me thinke it is better to passe the tyme with such a mery Jeste and laughe there at and doo no synne: than for to wepe and do synne."

The number of adventures in the English Howleglas is forty-

13   Adventure the 24th, pp. 38—39.
14   This should be M.CCC. & L.

six; but they are not numbered, one being a copy of verses (given in Appendix D), and forming an additional chapter, making forty-seven. Of this copy, Signature D is missing; otherwise, excepting the corner of a leaf, it is perfect. Signatures are from A–M, worked in sheets of eight pages, equal to fifty-two pages, of which the last is a blank. It belonged at one time to Garrick, and, with other portions of his library, was transferred to the Museum, where it will be found with the Press-mark C. 21. *c*.

Of this book a second copy exists, as above mentioned, also in the British Museum. It is a later edition (1530), but differing in nothing from the one already described. It is, however, very imperfect, wanting Signature B and the page marked K iiii, as well as all subsequent pages, comprising L and M. This has been completed from the other copy. On the fly-leaf is the following note, which I copy:

"Such is the rarity of this volume, that only *one* other copy is known, viz., that in the British Museum, which is of another edition, and is also slightly imperfect (*Note by the writer of the fly-leaf comment*: On a more accurate inspection of the above volume, I have discovered that it wants an entire sheet, viz. *c*[*d*]), wanting the corner of a leaf. *This* copy was purchased at the Roxburgh sale by the late Mr. Heber, whose note will be seen on the fly-leaf immediately preceding the title."

Mr. Heber's note is: "1812. Roxburgh sale £14 5 0. Mem. to examine the Museum copy."

In 1842, it was marked in Lilly's Catalogue; and the date placed upon it by the Museum authorities is sixth of October, 1857, with the press-mark 12316 *c*.

The only record of any other copy of this English Howleglas, also referred to in the preface, is in a paper of Mr. Halliwell's in the Papers of the Shakspere Society (vol. iv. p. 18, 26–28), where that gentleman describes the library of a certain Captain Cox, quoting from an account of Queen Elizabeth's entertainments at

Kenilworth, made by Laneham, clerk and keeper of the Council Chamber door.

That same Captain Cox is represented by Ben Jonson in the "Masque of Owls, at Kenelworth, presented by the Ghost of Captain Cox, mounted on his Hobbyhorse 1626," and is made to say:

> "This Captain Cox, by St. Mary,
> Was at Bullen with King Ha—ry;
> And (if some do not vary)
> Had a goodly library,
> By which he was discerned
> To be one of the learned,
> To entertain the queen here,
> When last she was seen here."

It has been stated, that Owlglass also existed as a Miracle Play; but this statement does not seem to refer to more than the Easter Play, to which reference has been made in the Preface.

5. 1532. This year we find the first French edition, stated to be translated from Flemish into French (probably from the Antwerp edition) printed at Paris, the title being as follows:—

Between four flowerets there is first an owl then the word: "Ulenspiegel," and after it a round glass. Next: "De sa vie de ses oeuures | Et merueilleuses aduentures par luy faictes | et des gran- | des fortunes quil a eux, lequel par milles fallaces ne se lais | sa tromper. Nouuellement translate et corrige de Flamant | en Francoys." The colophon is thus: "Imprime nouuellement a Paris en l'an Mil*ccccc*xxxii*." Sheets run to K iiij *b* in quarto, without pagination, and the type all Gothic. The only known copy exists in the Royal Library at Stuttgart.

6. In the same year, 1532, an edition appeared at Erfurt, printed by Melcher Sachsen. The following is the title: "Von Vlenspiegel eins bau | ren sun (son) des lands Braunschweick, wie | er sein leben volbracht hat, gar mit | seltzamen sachen." Ten sheets in

quarto, leaves in number 84, without pagination; the last being blank. There are 102 stories, with 86 woodcuts, some little merit belonging to the first few—the later ones having been considerably worn. Only four copies, nearly all defective, are known of this edition; one was bought for the private library of the King of Prussia, at the sale of the collection of the Viennese antiquary Matth. Kuppitsch, and presented by his Majesty to the Royal University Library of Berlin. There is another in the Royal Library of München.

7. Another edition, in every respect similar to the Erfurt edition of 1532, was printed between 1533–7; but from the last pages being lost, it is impossible to say by whom, where, or in what year. The copy is at the Royal Library of Berlin. The missing leaves are perfected in manuscript; and it ends with a strange note, to the effect that it was printed at Augsburg by Simon Gymell, and "translated from the old Saxon tongue into good German," in the year 1498. No such person is known to have existed at Augsburg at that time, and the words between inverted commas, first appear in 1539, in the Cologne edition.

8. In 1538, an edition was again issued, in every way similar to that of 1532, by Melchior Sachsen at Erfurt. Copies at Berlin, in the collections of Herr von Meusebach, and Professor J. A. Nasser.

9. Shortly after the 1532 edition of Erfurt, another quarto edition in forty pages was issued in French, by Alain Lotrian, at Paris. There are forty-six stories and twenty-six woodcuts. The copy examined by Dr. Lappenberg belonged to the Ducal Library at Wolfenbüttel, and contains an autograph of Duke Julius of Brunswick and Lüneburg, dated, July 17, 1567. The title is as follows, after four flowers, with the owl in the centre, and the looking-glass, and between them the word Vlenspiegel: "De sa vie & de ces oeuues[15] | Et merueilleuses aduentures par luy faictes et des gran- | des fortunes quil a euz, lequel par milles

15   Error *oeuues* for *oeuures*.

fallaces ne se lais | sa tromper. Nouuellement translate et cor-
rige de Flamänt | en Francoys." Colophon: "Cy finist les faictz
et merueilleuses aduētures | de Thiel Vlespiegle lequel a este
translate de | langage Flameng en Francoys, et nouuelle- | ment
imprime a Paris par Alain Lotrian demou- | rant en la rue neufue
nostre dame a l'enseigne de l'es | cu de France."

10. 1539. Ulenspiegel | De sa vie de ses oeuures, | et merueil-
leuses auentures par luy faictes: et des grandes fortunes quil a
eu: leql par nulles fallaces ne se laissa trom- | per: nouuellemēt
translate & corrige de flamēnt en francoys.

Colophon: Imprime nouuellement a Anuers en l'an M.CCCC
XXXIX.

The only copy known is in the Library at Wolfenbüttel. This
edition almost coincides with that of Alain Lotrian, with some
very trifling variations.

11. 1539. A German edition was this year published with the
following title: "EYn wunderbairlich | vnd seltzame History,
vonn Dyll Ulnspi | gel, bürtig auss dem land Brunschweig, wie
er sein leben | verbracht hat, newlich aufs Sachsischer sprach
vff | Teutsch verdolmetscht, seer kurtz- | weilig zu lesenn, myt
schö | nen figuren."

Colophon: "Gedruckt zu Cöln für Sanct Lupus, bey Ian von
Ach. Im Iar Dusent Funffhundert Neunund dreissig."

One copy of it is to be found in the private Library of the king
of Würtemburg at Stuttgart. The text is divided into one hundred
stories, each with its own heading. The signatures of the sheets
run from A to S, each containing four leaves. The name of the
printer was found by Dr. Lappenberg as Ian van Aich. One other
copy is known to be in the Royal Library at München.

12. 1539. "Wunderbarliche, vnnd seltzame Historyen Tyll
Vlnspiegels, ausz dem land zu Braunschweig bürtig, new auss
Sachsischer sprach auff gut hochdeutsch verdolmetscht. Stras-
zburg, Jac. Frölich. Mit Holzschnitten. 1539." This is in quarto,

and is mentioned in a catalogue of a collection of books which were to be publicly sold on 25th January, 1847, at Frankfort-on-the-Main. Lappenberg, who gives us this information, appears unable to give any more.

13. 1540. "Eyn wunderbarliche | vnd seltzame History, von Dyll Vln | spiegel, burtig ausz dem land Brunschweig, wie | er sein Leben verbracht hatt, newlich ausz | Sächsischer sprach auff gut Teutsch | verdolmetschet, seer kurtzweilig zu lesen, mit schönen | figuren." Colophon: "Gedruckt zu Augspurg, durch Alexander Weissenhorn | Im Iar Tausend Fünffhundert | und fiertzig."

This edition, in quarto, runs as far as S iii, seventy-three pages, without pagination. The book contains one hundred adventures (numbered) and is a reprint, word for word, of the Cologne edition of 1539 (see No. 11, *ante*, p. 224). There are forty woodcuts in all. A copy exists in the Ducal Library at Wolfenbüttel.

14. 1541. Under this year an Augsburg edition, now at Lemberg, is mentioned in San-Marte's Gross-Polens National Sagen (pp. 203 and 207).

15. 1543. "Wunderbarliche, Vnnd | seltzame historyen, Tyll Vienspiegels | ausz dem land zu Brunschweig bürtig, newlich ausz Säch- | sischer sprach auff gut Hochdeutsch verdolmetscht." Colophon: "Getrukt zu Straszburg, bey Jacob Frölich, | in M.D.XLIII Iar."

Woodcuts and pagination similar in almost every respect to the edition of 1519. A copy is in the Royal Library at Göttingen from the Gebauer collection.

16. 1545. "Seltzame vnnd | Wunderbarliche History- | en Dyll Vlenspiegels, eines Baw | ren son. Bürtig ausz dem landt zu Braun- | schweig. Newlich ausz Sächsischer | sprach auff gut Hochdeutsch | verdolmetscht, sehr kurtzwei- | lig, mit schönen Fi- | guren." On the title page is a woodcut of Eulenspiegel on horseback; in the left-hand, his owl; in his right, the mirror; upon his head, a hat with three feathers. Beneath: "M.D.XLV." Colophon: "Gedruckt

zu | Franckfurt am | Mayn, durch Her- | man Gülfferichen, in | der Schnurgas- | senn zum | Krug.”

Signatures to D iiii., one hundred and nine numbered pages, and one without pagination, in small octavo. There are one hundred and two stories, and some of the woodcuts are new.

17. 1551. “Seltzame unnd | wunderbarliche Historien | Tyll Vlenspiegels, eines Bawren Son | Bürtig auss dem land zu Braunschweiyg | Newlich ausz Sachszischer Sprach auff gut Hochdeutsch verteutscht, sehr | kurtzweilig zu lesen mit schö | nen Figuren.” Colophon: “Zu Strassburg | In Jahr | M.D.L.I.” This is preserved in the Grand Ducal library of Darmstadt; it is in octavo, sheets A–O without pagination; the stories are 102 in number, each with a woodcut.

18. 1554. “Eyn wunderbarlich.... History von Dyll Ulenspegel, Cöln. 4to. 1554.” Preserved at the Royal State Library at München.

19. 1558. “Triumphus | humanae | stultitiae, vel Tylus Saxo nunc primum Latinitate dona | tus ab Joanne Nemio. Vltraiecti. | Harmannus Borculous excudebat. | Anno 1558.”

Five sheets and a half in 8vo. This translation was made by the rector of the school at Herzogenbusch, and is in iambics. The copy examined by Dr. Lappenberg is preserved in the Town Library at Lübeck, and another exists at Göttingen.

20. 1559. “Les avantures joyeuses et faitz merveilleux de Tiel Vlespiegle, ensemble les grandes fortunes à luy avenues en diverses régions, lequel par falace ne se laissait aucunement tromper: Le tout traduit d’allemand en françoys. Livre fort récréatif pour réveiller les bons espritz. Lyon, par Jean Savgrain, 1559.”

One hundred and nine pages, in 16mo. Brunet mentions several copies of this edition.

21. 1557–1563. “Wunderbarlich | vnnd seltzame Historien | Tyl Eulenspiegels, eines Bawren | Son, bürtig ausz dem Land zu Braunschweig. Newlich ausz Sächsischer sprach, auff gut | hoch

deutsch verdeutscht, sehr | kurtzweilig, mit schö | nen figuren. Gedruckt zu Franckfurdt | am Mayn | durch Wey- | gand Han."

Signatures to Q, 127 pages, and one page without number, in small octavo. This is the earliest edition where Vlenspiegle becomes Eulenspiegel. Copies preserved at the Royal Library at Berlin, and the University library at Jena.

22. 1563. Another edition of the version of Nemius appeared in this year, and is preserved at Halle.

23. 1567. "Noctvae Specvlum. | Omnes res me- | morabiles, varias qve | et admirabiles, Tyli Saxonici | machinationes com-plectens, planè novo more nunc primum ex idiomate Germanico latinitate donatum adiectis insuper elegantissimis iconibus veras omnium historiarū species ad venum adumbrantibus, ante hac nunquam visis aut editis. Avthore Ægidio Periandro, Bruxellensi, Brabantino. Cum Gratia et privilegio ad decennium, Francofvrti ad Mœnum, M.D.LXVII." At the end: "Impressum Francofurti ad Mœnum, apud Georgium Corvinum, sumptibus Sigismundi Feyrabendt & Simonis Huteri."

Signatures A-Z, 210 pages, with 103 woodcuts. Copies at Dres-den, Göttingen, München, Hamburg, and two copies in the British Museum (Press-marks 243. a. 11 of the King's Library, and 1080. d. 33). The book is in elegiac verse, and was composed by Giles Omma, who was known as Aegidius Periander.

24. About 1571, a Danish translation of Eulenspiegel is men-tioned. See Nyerup Morskabs laesning, p. 269.

25. 1566–1571. We next have to record the title of a very remark-able versified edition, by John Fischart, as follows: "Eulenspiegel Rei | mensweisz. | Ein newe Be- | schreibung vnnd Le- | gendt desz kurtzweiligen Le- | bens | vnd seltzamen Thaten | Thyll Eulenspiegels mit | schönen neuwen Figuren be- | zieret vn nu zum ersten male in artige Rei-| men durch J[ohann] F[ischart] G[ennant] M[entzer] gebracht, | nützlich vnd lustig zu | lesen. Cum Gratia & Privilegio. Getruckt zu Franckfurt." Colophon:—

"Getruckt zu Frankfurt am Mayn, | durch Johannen Schmidt, in Verlegung | Hieronymi Feyrabends, vnd | Bernard Jobin."

This edition is in octavo, with 16 unpaged leaves and 307 numbered pages, and 98 woodcuts. The year 1571 is assigned to it by Ebert. In this versified edition, Fischart applied much of the satire of the book to the events and customs of his time, and he appears to have been well acquainted with the editions which had preceded him, and his knowledge of Rabelais, of whom he was the German translator, was also very great, but he did not know Eulenspiegel to be the work of Murner. Many copies of this edition exist; amongst others, the British Museum contains one, the press-mark of which is 11517. a.

26. 1571. "Evlenspiegels Wunderbarliche, abendtheurische vnd gar seltzame Historien, Geschichte, bossen vnd Fatzwerck, jetzt auffs neuwe mit schönen artlichen Figuren zugericht, so vormals im Deutschen nie gesehen. Getruckt zu Frankfurt am Mayn. M.D.LXXI." At the end: "Getruckt zu Frankfurt am Mayn durch | Johannem Schmidt, in Verlegung Hieronymi Feyerabends Anno M.D.LXXI."

Twenty-one and a half sheets in octavo, without pagination.

27. 1567–1574. "De sa vie [et] des ses oeuures, | Et merueilleuses aduentures par luy faictes. Et de grandes fortu- | nes quil a eues, lequel par milles fallaces ne se laissa tromper. Nou | uellement corrige & translate de Flament en Francoys. viii. c. A Paris pour la vesue Jean Borfons, demourant en la rue | neuue Nostre Dame, a lenseigne sainct Nicolas."

Thirty-two unnumbered pages, in quarto. This edition is almost identical with that of Alain Lotrian. A copy exists in the Ducal library at Wolfenbüttel.

28. 1571. "Les aventures joyeuses et faits merveilleux de Tiel Vlespiegle, trad. du Flamand. Orleans." An edition in duodecimo.

29. 1571. "Eulenspiegels Historien, mit newen Figuren zugericht. Frankfurt."

A duodecimo edition mentioned by Celsii, Elenchus librorum ab āo 1500–1602 editorum, II. 221.

30. 1571. "L'histoire joyeuse et recreative de Tiel Vlespiegle; nouvellement reueu et traduit du flameng en françois. Orleans, par Eloy Gibier."

No date is assigned to this book; but it has been seen by Brunet bound up with "Le Voyage de Panurge," issued in 1571. One hundred and seventy pages, in 16mo.

31. 1575. "Ulen Spiegel. | Van Ulespieghels leuen Ende schimpe- | lijcke wercken ende wonderlijcke auonturen.... Thantwerpen. Ghedruckt by my Jan van Ghelen in den witten Hasewint, 1575. Met Gratie ende Privilegie. Mit Figg."

A quarto in the library of Dr. Jacob Grimm; this appears to be the edition prohibited by Philip II. and the Duke of Alba, in 1579.

32 and 33. 1578–9. "Histoire joyeuse et recreative de Tiel Vlespiegle, ou est traité de ses faits et merveilleuses avantures et de grandes fortunes, quil a avés. Traduit de Flamand en françois. Anvers. 1579."

An octavo spoken of by Von Murr, Journal xiv. 353.

34. 1580. "Ulen Spiegel—Van Ulenspieghels leuen En | schijm-pelijcke wercken ende wonderlijcke auonturen | die hi hadde, want hie en liet hem gheē Boeuerije verdrieten | seer playsant en ghenuechlijck om lesen. | Ghedruckt Thantwerpen, | Opede Camerpoortbrugghe in den Schilt van Basele by my | Jan van Ghelen de Jonghe, ghesworen Drucker der Con. Ma. Met Gratie en Privilegie."

Title-page in black and red, and the name of the book in old Teutonic letters. Thirty-two pages, in quarto. Signatures A-H ij. Copy at Göttingen.

35. 1586. "Wunderbarliche & seltsame Historien Tyl Eulen-spiegels—[without place]—1586."

An octavo in the Royal Library at München.

36. An edition, bearing the date of the year 1588, is mentioned

in the Catalogue of the Kiel Library, but is not to be found there now.

37. 1592. An edition of this year, uniform with a Flemish edition of Dr. John Faust, is mentioned by Tross, in Naumann's Serapeum, vol. xi. p. 159.

38, 39. 1612–1613. "Historie van Thyl | UUlenspieghel | van syn schalke boeverijen die | hy bedreuen heest | seer ghenoechlije [om te lesen] met schoone figuren. Tot Rotterdam | By Jacob van der Hoeven Op de | Delffe vart. 1613."

Small octavo sheets A-F, forty-eight pages. Preserved in the Royal Library at Berlin. Another Dutch edition, the title of which need not be recapitulated, was also published about this time.

40. 1618. "Wunderbarliche und seltzame Historia | Tyllen Eulen- | spiegels, eines Bawren Son, | aus dem Land zu Braunschweig bür- | tig. Newlich aus Sächsischer Sprache auff | gut Hochteutsch verdolmetschet sehr | kurtzweilig zu lesen. Jetzundt wider frisch gesotten vnd new gebacken. Gedruckt im Jahr M.D.C.XVIII."

Thirteen sheets in small octavo, without pagination. The stories, 102 in number, with woodcuts. Preserved in a book, together with a song-book printed by Jacob Singe, and with which the Eulenspiegel is uniform, at the Town Library at Bremen.

41. 1636. This edition is not in the list of Dr. Lappenberg. The copy I have examined is in the British Museum (press mark 12315 c), and the title is as follows: "L'histoire de | Tiel Vlespiegle | contenant ses faits | merueilleux, & les grandes fortunes | quil a euës durant sa vie. | Nouuellement traduit de Flammand en François." (Beneath this a woodcut representing in a rude way Eulenspiegel with the glass in the right hand and the owl in the left, on horseback), a Paris, chez Iean Promé, en sa boutique au coin de la ruë Dauphine. 1636. 16mo. The stories are forty-six in number and the epitaph is thus given:—

> "Vlespiegle est icy gisant,
> Son corp est icy mis en terre,
> Pour-ce on aduise le passant,
> Q'aucen ne change cette pierre."

The pagination is only on one side, and extends to thirty-five, signatures A-E iij, and the rude woodcut at the commencement is repeated at the end. The chapters are not numbered, and the following prologue is printed at the back of the title: "Ayant esgard aux prieres d'aucuns miens familiers, ausquels ie n'ay osé bounement refuser, amy Lecteur, i'ay acteur du present Liure, amasse & compilé les plaisantes tromperies mocqueries & finesses, dont usa en sa vie Tiel Vlespiegle, lequel depuis mourut l'an mil trois cent cinquante. En quoy toutes fois ie demande d'estre excusé à l'endroit de toutes personnes, tant Spirituels, que Temporels, Nobles que Roturiers; attendu le dessein que i'ay tousiours eu de n'offencer aucun, l'ayant composé, non point au mespris de la gloire de Dieu, ou pour inuenter menteries & enseigner malice; mais seulement pour recreer & resueiller les esprit eunuyez, afin aussi que les simples se puissent garder de telles tromperies au temps aduenir." The copy in the Museum is well bound in a dark coloured calf.

42. 1637. "Wonderbaerliche ende seltsame historie van Thijl Ulenspiegel, van zijne schalke, listighe bootsen ende boeverijen, gedruckt by broer Jansz." Broer Jansz is known as the printer of the earliest Amsterdam newspaper, in 1628.

43. 1640 (?). "Het aerdig leven | van | Thijl Ulenspiegel | Waer in verhallt worden niet alleenelyk veel aerdige en kluchtige Poetsen en Boeveryen, maer ook besonderlyk syn wondere aventueren, die hem geduerende syn Leuen gebeurt zyn, zoo hier, als in andere Landen. T'Antwerpen. By J. H. Heyliger, op de groote Merkt in de Pauw."

Sheets A-D 2. Sixty-one sides without pagination, in octavo, with rough woodcuts. This edition varies considerably from all others, although founded upon the edition of Broer Jansz. New adventures and scenes are introduced, and the tone of the book much altered.

44. 1655. "La vie de Tiel Vlespiegle de ses faicts merveilleux et finesses par luy faictes, & des grandes fortunes qu'il a euës, lequel par nulles fallaces ne se laissa tromper. Nouuellement corrigée & translatée de Flamand en François. A Troyes. Chez Nicholas Oudot, demeurant en la ruë Nostre Dame au Chappon d'Or Couronné." Signatures A-E, in small 8vo. In the public Library of Ponikau at Halle.

45. 1657–63. In a volume, entitled "Recueil des plus illustres proverbes, mis en lumière par Jacq. Lagniet"—the Life of Eulenspiegel is given as the fourth book. Brunet, Manuel, Tom. III. s. v. Lagniet.

46. 1663. A French translation in "Les œuvres de Bruscambille. Rouen." Copy preserved in the Royal Library of Göttingen.

47. 1675. Tyll Eulenspiegel is referred to by Koch, as published this year without place.

48. 1677. "La vie de Til Eulenspiegel, a Troyes." An octavo, preserved at Göttingen.

49. 1683. This edition was not known to Dr. Lappenberg when his work appeared. The title page is as follows: "La vie | de | Tiel Ulespiegle | De ses farces & merveilleuses finesses, par luy | faites, & des grandes fortunes qu'il | a euës, lequel par milles fallaces | ne se laissa tromper. | Nouvellement corrigée & translatée de Flamen en François, avec des belles figures. | (Here a figure of an owl in a looking-glass). A Paris | Chez Pierre Clinchet, à l'enseigne du Dau-phin | M.DC.LXXXIII." In the British Museum (Press mark, 12315 *a*), small octavo, bound in paper. The woodcuts in this edition are of the rudest kind and the prologue the same as that in the edition of 1636. The stories are forty-six in number, and the epitaph; the number of pages are eighty-eight. Signatures A-F iij. It seems to be a close reprint of the edition above mentioned, No. 44.

50. 1690. "Historia Tillen Eulenspiegels." An octavo, named in Heise's Bücher-Catalog. Hamburg, 1827. Vol. I.

51. 1696. "Underlig oc selsom Historie om Tiile Ugelspegel, een Bondes Soen, barnfoed udi Lande Brunszwig, saare Kortvillig at laese, af Tydsken paa danske udsat. Sidste Gang prentet i dette Aar." At the end is the date of the year, 1696. Thirteen sheets in octavo.

52. 1699. "La vie | de Tiel Ulespiegle | De ses faits merveilleux, des grandes fortunes qu'il a | eues, lequel par aucunes fallace [sic] ne se laissa surprendre ni tromper. A Troyes | Chez Jacques Oudot, demeurant en la rue | du Temple, 1699. Avec permission." A small octavo, signatures A-C (query F), forty-eight pages, without numbers. The copy described by Lappenberg is preserved in the Imperial Library of Paris.

17th Century, without particular date.

53, 54. Without date, but belonging to the seventeenth century are two octavo editions mentioned in a catalogue published at Halle in 1846, p. 379.

55. An undated Dutch edition of this period in octavo has the following title: "Wonderlijke Levensgeschiedniss van Thyl Uilenspiegel, behelzende zijn schalkachtig en avonteurlijk leven, op nieuw verbeterd en vermeerderd, met zeldzaamheden welke noch nimmer bekent zijn geweest. Tweede Druck. Rotterdam." This is a second edition.

56. An edition without date appeared at Amsterdam about this time in octavo. "Wonderbarelyke en zeldzame Historien van Thyl Uilenspiegel, van zyn schalke, listige potsen en Boeveryen, di hy, zoo in zyn dood, als ook in zyn leven bedreven heest. Zeer tydkordig en geneuglyk om te lezen voor oude en jonge lieden."

57. A Rotterdam edition, with following title page, is in the Bodleian (Douce, v. 58): "Wonderbaarlyke en Zeldzaame | Historie

| van | Thyl | Ulenspiegel, | en van Zyn Schalke, Listig Bootzen en | Boerveryen, | die hy en zyn leven | bedreef. | Zeer tydkörtig en genoeglyk om te leezen | Verciert met Figuuren en zyn Lyk-Ceel. | Te Rotterdam. | By Johannes Scheffers, Boek- | Drukker in de Prinsestraat." Duodecimo, eighty-eight numbered pages, and eight without pagination. Rough woodcuts, and typography in black letter, except the headings of chapters, and the last eight pages. This edition is not mentioned by Dr. Lappenberg.

58. Without date: "La vie de Tiel Vlespiegle de ses faicts et merveilles & des grandes fortunes qu'il a eues, lequel par milles fallacies ne se laissa surprendre n'y tromper. A Troyes et se vend a Paris chez Antoine de Rafflé, Imprimeur Marchand libraire, Rue de petit Pont, à l'Image S. Antoine." Signatures A-D, small octavo. Preserved in the Royal Library of Dresden, and in the public Library of Ponikau at Halle.

59. A Rouen edition, without date, not mentioned by Lappenberg: "Tiel Vlespiegle de sa vie..... ne se laissa tromper. A Rouen chez Loys Costé, rue Escuyere aux trois croix Couronnées." Printed in double columns in quarto, without pagination, and bound in a volume, preserved in the British Museum (press mark, 12513 5, *g*), together with a number of publications by Loys Costé and others, comprising Melusine, Geoffrey a la grand Dent, Richard sans paour, Florimont, and Oliuier de Castille.

60, 61, 62. At this time several Polish translations seem to have appeared. See San Marte Gross-Polens Nationalsagen. Bromberg, 1842. p. 203.

63. 1701. "Tiel Wliespiegle, de sa vie, de ses faits et merveilleuses finesses par lui faites, et des grandes fortunes qu'il a eues, lequel par les fallaces, ne se laissa tromper, traduit du flamand. Rouen. Besogne, 1701." An octavo, on which see Brunet.

64. 1702. "Histoire de la vie de Tiel Wlepiegle, Contenant ses faits et finesses.... ne s'étant jamais laissé tromper par aucune personne. Amsterdam, chez Nicolas Chevalier." A duodecimo,

in the Royal Library at München, and in the possession of Herr Regierungsrath Blumenbach, of Hanover; as also in the British Museum, press mark, 12315 *a*.

65. 1702. "Histoire de la vie de Tiel Wlespiegle. Contenant ses faits et finesses, ses aventures, et les grandes fortunes qu'il a euës, ne s'etant jamais laissé tromper par aucune personne. Nouvelle Traduction de l'Alemand en François: où l'on a ajouté à cette edition, plusieurs pieces qui n'ont point encore paru en François jusques à present. A Middelbourg chez Ric. Parmenter. MDCCII." A duodecimo, at the Royal Library at Dresden.

66. 1703. The same title at Amsterdam, printed by Pierre Marteau, MDCCIII. 247 pages, and eight leaves, in duodecimo. In this edition, several adventures are added, which appear in the German Rogue (*vide infra*, No. 71). Copies in the British Museum (press mark 1079 *b*, 18); at the Royal Library at Dresden, and the Town Library at Hamburg.

67. "La | Vie de Tiel | Ulespiegle | (see edition of 1699, *supra*). Troyes, chez la veuve Jacques Oudot. 1705. Avec permission." In small octavo, with two rude cuts. Signatures extend from A-D ij, over fifty-four pages. Flemish names, as in some other editions, take the place of German. This edition is in the library of Dr. Lappenberg.

68. 1713. "Wunderliche und seltsame Historien Tillen Eulenspiegels, eines Bauren Sohn, aus dem Lande zu Braunschweig bürtig; neulich aus Sächsischer Sprache auf gut Hochteutsch verdollmetscht, &c., &c. Anitzo wieder aufs neue aufgelegt. Gedruckt in diesem Jahre (13) Mit Holzschnitten." Small octavo. Referred to in the Catalogue of the "Bibliothek der Maatschappij van Nederlandsche Letterkunde, te Leiden," vol. ii. p. 336.

69. 1714. "La Vie de Tiel Ulespiegle de ses faits... tromper. A Troyes, 1714." Duodecimo.

70. 1714. "Wunderliche & Seltzame Historien von Tyll Eulenspiegel.... Kurtzweilig zu lesen. Hamburg gedruckt auffm

Schaarsteinweg." Octavo, sixty-three woodcuts, numbered to 100 chapters, except that, by the omission of chap. 79, there are really only ninety-nine. This is the commonly received text constantly reprinted.

71. 1720. "The | German Rogue, | or the | Life and Merry | Adventures, | Cheats, Stratagems | & | Contrivances | of Tiel Eulespiegel. Let none Eulespiegle's Artifices blame, | For Rogues of ev'ry Country are the same. | Made English From the High Dutch. London: Printed in the Year MDCCXX." This edition is the only other version ever made of the work presented in this volume. It differs widely, however, from the popular German Owlglass; many stories are introduced which the original editions did not contain, and the taste for tales of the Decameron class has been consulted in the compilation of it. Dr. Lappenberg, in his bibliographical section, assigns to it the date of 1709; but the only two copies I have seen, one of which is in my possession, give the date 1720 as above. It is an octavo and of extreme rarity, the British Museum contains no copy of it; the only other copy is in the Douce Collection at the Bodleian Library, Oxford. That which I have was formerly the property of Mr. Bernard Quaritch, who priced it at £2 12*s*. 6*d*. A note on the fly-leaf states the rarity of the book, and that the annotator never met with another; and Mr. Thoms says, that he only saw the one in Douce's Collection. The number of pages is 111, and of chapters forty-four. Signatures B-P 4, with title and preface. The rarity of the book is not much to be regretted; for its contents are not in any way of a nature fitted for quotation or great remark.

72. 1736. "Lustige Historien oder Merckwürdiges Leben, Thaten und Reisen des Weltbekandten Tyll Eulenspiegels. Mit vielen Historischen, Politischen, und Moralischen Anmerckungen, Auch allerhand Tugend-, Staats und Sitten-Lehren, Nach aller Ständen durch und durch, bei jeder Historie, erläutert und beschrieben

(Dresden bei Hilscher)." An octavo, preserved at the Royal Libraries of Dresden and Göttingen.

73. 1774. "Wonderbaerlyke en zeldzame Historie van Thyl Ulenspiegel, van zyn Schalke..... Zeer teydkortig en geneuglijk on te lezen. Vor Oude en Jonge Lieden. Te Amsterdam, by Joannes Kannewet." A small octavo, of eighty-eight numbered pages, and four pages without numbers, preserved at München.

74. A popular romance on Owlglass appeared in two volumes in 1779 and 1784.

75. A Danish translation was published in 1787 at Copenhagen; twelve sheets in octavo without pagination.

76. 1794. "Leben und Sonderbare Thaten Till Eulenspiegels." An octavo of 136 pages.

77. 1795. The same, republished at Prague and Vienna.

18th Century, without particular date.

78. In the Bodleian at Oxford (Douce Collection, p. 280, press-mark TT iii) is a French Eulenspiegel, entitled, "Histoire | Plaisante | de | Tiel Ulespiegel | Contenant les faits & subtilités dont | il s'est servi. | Revue et Corrigée de Nouveau. | A Limoges, | Chez F. Chapoulard, Imprimeur-Libraire, | place de Banc." It is an octavo of twenty-nine pages, and the number of adventures far from complete. It is printed on very bad paper, and evidently with a view to cheapness.

79. "Wonderbaarlyke | en zeldame | Historie | van | Thyl Ulenspiegel, &c. Te Leyden. By P. van Leeuwen. In the de Pieters Choorsteg." Chiefly curious from a cut on the title, representing Eulenspiegel holding a mirror up for an owl to look in, with the inscription above it, "Broeder myn." Ninety pages duodecimo, with the ordinary adventures and rude cuts. Preserved in the Bodleian.

80, 81. Several stories of Eulenspiegel were translated into

Jew-German, and printed at Frankfort-on-the-Main, in octavo, according to Wolf, "Bibliotheca Hebraica," vol. iii., p. 86, 1727. Another Hebrew-German edition appears referred to in the same work, vol. ii., p. 1255, 1721.

82. Flögel mentions, in 1789, an old Polish version (p. 473): "Sowizrzal Krotochwilny Smiezny Poczatek, zywot y dokonanie iego." Without year or place, in octavo.

83. "La Vie | joyeuse et récréative de Thiel Ulespiègle... qu'il a eues. A Douai. Chez Deregnaucourt. Imprimeur-Libraire, rue Jacques, no. 45." Three sheets of forty-eight pages in duodecimo, in the Imperial Library at Paris.

84, 85. Of the eighteenth century. "Historien von dem wunderlichen & seltsamen Till Eulenspiegel. Hamburg." Twelve sheets in octavo. Another edition published by Solbrig of Leipzig.

86, 87. 1804 and 1806. Two Dutch editions, published at Amsterdam and Deventer.

88. 1807. A German Leipzig edition.

89. 1819. Dutch book of the Eulenspiegel character, but not containing the same Adventures. "Het | Leven | van den | Jongen | Ulenspiegel, &c. Te Amsterdam. By B. Koene, Boekdrukker in de Boomstraat." 12mo. in ninety-six pages, in the Bodleian (v. 58, Douce Collection).

90, 91. A quarto edition, consisting of fifty-five plates, published by Ramberg at Hanover. In the Museum (press-mark, 554 *b* 40). At Rotterdam in the same year an edition in Dutch appeared, which contained several adventures differing from the common version.

92. 1830. Baron von Halberg in this year published a versified edition in octavo at Crefeld. In the Museum, with the press-mark 11526 *d*.

93–96. "Der ganz neue wiedererstandene Till Eulenspiegel," in 100 chapters, with 102 woodcuts. "München, 1833, 1836–7, 1844." This edition has been used in the preparation of this volume.

97, 98. "Avantures de Tiel Ulespiegle et ses bon mots, finesses et amusantes inventions. Par Joseph Octave Delepierre. Bruges. 1835." Ninety pages in octavo. Only fifty copies of this edition printed.—1840. "Les Aventures de Tiel Ulespiegle. Par Delepierre." An octavo of 222 pages. This edition of M. Delepierre affirms with amusing mock gravity the entirely Flemish origin of Owlglass, and the names are ingeniously altered to suit Flemish localities. Use has been made of the edition in this version.

99, 100, 101. In the years 1838 and 1839, several editions appeared, one of them that of Cornelius, which, together with the 1519 edition and the preceding, has been consulted in this edition.

102. 1841. An edition belonging to Dr. Simrock's Collection of German Folkbooks, at Berlin.

103. "Tyll Eulenspiegel's wunderbare und seltsame Historien. Von Carl Frölich. Reutlingen, 1849."

104. 1854. Dr. Thomas Murner's Ulenspiegel. By Dr. J. M. Lappenberg. Leipzig, Weigel. This is the best and completest edition yet published of Owlglass, and one which has formed the groundwork of the translation now published.

Several editions have appeared since, but none of them possessing value sufficient to render notice necessary; the only one which need be mentioned being—

105. "Histoire Joyeuse et Récréative de Tiel L'Espiègle. Nouvelle Edition. Avec une étude littéraire sur Tiel L'Espiègle par Pr. van Duyse. Gand, 1858."

We have thus, without referring to the numerous badly printed versions of the illustrious Eulenspiegel, given here a complete review of all the editions of this remarkable book, which, from its length, will serve to show how popular it has been from its very first appearance.

In connection with Eulenspiegel literature, it may be interesting in this place to give a description of a curious work, of which three copies are preserved in the Bodleian Library at Oxford (Douce Collection, Catalogue, page 290 A. Press-marks, R 328, 90), and which, by the kind permission of Dr. Bandinel, and of my friend, the Rev. A. Hackman, M.A., Precentor of Christ Church, I have been permitted to examine. It is entitled—

"The | French | Rogue. | Being a pleasant | History | of | His Life and Fortunes | adorned with variety of other | Adventures | of no less Rarity | With | Epigrams | suitable to each Stratagem | London: | Printed by T. N. for Samuel Lowndes, | and are to be sold at his Shop, over against | Exeter House in the Strand, 1672."

The two copies which I saw are well preserved, especially the one marked "R 90," which is bound up with the letters of Monsieur De Bergerac. The book is a small 12mo, with 197 pages and two pages of advertisements. The Signature A is formed of title page and six sides (without pagination) of preface and lines to the author. It is one of those dull books so common about that time, and contains the adventures and travels of a personage who, like Owlglass, but without his wit, cheats and robs those whom he encounters. He journeys over France, and becomes a member of a society of thieves, and swears to abide by certain rules of their order, tedious to be recapitulated here. The book is curious as an example of the taste of the time. The chapters are twenty-nine in number, and, as the title page says, epigrams appropriate to the adventures are inserted. Other works, ancient and modern, akin to Eulenspiegel literature, will be found in a subsequent Appendix.

APPENDIX B.

The historical Eulenspiegel and his gravestone.

It is scarcely necessary to enter upon the question of the historical Eulenspiegel. That there was such a person seems unquestionable. The names of his parents were Saxon names, not unfrequent, and the name of Ulenspiegel appears as early as 1337, being the name of a widow living at Brunswick, and again in 1473, in conjunction with another name. The widow Ulenspeygel has even been supposed to be the mother of our hero. But what little is known of him, is more easily to be read in the book itself than gathered from other records.

Among the objects of interest which remain to the present time, a testimony of the real existence of Eulenspiegel, is the gravestone at Möllen, the place assigned to him as his last resting-place, both by historical tradition and in the folkbook. Caspar Abel, who in 1729–32 published a collection of old German chronicles, gives one which he describes as having been the property of the family of Hetling, at Halberstadt, and which seems to have been written about 1486. In this chronicle, mention is made under the year 1350 of the ravages of the Black Death at Braunschweig, and it continues: "Thereof died Ulenspeygel at Möllen, among the Gheyseler brethren" ("*Dosulffest sterff Ulenspeygel to Möllen unde de Gheyseler Broder kemen an*"). Yet it is necessary to remark, that this statement, later than the first presumed edition of 1486—of which little is known—is not supported by any other Saxon chronicle of the fifteenth century. The next reference to the grave at Möllen, is in Reimar Rock's *Lübscher Chronik*, in the following jest concerning the Cardinal Raymond; being the original hint, indeed, which I have amplified in the present book, in adventure the hundredth and tenth: "The Cardinal abode in the first night at Möllen. And when he comprehended the German speech, and heard of the holy-living saint Ulenspegel, an if there had been money in store—after which do all Italians and Spaniards thirst—Ulenspegel could have been entered on the Pope his calendar." This jest, as Dr. Lappenberg well notices, is at any rate a proof, that at this time the grave was often sought out by visitors. Michael Heberer, in his voyage to Sweden and Denmark, in 1592, describes the gravestone, but not in the way depicted in our cut. He makes no mention of the figure, but only of the owl and glass; and the same description occurs in Merian (*Topographie von Nieder Sachsen*) as being there in 1614. But in 1631, in the manuscript Chronicles of Dethlev Dreyer, a description of the stone, nearly as it now stands, is given; but a basket of owls is mentioned, so it could scarcely be the same. Dreyer and Zeiller (*Reiszbuch durch Hoch und Nieder Teutschland*, 1674), both speak of the gravestone having been renewed and fenced off from the attacks of boys, and other wilful destroyers of antiquities. But the most interesting account is given by Zacharias Conrad von Uffenbach, who visited Möllen in the year 1710, and I shall, therefore, offer a translation of it:—

"We first," says the writer, "examined at the church, which

stands upon a slight hill, just by where one goeth up by steps into the churchyard, near the door, the little hut in which the gravestone of Eulenspiegel is set up and leans against the wall of the church. Formerly it had lain in the churchyard not far from the church, under the elm tree, which still stands in its place, but as by bad boys it was often damaged and went hard to be destroyed by rain and weather, a most worthy and benevolent magistrate of this town, a long time ago, had it placed against the wall of the church, and a small house erected round about it, and closed in, with only an open window, or hole, in front. The stone is more than four ells high, and only about one broad. There is not alone an owl and glass sculptured on the two sides, as Merian or Zeiller says in *Topog. Sax. infer.* p. 184, but the noble [*vornehmes*] likeness of Eulenspiegel is upon it in the size of life, although not quite equal to his stature and tallness, and the above-named things are in his hands. That he wears bells, may not arise from the fact that he plays the part of a wise fool or a jesting knave [*Schalksknecht*], but that in those times the bells were greatly in the fashion, and even worn by great lords (as see in *Observat. Hallens. ad rem liter. spectant. Germanicas* concerning Schellen-Moritz). The inscription on the lower part of the stone, is somewhat damaged by rain and carelessness; so that it is somewhat difficult to be read by those who know it not. In the wood of the hut very many Owlglasses [*Eulenspiegels*, used in the sense of rogues] have cut their names."

The expression, that the figure was the size of life, but not quite equal to the stature and tallness of Eulenspiegel, cannot be otherwise understood than that the figure was not entirely cut in the stone, but perhaps only to the knee. It would seem, however, that the figure was repeatedly replaced, for the one now existing differs from the account given by Uffenbach. It stands upright at the wall of the tower, with a wooden shed round it, the lower part of which hides the inscription. Other relics of this apostle of knavery are mentioned by Uffenbach, such as an old shirt of mail, preserved in the council chamber at Möllen. His sword, beaker, and money-pouch, all of a later period, are also shown. With the beaker, a very narrow and deep one, a sorry joke is connected, that he had it so made because his mother bade him never to dip his nose too deep in a glass.

In respect of the gravestone, it is yet to be mentioned, that in a little descriptive work which appeared some years ago, the figure is attributed to a certain knight, Tilodictus Ulenspegel, who, in Westphalian annals of the fourteenth century, is not unknown. Yet for the sake of romance, and also from historical probability, it is best to adhere to the story which remains to us. The inscription on the stone is as follows:—

> "Anno 1350 is dŭss
> -en vp gehauē ty-
> le vlenspegel ligt
> her vnder begrauen
> marcket wol vnd
> dencket dran. wat
> ick gwest sivp.. e
> ... de her vor...
> ... an moten mi
> glick wer....."

"Anno 1350 is this sculptured, Tyle Ulenspegel lies here under buried. Mark well and think thereover what I have been...." (rest too fragmentary). But to be restored thus:

> "Gedenk daran
> Wat ick gwest sivp... e
> ... de her vor (uber)
> (Gh) an moten mi
> glich wer (den)."

"Think thereover, what I have been... who passeth by may to me become alike."

At Damme, in Belgium, there is another gravestone with which tradition connects our hero, but unsatisfactorily. A writer in Meyer's "Conversations Lexicon," vol. ix. p. 331, thinks this gravestone is that of Eulenspiegel's father, who might have died at the date of it, 1301.

APPENDIX C.

Of Dr. Thomas Murner, the author of Eulenspiegel.

As the author of Eulenspiegel, and also as a not unknown man in his own country, as well as in England, it may be not unwelcome to print here a few brief notes concerning Thomas Murner. He was born at Ehenheim, south of Strasburg, the 24th December, 1475, his father being a cobbler at that place. He was educated in a school of the Franciscans at Strasburg, and seems afterwards to have visited, in the capacity of travelling student, the Universities of Paris, Freiburg, Rostock, Prague, Vienna, and Cracow, and in his nineteenth year (1494) appears already to have taken orders. In 1499 he published his first work, his *Invectiva contra Astrologos*, and another piece, the *Tractatus perutilis de phitonico contractu*, and thenceforward lived a life of extreme literary activity. Having similar tastes to Sebastian Brandt, author of the "Ship of Fools," we find Murner printing similar works—works of a satirical kind, such as the *Narrenbeschwerung* ("Conjuration of Fools"), the *Schelmenzunft* ("Knave Corporation"), and the *Gäuchmatt*, in which the various classes of society are bitterly treated, but in a way not interesting to modern persons. The most memorable thing which can connect Murner with England, is the part he took in the dispute between

Henry the Eighth and Luther; and a book which he published under the title of "Is the King of England a liar or is Luther?" (*Ob der Kunig usz Engelland ein lügner sey oder der Luther?*), obtained favour for him from Henry.

The following letter from Sir Thomas More to Cardinal Wolsey, dated the 26th August, 1523, will tell the story of Murner's visit to this country better than any other mode of narrating it. Cardinal Wolsey was then staying at Easthampstead. The spelling, which is quite intelligible enough, has been left in its original state, to give the reader an idea of the unsettled condition of English at that time.

"It may ferther lyke Your Good Grace to be advertised that one Thomas Murner, a Frere of Saynt Francisce, which wrote a booke against Luther in defence of the Kinges boke, was out of Almaigne sent into England, by the meane of a simple[16] person, an Almaign namyng hymselfe servaunt un to the Kinges Grace, and afferming un to Murner, that the King had gevyn hym in charge to desyre Murner to cum over to hym in to England, and by occasion ther of he is cummen over and has now bene here a good while. Wher fore the Kinges Grace, pitiyng that he was so deceived, and having tendre respecte to the goode zele that he bereth toward the feith, and his good hart and mynd toward His Highnes, requyreth Your Grace that it may lyke you to cause hym have in reward one hundred pownde, and that he may retourn home, wher his presence is very necessary; for he is one of the chiefe stays agaynst the faction of Luther in that parties, agaynst whom he hath wrytten many bokis in the Almayng tong; and now, sith the cumming hither, he hath translated into Latyn, the boke that he byfore made in Almaign, in defence of the Kinges boke. He is Doctour of Divinite and of bothe Lawes, and a man for wryting and preching of great estimation in his cuntre.

"Hit may like Your Grace ferther to wite, that the same simple

16   "Simple" is here used in the sense of "cunning," "bad."

person, which caused Murner to cum in to England, is now cummen to the Court, and hath brought with him a Barons son of Almaygn, to whom he hath also persuaded, that the Kinges Grace wold be glad to have hym in his service. He hath also brought lettres from Duke Ferdinand un to the Kinge's Grace, which lettres J send un to Your Grace, wherin he desireth the Kinge's Highnes to take in to his service, and to reteyne, with some convenient yerely pention Ducem Mechelburgensem; of which request the Kinges Grace greatly merveileth, and veryly thinketh that this simple felow, which brought the lettres, lykewise as he caused Murner to cum hither, and persuaded the Barons sone that the King would be glad to have his service, so hath by some simple ways brought the Duke of Mechelborough in the mynd, that the Kings Grace wold, at the contemplation of Duke Ferdinandis lettres, be content to reteign the Duke of Mechelborough with a yerly pention. The felow hath brought also fro the Duke of Mechelborough lettres of credence written in the Duche tong. He bare hym selfe in Almaign for the Kinge's servaunt, and bosted that he had a yerely pention of fiftie markes, and that the King had sent him thither to take upp servauntes for hym; and now he saith, he is servaunt un to the Empereurs Majeste, and is going into Spaigne, with lettres to hym; and in dede he hath diverse lettres to his Magestie, and so it was easie for hym to gete, if he entend to deceive and mocke; as the Kinges Grace thinketh that he doth. For His Grace never saw hym byfore, but he understandeth now, that before this tyme he was in England, when th Empereur was here,[17] and slew a man and escaped his way. Wherfor His Grace requyreth Yours to give hym your prudent advice, as well in a convenient answere to be made both to Duke Ferdinand and the Duke of Mechelborough, as also in what wyse hit shal be convenient to ordre this simple felowe, that so hath deceived menne in the Kinges name."

17   Charles V. was in England from the 26th of May, when he landed at Dover, till the 1st of July, 1522.

However agreeable to the vanity, and useful to the cause, of the King, the book is a somewhat dreary book to read now; and save that it consists of a long dialogue between the King, Luther, and Murner, there need be little more said of it. Those who wish to read it will find it in its original German in that valuable collection of Middle Age literature made by Scheible, and entitled *Das Kloster* (the Convent) Volume IV. pp. 893–982. The dispute continued to give a tone to his life henceforth, and all his later years were spent in empty and angry controversy. Indeed, we lose sight of him altogether in the year 1530; and it has been suspected that he was murdered at Lucerne, though we hear the last of him at Strasburg. His death was certainly before 1537.

APPENDIX D.

The verses inserted by William Copland in the English black-letter Howleglas of 1528.

How Howleglas came to a scoler to make verses with hym to that vse of reason. And howe that Howleglas began, as after shal folowe:—

HOWLEGLAS.

Mars with septer[18] a king coronate,
Furius[19] in affliction, and taketh no regarde.
By terrible fightyng he is our prymate
And god of battell, and person ryght forward,
Of warries[20] the tutor, the locke and the warde.
His power, his might, who can them resyst?
Not all this worlde, if that him selfe lyst.

18   *Septer*, sceptre.
19   *furius*, furious.
20   *warries*, wars.

The Scholer.

Not all this worlde, who told the[21] so?
Where is that written, ryght fayne wold I see?
Ye came lyke a foole and so shall ye go.
By one person only deceived ye may be
And by astronomy, I tell vnto the.
If that will not helpe, some shyft shal I fynde
By craft or cunnyng, Mars for to blynde.

Howleglas.

Venus a god of loue most decorate,
The floure of women and lady most pvre,
Louers to concorde she doth aye aggregate
With parfyte loue, as marble to dure,
The knot of loue, she knittes on them sure
With frendly amite[22] and neuer to discorde
By dedes, thought, cogitation, nor worde.

The Scholer.

Not to discorde? yed[23] did I never see,
Knowe not here tell of louers suche twayne,
But some fault there was, learne this of me.
Other in thought, or yet in wordes playne
Your reasons be nought, your tongue goeth in vayne.
By naturall person such loue is not found
In Fraunce, Flaunders, nor yet in Englysh ground.

Howleglas.

The God of wyne, that Bachus hath to name,
The sender of fruytes, that maketh wynes all,
May slake or make or put them in frame,
All at his pleasure and use dynyall.[24]
He may the[25] exalt in lyke wyse to fall,

21   *the*, thee.
22   *amite*, French *amitié*.
23   *yed*, yet.
24   *dynyall*, denial.
25   *the*, thee.

Their lorde and meister,[26] and chief gouernour
He may then destroye and make in an houre.

THE SCHOLER.

All to destroye it is not by his myght,
Nor yet for to make, of that be thou sure.
"Omnia per ipsum," Saint Johan sayes full ryght.
Than we call Christ our god and our treasure.
Presume not so hye,[27] you fayle of your measure,
Rede, heare and see, and here well a waye,
Unknowen, vnsayde and for grace thou pray.

APPENDIX E.

The Bakâla legend of the Valacqs analogous to Owlglass.

The most interesting fiction with which I have met, approaching in intention and construction to the German Eulenspiegel, is a legend current among the Wallachians, entitled "Bakâla." The hero goes through a few adventures savouring much of the wily malice of Owlglass; but there are only thirteen of these adventures in all. The first introduces us to Bakâla, at the death of his father, who leaves a single cow behind him. The question arises between Bakâla and his two elder brothers, as to which is to become possessor of the cow. They agree at last to build three sheds, and, placing the cow in the middle, give her the opportunity of deciding the ownership. Bakâla builds his shed of a grassy material, which the cow perceives, and instead of entering the sheds of stone built by Bakâla's brethren, enters his, and thus becomes his property. He then sells his cow to a tree, which agitated by the wind, appears to bargain with him. His brethren mock at him for

26 *meister*, master.
27 *hye*, high.

244

a fool in selling the cow to a tree; and next day, when payment is to be made, the cow has broken loose and departed, and when Bakâla asks for the money, there being no wind, the tree is silent. Then Bakâla cuts down the tree and finds a pot of money in the roots; thereof he takes the agreed price, and goes home, and his brethren are astonished at his receiving money from a tree. The two brothers plague him until he tells them the whole story as to the treasure, which they go and take. Bakâla is then sent to borrow a fruit measure from a neighbour, who asks him what he wants it for, and Bakâla tells him that it is to measure his money. So the neighbour follows him, and peeps through the window. This is seen by the inmates of the house, and Bakâla is told to go and kill him, which he does; the brothers only meaning that Bakâla should give him a beating. When they find, however, that Bakâla has killed him, they are obliged to depart from that place.

An adventure by which Bakâla becomes possessed of a sack of incense, obtains him a gift from the Almighty (who, as in the ancient miracle-plays, is brought into the story) of a marvellous bagpipe, which causes every one to dance. When a shepherd the sheep dance; and his master, who is watching him, is obliged to dance also; and afterwards his master's wife dances herself to death. Other mischief Bakâla also contrives to do. After cutting the tails of his master's dogs off, and killing the youngest child by washing it and hanging it up to dry, the master resolves to depart; for he is bound by a treaty to Bakâla. But Bakâla gets into the sack, which the master prepares to carry books in, and is discovered at last. Then the master and his son conspire to drown Bakâla; but he overhears them, and the son gets drowned instead. Bakâla appears here to be analogous to the Old Man of the Sea, of whom Sindbad cannot rid himself. At last the contract between them, to the effect that either on breaking it should forfeit a long strip of skin in the back, has to be completed by Bakâla on the body of his master, who has broken it by the attempt to drown his servant. And as the master's back is sore, he takes the book-wallet and departs. This story, as our authority, Schott, says (*Walachische Mährchen*, p. 362), reminds us of the agreement between Apollo and Marsyas. Then he sets a bride free from a disagreeable bridegroom by a stratagem, and after acting the bride's part himself, escapes.

The last story in the series is worthy of translation entire, therefore here it is:—

"How Bakâla findeth a fellow, and thereafter is not any other news heard of him.—After that Bakâla had in such wise departed from the bridegroom, he gat, whence I know not, a sack filled with sawdust. No longtime had he journeyed, when he encountered by the way another man, who likewise bare a sack. Then did they greet each other, and after awhile proposed that they should change sacks. And so did they; then they hasted to open the sacks, and in that which Bakâla had received lay nought but flint stones, and what the other received that do we know. For a time they looked upon their prizes with great wonder; but thereupon laughed hugely. 'Truly,' quoth Bakâla, 'we have beguiled each other!' 'That is truth indeed!' cried the other. And great content had these twain one of the other, and embraced thereupon, and made agreement that thereafter would they journey everywhere in company. From that time hath no more been heard of Bakâla."

Schott, in his work, finds analogy between the various adventures of Bakâla, and the course of the sun through the months of the year; but it is foreign to our present purpose to enter upon such a speculation. Yet, as a curious exemplification of the love of trickery to be found among all races, this Wallachian Owlglass is worthy of mention.

APPENDIX F.

Works akin to the Eulenspiegel literature.

Although the Eulenspiegel folk-book has become the best known of the special class of books in which the middle age took such pleasure, there are many other compositions of a kindred nature worthy of mention, and of these I shall here describe the most important. The first on which any remark is necessary is the celebrated legend of Salomon and Marcolphus, which, in Latin, German, Anglo-Saxon, and French, has survived to the present time. Marcolphus is a jester in a more sober sense than is Owlglass; the jests of the former, though some of them are analogous to those of the latter, rarely touch upon the humourous. They are capable of application to far more serious things, to matters of speculative philosophy and science. Luther, for instance, applied a story of Marcolphus in reproof of persons who shut their eyes to the good, but afterwards were compelled, whether they would or no, to behold the evil.[28] But the Marcolphus legend is an exemplification rather of the combats of wit and wisdom common to the earlier part of the middle age, than a vivid reflex, as is the Owlglass, of the manners and customs of the time to which it belongs. One story borrowed from the Marcolphus, or from Morlini, at an early period, appears in Owlglass, being the second adventure in this edition, p. 3.

The *Narrenschiff* ("Ship of Fools") of Sebastian Brandt was

28   The curious reader will find this duly set forth in Mr. Kemble's critical history of the Salomon and Marcolphus tale (Salomon and Saturnus, p. 70). And in the preface to Dr. Luther's "Table Talk," where this application is made, Stangwald complains of the great number of people who prefer Marcolphus, Eulenspiegel, and such books, to these *Colloquia Lutheri*.

published in 1494. It is also called the *Welt Spiegel,* or "World Mirror," and it enjoyed a great and deserved reputation in its time, but was far too pedantic and tiresome to survive to the present age, or be profitable now. A few remarks upon it, extracted from Hallam, will be found in the Preface.

Murner himself published a satirical work in 1517, entitled the *Schelmenzunft* ("Corporation of Knaves"), but from a want of entirety it has fallen into little repute. So also the *Gäuchmatt* has been forgotten, while Owlglass, published in the same year (1519), will live a companion to many.

Similar books had preceded Master Owlglass, but not with the same success, although from them the frequent editors of the latter abstracted stories to add to the deeds of the wandering knave; from the legend of the "Priest Amis," for instance, Murner took the story of the invisible picture, the reading ass, the wise university examination at Prague, and the history of the pardoner with the holy head of Saint Brandonus. Another work, the "Priest of Kalenberg," preceded Owlglass, having appeared before the year 1494 at Vienna, being written by Villip Frankfurter; the only copy known is preserved in the Hamburg Town Library. The "Priest of Kalenberg" is mentioned by Sebastian Brandt in the "Ship of Fools;" and Murner, in his *Narrenbeschwerung*, tells a story concerning him. The book is alluded to by Fischart in the preface to his Eulenspiegel, as having been a great success. The latest edition of the "Priest of Kalenberg" appeared under the title of *Der geistliche Eulenspiegel, oder der Pfarrer vom Kalenberg, nebst Schwänken einiger anderen lustigen Gesellen* ("The Clerical Eulenspiegel, or the Parson of Kalenberg, with the quips of some other merry fellows"). Leipzig, 1818.

Another book which supplied the editors of Eulenspiegel with materials for its extension was the Jests of Gonella, Court Fool to the Margrave Nicolaus of Este (†1441), and to his son Borso, the Duke of Ferrara (†1471); indeed, it is far from unlikely that

Murner himself was acquainted with it, as it was published in 1506 at Bologna. So rare is this work, that in an appendix Dr. Lappenberg has reprinted it.

The "Jests of Poggio Bracciolini" (1381–1459), a man to whom we owe the recovery of Quintilian, eight orations of Cicero, twelve comedies of Plautus, and other classics, also furnished Murner with matter for the Eulenspiegel. In fact, Murner and his successors must have very diligently sought out all the literature of the class likely to serve their purpose in adding to the adventures of their own hero. Thus several stories are adapted from the "Cento Novelle Antiche" (printed at Bologna, 1525), from Morlini (Naples, 1520), from Bebel, and from François Villon.

There are a few books later than Eulenspiegel having a family resemblance to it; of these the *Schimpf und Ernst* ("Abuse and Seriousness") of John Pauli Pfedersheimer, published in 1522, is the most noted. The following is the title of the first edition: "Schimpf vñ | Ernst | heiset | das Buch mit namē | durchlaufft e d' welthandlung mit | ernstlichen vnd kurtzweiligen exem- | plen, parabolen vnd hystorien | nützlich vnd gut zu besse- | rung der menschen." This title is in an oblong tablet surrounded with woodcuts. Below is Herodias bringing the head of John the Baptist to her father; to the right is Adam and Eve; to the left, Bishop Martin; and at the top is St. George with the dragon. Sheets run from A-X iiii, 124 pages in folio, double columns. Colophon: "Getruckt zu Strassburg von Johannes | Grieninger, vnd volendet vff vnser lieben frawentag der geburt, | in dem iar nach der geburt Christi vnsers herren. Tausend | fünf hundert vnd zwei vnd zwantzig." Then follows sheet Y, with six pages of contents. Copies in the Royal Libraries at Dresden, Berlin, and München. Forty-nine editions are specified by Lappenberg in "Ulenspiegel" (pp. 368–378), besides several translations. Pauli, in turn, has borrowed from Eulenspiegel, and that he understood the spirit of the book is plain from a reference he makes to it.

Another work akin to the Owlglass is the popular folk-book of Friar Rush, which is sufficiently well known to need no further description here. Mr. Thoms has reprinted it in his "Collection of Early Prose Romances." Claus Narr von Ranstedt is another successor to Eulenspiegel. This worthy was court-fool to the Elector of Saxony from 1486 to 1532; thus a contemporary to Murner, who, indeed, mentions him in the treatise, "Whether the King of England be a liar or Dr. Luther?" The earliest edition appears to be of 1572, and its author was Master Wolfgang Büttner, Priest of Volfferstet. In the preface, Büttner sneers at Eulenspiegel, and asks why the pure words and good sayings of this good man should not be preferred and esteemed rather than the shameless stories of Owlglass.

Noteworthy also is a book containing the adventures of Hans Clauert of Trebbin, who in a humble manner, yet not without humour, follows in the footsteps of Owlglass. The only edition of it which I have seen is an undated folk-book, published in the series of Otto Wigand at Leipzig. This hero goes to Hungary and other places; but his adventures contain none of the satiric intention evident in the Owlglass. With these elucidatory remarks touching Owlglass, and the literature of which his adventures form the completest example, I bid the reader

A HEARTY FAREWELL.